CALIFORNIA DREAMING

Also by Harlan Hague

CALIFORNIA DREAMING

HARLAN HAGUE

WOLFPACK
PUBLISHING
— EST 2013 —

CALIFORNIA DREAMING

Chapter One

THE *YANKEE ENTERPRISE* sailed into a light headwind, heeling gently to port. Sailors not on duty lined the starboard railing, staring at the rugged coastline of headlands and sandy coves. They wore no uniform, simply clothing of their own choosing, rumpled, coarse, worn, and soiled. Jacket collars were pulled up, stocking caps pulled down over ears. They looked up, eyes closed, smiling, smelling the faint odors of land in the soft cold offshore breeze.

Jess and Reuben stood near the bow, apart from the others. Jess's hair, wavy, unruly, and uncovered, flew about his face and ears. He looked younger than his twenty-eight years, often described by friends as a nice-lookin' fella. Reuben, at his side, was younger. Eighteen? Nineteen? He didn't know for sure. His face was cherubic, smooth, black. His hair was coal black, kinky curly.

"Does the captain know where he's going, Reuben?" said Jess.

The only black man on the ship, Reuben was generally ignored by most of the crew, but Jess often sought his counsel. He belonged to Captain Harris and was privy to conversations overheard when he was with his owner. The captain made no attempt to hide comment around his chattel, considering him essentially mindless.

"Well, yes and no," said Reuben. "He plan to get the upper hand on the other hide and tallow ships on the coast. Remember when he talk to the crew about the trade just after we left Boston? Ships in the trade call mostly at San Diego or Monterey, he say, so they're in competition with all the other ships who call at those ports.

"Captain say he gonna find a landing where nobody else go, somewhere between San Diego and Monterey. That's why we sailing slow along the coast, pokin' into bays, sailin' out, then up the coast and poke in again. He say when he see a likely bay and see some people on the shore, he gonna sail in as far as possible, anchor and send in a scouting party. It shouldn't take those boys long, he say, to go inland and check out the country. He needs to see people ashore so the sailors can get horses."

"Seems pretty chancy to me."

Reuben pulled back and made a face, grinning. "Don't let Captain hear you say that. He think he knows everythin' there is to know about everythin'."

Jess smiled, a wry sort of smile. "I hope he settles on a cove soon. I'm itching to stand on some solid ground. It seems like ten years since we left Boston. I was so sick of this ship by the time we reached

Chile, I thought about going ashore and getting lost."

"No!" said Reuben, open-mouthed.

Jess chuckled. "Then I was reminded that Juan Fernandez where we landed was an island. Captain probably could have found me with no trouble. On the other hand, I was so fatigued with the voyage, I might have taken a risk. I heard crickets and bird song for the first time in months. And the wonderful smells! Remember the fruit, the melons, strawberries, grapes, cherries? Beautiful place, the mountains, beaches, streams..." He looked toward the coast, sighed deeply. "Might have been worth the risk."

Reuben frowned. "Oh, Jess, don't let Captain hear you say anything about gettin' away! He'll have you flogged for sure. He 'spects you signed on for the whole trip, out and back, you know."

Jess looked at the mountains beyond the coast, their peaks shrouded in clouds. He sighed, leaned on the rail. "Yeah, signed on, if you want to call it that. You also must know by now that I'm not a serious sailor. I keep cows with my daddy in Kentucky. I went to Boston out of curiosity, just to have a look. Then I got drunk and signed on for this trip, right there in the pub. I had no idea what I was signing. It might have been for a marriage license, for all I knew. I woke up in a bunk, staggered up on deck and saw Boston harbor in the distance. Then I found out where we were bound. I don't think I would have been drunk enough to sign on if I knew we were headed for California."

"Yeah, you've told me a dozen times." Reuben pulled a face.

"Well, just want to be sure you understand I'm a cow man, not a sea man." He turned back to the coast. "I sure don't look forward to the sail back to Boston."

"What th' hell you two doin', leanin' on the rail? You think this is a playground?" Captain Harris stood behind them, glaring. They had not heard him coming.

"No, sir, Captain, just getting a look at the land," said Jess. "Sure is pretty."

Harris fumed. "By god, I might give you a chance to look at the land from the water if you don't get back to work! We're heading in pretty quick, and everbody needs to be at his post!"

Jess stepped away from the rail. "Yes sir, I was just—"

Captain's face turned hard. "By god, you don't talk back to me! Get forward! I don't want talk! I want work!"

Reuben stepped up beside Jess. "Aw, Cap'n, Jess was just—"

Harris jerked aside to glare at Reuben. He spoke softly, slowly. "You speaking to me, you black scum? You don't never speak to me unless I say somethin' to you."

Reuben winced. "Well, Cap'n, we talk everday and—"

The captain whipped around, shouted at the ship's officer standing above on the quarterdeck, listening, watching. "Wilson! Put this man in chains and bring me the whip!" He turned back to Reuben.

His face was contorted in anger. "I'll teach you some manners."

Reuben and Jess looked at each other, frowning. Reuben shook his head, the slightest movement.

Wilson and a seaman carrying chains hurried down the ladder. The officer took Reuben by an arm, moved him forward, threw the chains around a mast and clamped them at Reuben's waist. Reuben looked at Jess in dismay, then acceptance. Jess almost stepped forward, but the officer warned him off with a slight shake of his head and a look that told Jess that he did not agree with the captain's intent to flog Reuben.

"Bare his back!" said Captain.

Wilson gripped the shirt at the collar and pulled down, ripping it off Reuben's back and revealing a crisscrossing of scars.

Harris, his face hard and eyes squinted, took the whip. "I'll teach you to know your place, you black demon. And to speak only when I speak to you." He spread his feet, drew back, and struck Reuben's back hard with the whip. And again and again, swinging the whip as hard as he could. After twenty lashes, he stopped, breathing heavily.

"There, by god," said Harris. He dropped the whip and strode to the ladder and up to the quarterdeck. Wilson went to Reuben, leaned close to Reuben's ear while unshackling him. He picked up the whip and climbed the ladder.

Jess went to him. The chains were gone, but his arms still encircled the mast. His eyes were closed. "Reuben?"

Reuben opened his eyes, turned his head slowly

and looked at Jess through half-slit eyes. He dropped his arms, bent and picked up his shirt from the deck.

"What did Wilson say to you?" Jess said.

Reuben blinked, looked at him through slitted eyes. He almost smiled. "He said, 'mind how you go.' He's good man. He knows not to cross the boss."

"Let's go below and find some water," said Jess.

They walked to the ladder, down the steps, and forward to their quarters in the forecastle. Jess found a rag, wet it from a bucket of water and gently moistened the bloody stripes on Reuben's back.

Reuben, bending forward, winced from the cloth's touch, his eyes closed tightly.

"You okay?" said Jess.

Reuben, his eyes glazed, half-opened, turned his head aside to look at Jess. He said nothing a long moment. Then he smiled, hardly a hint of a smile. "I expected more. He gave me fifty lashes last time. Remember?"

Jess nodded.

"You won't believe this, Jess, but I feel better now than I did before the flogging."

"What? There's something I don't know?"

Reuben straightened, leaned against a post. He looked each way in the compartment, saw only Jess. "I been thinking of leavin' the ship, runnin'. I was just thinkin'. Now I'm not thinkin'. I'm gonna do it. I'm not goin' back to Boston," he said, almost a whisper. "I ain't tellin' nobody but you. I want somebody to know what happened to me, and I don't trust nobody but you. If Captain finds out, he'll flog me near death, or he'll kill me on purpose."

Jess leaned back and stared at Reuben.

"Are you okay with this?" said Reuben.

Jess said nothing while Reuben fidgeted. "I'm not just okay with it, Reuben. I'm gonna help you." He paused, frowning, pondering. "Captain told me that I would be in charge of one of the boats that go back and forth to the beach, bringing hides to the ship and transporting people who come out to buy our goods. I'll arrange for you to be assigned to my boat. I'll fix it so my boat one day leaves the shore near sundown. I'll tell Captain that when it came time to leave, you weren't there. You went to the bushes or something. You disappeared. It was almost dark, and we didn't have time to go inland to search. I'll tell him I asked the vaqueros to keep an eye out for you. Course, I'll say nothing of the sort to anybody ashore. They will know nothing about you jumping ship. I don't think they would help chase you anyway. They would probably help you."

Reuben took Jess's hand in both of his. His eyes misted. "You are a saint, Jess. I will pray for you. I hope Captain will believe you. If he don't, you're in trouble."

"I'll not worry about that. But we're getting ahead of ourselves. When the captain finally settles on a landing, he'll send boats ashore to talk with locals about the prospects for gathering hides. Once he's convinced that he's found a good landing, we'll anchor and start business. He'll make contact with ranchers who probably will have done business with Boston ships in the past. They'll have to get busy slaughtering the cattle, cleaning and drying the hides and storing them for transfer to the ship. Also preparing the tallow by boiling fat.

"It will likely take a year or more to gather a load. During that year, locals from miles around will come to the ship to buy and barter the goods we're carrying. I understand the locals are real happy to get Boston's manufactured goods, and we've got a bunch. Clothing, cotton and silk goods, tobacco, sugar, wine, tea, manufactured kitchen and household goods.

"Captain says I'll be in one of the boats that go ashore at the outset, contacting the locals. Each boat will have one of our Spanish-speaking crewmen. You won't go in with these boats. It would be too hard to run from these groups. You'll go in later on one of the boats that are transporting people and picking up hides. I'll let you know. Be sure you pack food and your personal stuff among the goods. Carefully. Sit on your goods in the boat. If you are caught before you get away, we're in big trouble."

Jess pointed in Reuben's face. "The important thing for you is to be a good boy until we can bring all this off. We can't very well get you on shore and away if you're in the brig."

Reuben smiled. "I'll be a good boy."

Jess patted him on an arm, left the cabin, and went up on deck. He looked westward, where the sun hovered just over the horizon. He stared at the rocky headlands and sandy beaches, the dark forested hillsides beyond. He shifted when the ship turned slightly to starboard, and the sails came about as the ship heeled to the right. He looked forward at the coast.

Looks like a nice cove ahead. Captain's going in for a look.

————

Jess and the other oarsmen of the ship's boat pulled hard for the beach. Half a dozen men stood on the beach near the waterline watching the boat coming. Eusebio, the crewman standing in the bow, called to the men and waved. A couple of the men returned the wave. As the boat neared the shore, the men on the beach ran to the likely landing spot. Near the waterline, the bow lifted gently in the swell, dropped and touched bottom, sliding in the sand. Eusebio and another crewman jumped out. The crewman took the coiled line from the bow, dragged it up the beach, pounded a stake in the ground and attached the line to it.

Eusebio was one of only three aboard the *Enterprise* who spoke Spanish. He went to the men and extended a hand. A smiling vaquero took the hand, and they shook, chattering in Spanish, pointing at the boat and the ship, now anchored and sails down.

Robert, the officer in charge of the boat, clambered over the side into the shallows, followed by the oarsmen. Robert walked over to stand beside Eusebio and the Californios, as Eusebio called them, Californians of Mexican descent. The Californios clustered around the two sailors, leaning in and listening intently. Eusebio spoke rapidly, gesturing toward Robert and the ship.

Jess jumped from the gunwale to the sand. He stamped, stretched, closed his eyes, threw back his head, and grinned, ecstatic to be standing on solid ground once more. He opened his eyes and saw the Californios staring at him, frowning. They smiled when they saw his smile, then turned abruptly back toward Eusebio and their leader who spoke rapidly, smiling often, pointing at the ship and inland.

Jess studied the Californios. Eusebio had told him that those they would see on the beach would be vaqueros, Californio cowboys. With bronzed, creased faces suggesting a life in the elements, they wore shirts loose in the arms and tight at wrists, cloth trousers covered with leather leggings, billowing below the knee and stitched with leather thongs. They wore broad-brimmed hats with a strap under the chin. Some sported a leather cape, fringed at the bottom and a hole at the top for pulling over the head. Jess decided he liked the outfits, thought he might like to own one.

Robert, through Eusebio, asked about the locations of ranches, cattle populations, whether the local rancheros had experience in the hide and tallow trade, and would they be willing and ready to open trade with the *Yankee Enterprise*. The men listened intently, nodded sharply. The conversation ended with grins, handshakes, and back-slapping. The vaqueros hurried to their horses tied to bushes just off the beach. They untied reins, mounted and kicked their horses into a furious gallop up the grassy incline and into the forest.

Robert, a bit puffed up and smiling, turned to the sailors who had watched the conversation silently. "Boys, this is your home for the next year.

Or two. I hope you like the view. San Simeon Bay, the vaqueros called it."

Jess indeed liked the view. The difference between San Simeon Bay and the ship was akin to the difference between Heaven and Hell. A forested peninsula on the north side of the bay jutted out into the swells. The peninsula would serve to shield the anchorage from cold northerly winds. The sandy beach stretched southward from the peninsula for miles along the arc of the bay. Beyond the beaches, broad meadows rose to a line of trees along the distant crest. He wondered what lay beyond that wooded crest. He knew virtually nothing of California. Suddenly he was filled with a strong desire to know.

———

JESS STOOD with two others at the rail, watching the sun ball drop slowly until the top rim vanished, coloring the lacy cloud layers at the horizon shades of red, blue, and gray. Jess shivered, pulled his coat tight and raised the fur collar.

"Very strange, crossing the equator and changing seasons like that, from summer to winter. First Christmas I've been away from home," Jess said, staring at the darkening horizon.

"Hard to remember when I spent a Christmas at home," said Andy. "No captain I ever sailed with paid much attention to family matters."

"Andy, I saw you talking with Eusebio. Did he learn anything about the war from the vaqueros? The people we talked with at Juan Fernandez knew the United States and Mexico were at war, but that's all they knew."

"The vaqueros talked about it, but they didn't know much either. They said American ships were at Monterey last summer. Sometime during the summer, August they thought, American ships were in Los Angeles under an officer named Stockton. They said they hadn't heard about any fighting anywhere after that. They think the war, if you want to call it that, is over. One of them said that they may no longer be Californios; they may be Americanos. Eusebio said the man wasn't smiling when he said it."

"Hmm, sorta sad. I understand, but real glad to hear the war is over. As boring as this year is going to be, I sure don't want to make it exciting by getting caught up in a war." The others murmured their agreement.

———

DURING THE NEXT TWO WEEKS, Robert and a trio of selected crewmen rode with vaqueros to ranches inland from the landing place to investigate prospects for buying hides and tallow and selling the manufactured goods the ship offered for sale. They learned quickly that the rancheros, as the vaqueros called their employers, were delighted to trade with the Americanos at this beach, cutting off time wasted doing business with ships at more distant landings. They said the *Yankee Enterprise* was the first hide and tallow ship to anchor in San Simeon Bay.

Landing parties from the ship occasionally

camped in the open, but more often were invited to stay the night at a ranch house. The sailors were invariably delighted with the overnights, especially when the host family included a pretty señorita. When they returned to the ship, they couldn't stop grinning.

Jess was among the crew taking part in the exploratory excursions in the hinterland. Vaqueros furnished horses to the crewmen. Some of the sailors had never been astride a horse and had considerable difficulty. The vaqueros tried to help crewmen and were at a loss how to react to the sailors' difficulties. Probably they had never encountered a man who did not ride. They looked at each other, embarrassed. Then they saw Jess and the hapless sailors laughing out loud. The vaqueros relaxed and joined in the hilarity. Jess decided he liked Californios.

Jess was impressed with what he learned on these excursions. He had heard about the large cattle populations in California, but he was still surprised at the huge herds of almost wild cattle and horses.

Evenings, the Americans sat around campfires with the vaqueros, sometimes joined by ranch owners. Jess was particularly intrigued by what the Californios told about the missions. Founded by the Spanish in the eighteenth century, the missions and the native people attached to them at one time were principals in the hide and tallow trade. This ended in 1834 when the missions were secularized, the native people scattered, and mission properties were passed from the church to private hands. Some new owners converted the missions from religious sites to private enterprises that offered rooms and food. Other missions, empty and unused, simply deteriorated. The hide and tallow trade then was totally in the hands of the rancheros.

Most interesting. Wonder if I can steal some time to visit a mission?

———

ARRANGEMENTS WERE COMPLETED with local rancheros who began the long process of preparing hides and rendering tallow. Sheds to hold processed hides were built at the landing. Arrangements finished, the ship was prepared for the sail north to Monterey. Every ship planning to do business of any sort in California was required to check in with customs officials in the provincial capital and pay the required fees.

Crewmen who had visited Monterey on previous voyages were anxious to visit again. At supper the evening before the planned departure, a grinning middle-aged crewman leaned over the table. "Boys, the cantinas are somethin' you never seen. And the senoritas, ooooh." He closed his eyes, smiling. He opened his eyes wide. "If the captain don't give us leave to go ashore, I'm for throwin' him overboard." He laughed, sobered quickly, looked around, pulled a face, suddenly aware of what he said. The others at the table laughed. One slapped him on the back.

———

THE SAIL NORTHWARD into the prevailing winds was without incident. The *Yankee Enterprise* dropped anchor in placid Monterey Bay. The town was located at the south end of the enormous bay. Thick woods lay above the broad sandy beaches.

Jess and Reuben were assigned to the first boat ashore, which prompted some grumbling among the old hands until Jess explained that they were picking up personal items for the captain and were ordered to return to the ship by the first available boat. No dallying ashore.

Old hands had described the landings at Los Angeles where oarsmen had to pull frantically until the boat was almost to the beach, then throw oars overboard when the boat's bow lifted high in the wave and slammed to the sandy beach. The landing at San Simeon Bay was not nearly as dramatic. The Monterey landing was even easier. Here, the boat coasted slowly in a light swell until the bow scraped gently on the bottom at the beach. Passengers climbed over the gunwale and stepped onto dry sand.

Jess and Reuben walked to the top of the beach onto green grass. Lining the beach, stands of huge pines leaned shoreward in the prevailing easterly winds.

"I'll take care of Captain's stuff," said Reuben. "You go see the town. I'll be back at the landing in a couple hours. If you aren't there, I'll tell Captain you jumped ship and are halfway to Kentucky by now."

Jess smiled and pointed at Reuben's face. "You better not even think about saying anything about jumping ship to anybody, young friend, even as a joke. You'll get some sailors to thinking."

"Yeah, guess you're right."

Jess watched Reuben walk down what appeared to be the main road toward a cluster of buildings. Reuben turned and waved. Jess returned the wave. He looked around. There were few roads. Houses and shops of wood frame and whitewashed adobe, both with roofs of red tiles, were sited haphazardly in the broad flat. Few people were about. They ambled, heads down. A vaquero rode slowly on the road toward the buildings. Jess waved to a walker who returned the wave. It was so quiet Jess distinctly heard the soft cooing of an unseen mourning dove.

He set off down the dusty street where Reuben had disappeared. After but a hundred yards, he stopped abruptly. Across the road was a two-story house that looked strangely out of place. He didn't know what to make of it. Featuring covered wrap-around porches on both stories, it looked like New England houses that his parents had described. The Stars and Stripes flew from a flagpole in the front yard. He frowned, staring.

"Bonito, no?"

Jess turned sharply to see the speaker who had walked up behind him. He was smiling, nattily dressed in clean, pressed trousers, cravat, and coat. "Uh, sorry, I don't speak Spanish."

"I just said it's pretty. I take it you are American. So am I. Well, I was."

"Yes, I'm American. I'm a hand on the *Yankee Enterprise*, there." He pointed to the ship anchored in the bay. He turned back, frowning. "What do you mean, you were American?"

The man smiled. "I married a California woman, became a Catholic, and received a nice land grant from the California government. And became a Mexican citizen. If you are long in California, you'll find a good many Americans in similar circumstances. Would you like me to introduce you to some young women? I know a few who would be delighted to meet you. You'll learn Spanish real easy." He smiled.

Jess laughed. "Sounds interesting. Gotta think about that." He pointed across the street. "Why's the American flag flying at that house?"

"Ah, that is the residence of the United States Consul, Thomas O. Larkin. He's the most influential American in California. Good man. He's also a businessman. His front room is a store. I pointed a young black man to the store a few minutes ago. You probably know him. He said he was from the *Enterprise.*"

"Yes, I know him. Reuben." Jess frowned. "Just had a thought. Is slavery legal in California?"

"Ah, good question. Do you know about the California missions?"

"I've heard talk about them but know little."

"Indians were forced to live and work in the missions. They weren't called slaves, but if they ran away, they were chased and returned to the mission. And punished."

Jess frowned. "Sounds like slavery to me."

The man nodded. "Do I take it correctly that the young black man in Larkin's store is a slave?"

Jess paused, nodded. "He belongs to the captain of the *Enterprise*."

"Ah. Well. Hmm. Slavery isn't talked about much in California. If the subject comes up, it's passed over as a problem back East between the North and the South. I must say that though the missions are no longer functioning, the treatment of Indians in California still borders on slavery." He inhaled deeply, frowned. "That is a complex subject, which few around here will wish to discuss. And I must be on my way. By the way, I'm John Cooper." He extended his hand, and Jess shook. "Larkin is my brother."

"Jess Winslow, Mr. Cooper. Thanks for the information. I'm finding California most interesting." Cooper smiled, touched his hat to Jess as he walked away. Jess touched his cap awkwardly in imitation. He watched Cooper, a self-assured, well-dressed Americano, as Eusebio would call him. *Americano? Or Californio since he's a Mexican citizen?*

Hmm. Marry a California woman, became a Catholic and receive a land grant. Seems to be the pattern for Americans in California. Hmm.

Jess walked across the dusty street to Larkin's house and stopped at the open door. He looked inside and saw Reuben talking with a man across a counter. Reuben was filling a bag with goods from the counter.

"Come in, come in. I can't sell you anything if you're going to stand on the porch." It was the man behind the counter, smiling and beckoning. Jess went inside. "I s'pose you two know each other."

"Hey, Jess," said Reuben.

"We do, Mr. Larkin," said Jess. He walked to the counter, put a hand on Reuben's back and looked around. Each wall was lined with loaded shelves, goods were stacked on almost every foot of floor space, and implements of all sorts hung from hooks in the ceiling beams. "I haven't seen such a store since leaving Kentucky."

"We've got what you need. By the way, I'm not Mr. Larkin. I'm Talbot Green, his trusted accomplice and consultant." He grinned.

"I heard that, Talbot!" They turned to see a man stride into the store through a door in the back wall. He wore a dark wool suit and a stern look that gave way to a faint smile. "Talbot, are these two fellows going to buy enough to push my net worth to a million dollars by closing time?"

Talbot smiled. "Not by closing today, boss. Maybe next week. These boys are from the *Yankee Enterprise*, a hide and tallow ship anchored in the bay. They'll do business down the coast after clearing customs."

"I suppose customs agents are aboard by now examining cargo," said Larkin, "so they can levy their inflated taxes. Don't tell anyone I said that." He smiled. "Give your captain a message for me. Tell him you met Thomas O. Larkin, United States Consul to California. Tell him Larkin is a supplier of ships of all sorts, whalers, hide and tallow, traders, all sorts. I can supply whatever he needs. If I don't have it in stock, I can get it in a matter of days. If he needs to sail before I get something he wants, I'll have it sent down to the anchorage. He won't find a more reliable supplier anywhere in northern California. Will you tell him for me?"

"Yes, sir, sure will," said Jess.

"As a matter of fact, why don't you suggest to your captain that you stay in Monterey to act as his agent, and you and I will handle all matters involving supplying the ship?"

Jess grinned at Reuben, then sobered. "I sure would like that, but I'm as sure the captain won't like it. Captain is reluctant to give anyone under him a responsibility that seems to offer free rein, an opportunity to think for himself, even if he is working for him. Does that make sense?"

"Oh yes, it's common with men who feel threatened because of their own inadequacies. Does that sound like your captain?"

"Oh, yes. You described him. He uses the whip often to prove he's the boss, and don't you forget it."

Reuben was clearly troubled. "Jess, Captain would flog you till tomorrow if he heard you say that."

Larkin laughed. "Well, no one in this room will talk," he said to Reuben. He turned to Jess. "Just tell him you found the principal supplier for ships in Monterey and mention my name. He will have heard of me.

"One more thing. Have you heard about the gold discovery in the mountains of central California?"

Jess shook his head.

"Seemed at first that this was like other discoveries in past years, more hope than reality. But this one seems real, so real that Californians of all stripes are running to the diggings. That includes deserters from ships moored in San Francisco Bay. If the sailors on your ship hear about this, they may decide their chances in the diggings are better than on that ship with that captain. Think about it, and I leave it to you whether you tell your captain or your shipmates."

Jess looked aside at Reuben, back to Larkin. "Mighty interesting," said Jess, frowning. "I'll think on it. But I sure won't mention it aboard ship."

Larkin smiled, turned to Green. "Talbot, Rico will be in this afternoon for his boards. I'm talking with John Black on Thursday. He should be able to give me some late word on our Honolulu shipment." He walked to the front door, turned back, "hope to see you boys again," and went out.

"Okay, fellas, if you need anything else, I'm here sunup to sundown," said Green.

Reuben shouldered the bag, nodded. "Thanks for everything."

"Take care of your own self, Reuben," Green said, pointing at Reuben.

Reuben and Jess went out. They stopped at the flagpole. Jess looked up at the Stars and Stripes, back to Reuben. "I take it you two had a talk before I arrived."

"Yeah, we did." Reuben looked around. "We talked about a lot of things, me and him and where we both come from." His eyes opened wide, he looked both ways on the street and leaned toward Jess. He spoke softly. "He don't hold to slavery, Jess! I hope I didn't mess up, but I told him I'm runnin' from the ship. He said if I come this way, he'll help me. And he said if I come this way to be real careful 'cause not everbody around here feel like he does. But he said he would help. When I leave the ship, I'll be on my own, and somebody on my side could give me a start. Maybe I'll go to the gold country. Do you think the people up there would let a black man try his hand at huntin' gold? What do you think?"

"Sounds good to me. I had worried about your chances once you left the ship. You know the captain. He'll take your running away personal, and he'll send a party to hunt you down. You're gonna have to get as far away as possible real fast. By the time we do this, we're going to be well into the hide business and I can't see the captain sparing men very long to search for you. On the other hand, knowing something about his temperament, he may decide you are more important to him personally than hides and tallow. He's not rational. If he comes after you, Reuben, you're not going to be hard to trace. I haven't seen many black people in California."

Reuben nodded. "Yeah, I've thought about that."

They went out to the road and walked in the sandy center toward the beach. Two Californio men walking toward them in the road dropped their heads and went around them. Reuben turned toward Jess.

"I'll disappear so fast," Reuben said, "you'll forget you ever knew me. Reuben? Who's Reuben?" He grinned.

Jess looked aside at him. "Not likely."

―――――

WEEKS PASSED, and the approach of winter brought colder temperatures and occasional rain squalls. Yet rancheros said this was the mildest winter they had seen in years. They and their vaqueros and the ship's crew were pleased since the process of preparing hides for the trade was well underway. "California banknotes," old hands called the hides. It took longer for the cleaning and drying than it would later in warmer weather, but all were content that they would do what they could in the cool weather.

Rancheros and their ladies were transported regularly by ship's boats from the beach to the *Enterprise* to investigate the goods offered by the Americanos. A cargo hold had been converted to a general store. The visitors saw tools of all sorts, bolts of silk and cotton, clothes for men and women, pins and needles, teas and coffee, spices, molasses, crockery, jewelry, combs, whiskey in abundance.

This late evening, Jess and Reuben stood at the top of the ladder at the ship's rail. They had just unloaded a half dozen prospective buyers and directed them to the store. Now they waited for a contingent of customers to finish their shopping and come to the rail for a return to the beach. A nattily dressed man with his wife and young daughter stood nearby at the rail, waiting for the departure of the next boat. Each held bulging bags.

Jess leaned on the rail beside Reuben, frowning, staring at the beach. He spoke softly to Reuben, still looking at the dusky coastline without looking at him. "Reuben, let's do it now. I always thought we would wait till we were collecting hides for you to get away, but the boats are going regularly to the beach for prospective customers. Sometimes we take a bunch in at near dark, and that's when you'll disappear. How about it? Tomorrow about this time of day?"

Reuben recoiled. He glanced sharply at Jess, then to the beach. "Been thinking 'bout it every day, but...tomorrow?" He nodded grimly. "Yeah. Tomorrow."

Chapter Two

JESS STOOD at the rudder while Reuben and three other crewmen pulled hard on the oars toward the beach. The sun behind them hovered over the horizon. A half dozen ship's customers huddled together on seats in the middle of the boat, looking nervously at the swells that lifted the boat at intervals. They clutched bags of purchases in their laps.

As they neared the shore, Jess called out: "Brace yourselves, folks!" realizing at once the absurdity of his warning since his English likely would be understood by no one.

When the bow lifted in the swell and gently touched bottom, Reuben jumped over the gunwale, waited for the next swell and pulled the boat as far forward as possible. The crewmen scrambled over the side into the shallows and helped passengers climb down. A couple of women shrieked, then laughed, when they stepped into water rather than sand as they had expected.

Reuben reached into the bow of the boat and

pulled out the boat's line and a canvas bundle. Tucking the bundle under an arm, he walked the bow rope toward a stake at the edge of the sandy beach, dropped the bundle at his feet in the tall grass and tied the bowline to the stake.

Jess looked back past the ship at the horizon where the glowing sun disc had just disappeared, coloring the lacy horizontal clouds hues of red and gray. He called to the boat oarsmen who sat and stood at the top of the sandy beach, smoking and chatting. "Half hour, boys. I need to find a bush." A couple of sailors waved to him. He walked past Reuben who looked up and continued fussing with the line at the stake.

Jess went to the small shack that served as a tack room for the horses Captain had procured from a ranchero in exchange for a few bottles of whiskey. The six horses stood quietly, heads hanging, in the corral behind the shack. Jess walked back to the building, looked around and confirmed that no one was watching. Out of anyone's view, he pulled a single key from his pocket. Each sailor who was assigned as landing boat supervisor was issued a key to the shack.

He unlocked the shack, went inside and quickly came out carrying a saddle and bridle. He looked around again, lowered the saddle and bridle silently to the ground and locked the door. Retrieving the bridle and saddle, he walked into heavy brush behind the tack room and deposited the saddle and bridle out of sight. Walking back into the open, he fussed with his pants, brushed his clothes and strolled to the landing.

"Okay, boys, let's go." The crewmen dropped smokes and followed. Jess untied the boat's line and coiled it as he walked to the boat. The others had taken up their positions in the boat. Jess dropped the line in the bow and began to push off.

"Wait a minute," said a crewman, "where's Reuben?"

"Ah," said Jess. He looked back to the shore. "He said he had to find a bush and wanted to talk to a couple of vaqueros at their camp. I told him we wouldn't wait on him if he wasn't here when we leave. He'll have to take the last boat."

He pointed at a boat that was just pulling away from the ship. "There it comes, last boat."

He grasped the bow, waiting for a swell. When the bow lifted, he pushed off and climbed over the gunwale into the boat. He bent and, hands on crewmen's shoulders, walked to the stern and took the rudder. Crewmen dipped oars into the surf and began to pull away from the shore. Jess looked back at the coast, the line of trees showing as a long shadow on the dark land.

Good luck, my friend.

———

CAPTAIN HARRIS WAS NOT long in learning that Reuben had not returned. He was accustomed to being attended at a moment's notice by his property. When the evening roll call confirmed Reuben's absence, the captain was furious. A few questions and threats revealed that he was last seen talking with Jess who the captain knew was Reuben's closest friend and confidant. Jess was summoned to the captain's cabin.

Jess stood before a glowering captain, seated at his desk.

"Explain," Captain said.

Jess swallowed. He had expected this confrontation and had rehearsed his reply a dozen times in his head. "He said he had to find a bush and then wanted to talk with some vaqueros at their camp. I told him that was not a good idea. He said he would hurry. I told him if he missed our boat, there was one more, and he better make that one."

The color and scowl on Harris's face had increased at Jess's every word. "Poppycock!" he shouted, banging his fist on the desk. "You knew! I've seen you two huddled and talking soft so nobody could hear. You probably planned it all! That black scoundrel doesn't have the brains to plan it. You're responsible! I'll have your hide for this!"

Both men jumped at a sudden loud knocking on the door. "What is it?" the captain shouted.

Through the door: "A ranchero who is leaving on his boat says he's coming back tomorrow morning and says he needs to ask you a question."

Harris pounded his fist hard on the desk. "Dammit!" He shook his head, pointed at Jess, mumbled incoherently. "Wait there!" He opened a drawer, fumbled with the contents and pulled out a key. He stood and strode to the door.

He opened the door, handed the key to the officer standing there. "Bennett, take this key. Lock that man there in the rope compartment." He pointed at Jess and spoke to him. "Damn you! I'll deal with you later." He strode down the passage-way, turned the corner.

Bennett motioned Jess to follow him. "Guess you got his ire up. I don't envy you a little bit." They walked in the passageway until Bennett stopped, unlocked a door and motioned Jess inside. "Good luck." He closed the door and locked it.

Well. You invited me to go with you, Reuben. Too bad I declined. Now what?

He fumbled in his pocket and pulled out a set of keys he used routinely when cleaning spaces. That was when he was in the captain's good graces, when he said Jess was the only crewman he could trust to have access to every compartment on the ship. *Guess he forgot he gave me the keys.* He tried a few keys until he found the one that unlocked the rope compartment door. He pushed the door open a crack, confirmed no one was in sight. He went out, relocked the door and crept down the ladder and passageway to the crew cabin in the forecastle.

He gathered a few pieces of clothing, pants, shirt, cap, and rolled everything in the shirt. Looking around to be sure no one else was in the cabin, he reached behind a bulkhead to retrieve a bundle of rags. Unwrapping the rags, he held his Colt Pater-son. He bought the new single-action pistol in Boston the same day he visited the pub and became a sailor. He shook his head, remembering. He recol-lected he was grateful that he had fortuitously carried the handgun with him in a bag that evening, also four loaded spare cylinders. He opened the bundle and pushed the pistol and cylinders inside.

Holding the rolled shirt, he went to the door of

the compartment, looked each way, then walked slowly in the passageway. He climbed the ladder carefully to the deck above. Turning a corner, he stopped before the captain's door. No light from inside showed under the door. He leaned against the door, his ear at the door edge. He heard nothing, then looked both ways in the passageway.

Do I dare? He reached into his pocket and pulled out the ring of keys. He leafed through the keys until he found the captain's. Looking both ways again, he pushed the key into the lock and opened the door slowly. When it creaked, he stopped, looked both ways in the passageway, tried to ignore the bead of sweat rolling down his cheek. He stepped inside and quickly, silently, closed the door.

Moonlight through the stern windows dimly illuminated the cabin. He went to the desk, pulled out the upper right drawer, picked up the pewter container he had seen the captain so often absent-mindedly swirling the coins inside. He lifted the container and emptied the coins slowly, silently, into a pants pocket. Replacing the container, he closed the drawer slowly. Going to the door, he opened it a crack, looked both ways and stepped outside. He closed the door and locked it.

Now he hurried. He climbed a ladder until his eyes were barely above the deck. He looked around, saw no one, climbed out to the deck. Bright moonlight cast shadows on the polished planking. He looked fore and aft, still saw no one, confirmed that no passenger boat was in sight and that other crewmen on board had likely gone down to the mess hall.

He walked quietly to the ladder and descended. He went to the boat that was always tied at the bottom of the ladder in case of unusual need. It was smaller than those used to transport passengers, but it still required four men at the oars.

I'll just have to pretend I'm a party of four. Stepping into the boat, he untied the line and pushed away. He sat down, took two oars and pulled toward the beach. *Bless the officer who only yesterday found a spot to anchor the ship considerably closer to the beach than the earlier anchorage.* He grunted as he pulled on the oars. *Uh-oh, just remembered. Gotta pull away from the direct route to the beach to be sure any boat coming to the ship doesn't see me. Damn. Hope I make it before sunrise.* He was too tired and stressed to smile at his attempt at humor.

He rested often, perspiring from the exertion, then shivering in the cold breeze, as the boat drifted slightly to starboard. Then he pulled again, grunting and breathing heavily. Finally, the bow touched the sandy beach a hundred yards north of the usual landing. He pulled the boat up as far as he could and tied the bow line to a low bush. *Don't want to deprive my shipmates of this little boat.*

He walked toward the main landing spot, saw the vaqueros' campfire a short distance inland. He crept past the landing to the tack shed. Reaching into a pants pocket, he found the shed key. He unlocked the door, went inside, felt around in the dark and located a saddle and bridle. Carrying them outside, he dropped the load beside his clothing bundle and relocked the door. He went to the heavy brush, dug a hole with his heel and dropped the shack key and the ring of ship's keys into it.

Covering the hole with loose soil, he pushed leafy debris over the hole.

He picked up the rolled shirt and went quickly to the corral. Searching in the near darkness, he located the mare he had ridden a number of times on visits to ranchos. He saddled and bridled her and tied the shirt bundle behind the cantle. Walking the mare from the corral, he closed the gate carefully.

We're gonna become good friends, little lady. Be good to me, and I'll be good to you.

Mounting, he rode into a thick pine wood, bending forward and pushing low boughs away, avoiding the vaqueros' campsite, the embers in the fire circle still visible.

Wish I could see Captain's face when he sees the empty pewter can. It wasn't theft. It was pay. Doubt Captain will agree. He smiled, but quickly sobered.

What now?

––––––––––

FIRST LIGHT. A band of golden light at the eastern horizon signaled the new day, a cold day. Jess reined up at a narrow, shallow stream. The mare dipped her muzzle into the water. Dismounting, he knelt and drank from his cupped hand. He wiped his face with a neckerchief, looking around. Since leaving the coast, he had seen thousands of cattle and horses, seemingly wild though he also lately saw a few vaqueros riding in the plain in the half light. Now he saw not a living soul or animal but his mare. He mounted and rode on a lightly-traveled trail that led inland.

The land on this early winter day was carpeted by green grasses surrounded by pine and oak woods. Clusters of bushes, some bare of leaves, others covered with brittle green leaves, dotted the landscape.

He looked behind, as he had scores of times since leaving the coast, to confirm that he was not being followed. He squinted at the sun ball that he had watched move from the eastern horizon almost to the western where it rested on the canopy of a line of oaks. He looked aside at a dozen cows that grazed only a few yards away. He was so hungry he had considered the prospect of killing a cow and enjoying a beefsteak. But he had no way to cook a beefsteak. Nor a knife to butcher a cow. His only nourishment since leaving the coast two days ago were some dry berries he couldn't identify. He hoped they weren't poison. His horse had fared better than he since there was good grazing every place he stopped.

Now he rode on a lightly traveled dusty road toward a cluster of structures that suggested a village. They proved to be small houses of adobe, some with fenced gardens and corrals enclosing one or more horses or mules. A man rubbing down a horse in a corral stopped, his hand on the animal's back, and watched Jess riding by. The man waved, and Jess responded with a wave.

Jess pulled up when the road turned in front of a substantial adobe building. It had a long covered porch fronted by a series of arches. One of the arches bore a crudely painted message: Wines Liquors Cigars.

In the dusty yard in front of the porch was a stone marker that read: Mission San Miguel Arcángel. The sign was crumbling at one end. Jess recalled a discourse by one of the crew who had been to the California coast twice before. He told about the string of missions that the Spanish had built in California a short distance inland from the coast.

"They ain't churches anymore," said another sailor. "They been closed and sold off. All the Indians that used to live at the missions have gone away. All the land the missions owned were given to ranchers."

Others at the table had listened with interest to this learned comment from one who always had little of interest to say.

Of more interest to Jess at this moment was the small wooden sign in front of the entrance to the building. The sign read: Mission Hotel - Rooms - Food, in Spanish and English. He decided at that moment he would say a prayer in the mission if it would get him a good meal and a place to sleep indoors that night.

He tied his reins to the rail, untied the small shirt bag from the cantle and walked to the double doors. Pushing a door open, he stepped inside and gaped. The long high-ceilinged room undoubtedly was the sanctuary when the building operated as a mission. The walls were covered with colorful paintings, and the ceiling arches were the color of gold. The floor at the far end stepped up, probably where the religious articles were displayed and where the padre stood to conduct services.

Instead of a church, the space now was a

cantina. A half dozen tables and chairs were arranged in the middle of the room, with a short bar against a wall. He guessed that a door behind the bar led to the kitchen. Only two tables were occupied. Two oldsters sitting at a table near the bar had stared silently at Jess since he came through the door.

Six men sat huddled at a table in front of a crackling fire in a brick fireplace. They did not appear to be vaqueros. At least, they were not dressed like the vaqueros he had encountered at the landing, those who were bringing hides and tallow to transport to the ship. He could not decide whether they were Californio or White. Their faces were brown, either from race or hard work in the sun. One appeared to be an Indian. The men looked at Jess standing at the entrance, then returned to their plates, eating slowly, stealing quick glances at the newcomer, mumbling softly.

"What can I do for you, young man?" Jess was startled by the voice behind him, English with what he guessed was an English accent.

"I could use a good meal and a room, if that's possible."

"We got both. Have a seat anywhere. What are you drinking? We got wine and aguardiente." He smiled.

Jess pulled out a chair at a round table, sat and exhaled deeply. "I'll have a plate and coffee, if you have it. I'll also try the ah-gar-dentee, whatever that is, as long as it doesn't take off the top of my head."

"National drink, translates to firewater in English. It's made from sugar cane, but it's not sweet. It'll make you feel good, or it'll make you feel bad, depending on your mood. On an empty stomach, it may erase all feeling whatsoever. Better drink your coffee and eat your meal first."

Jess nodded, and the man walked through the door to what Jess assumed was the kitchen.

He looked up at the vaulted ceiling and the wall paintings. *Pretty. Must have been even prettier when it was a church.* He was startled at raucous laughter from the men sitting before the fireplace. They talked with the young woman who stood there, holding an empty tray at her side.

Jess stared. She wore a loose simple dress that had been raised to a hem just below the knees, unlike the more common dress that almost touched the floor. She wore sandals, unlike the other older serving woman standing near the kitchen door, who was barefoot. The young woman's hair was shorter than that of other women he had seen on the coast, hardly reaching her shoulders. When she turned, he glimpsed a pretty face and a hint of a shapely body before she turned back to the patrons.

"Here you are, my good fellow."

Jess started at the voice. The man who had greeted him set a coffee cup and a filled plate of beef, potatoes and fried eggs on the table.

"And your introduction to aguardiente. Good luck. As I noted, eat first."

"Uh, may I ask, you're English?"

"Good ear, thought I'd lost it. Yep, been in California just a few years, long enough to learn some Spanish and corrupt my English. You know any Englishmen around here?"

"Not here, Boston."

"Boston! You're from Boston! I landed in Boston before coming to California." He pulled out a chair. "You mind if I join you for a little chat?"

"Please do."

He sat, raised a hand and called to the young woman standing at the other table. "Aguardiente for me, please." She waved, walked toward the kitchen door.

The man motioned toward Jess's plate. "Eat, eat, then we'll drink together. Boston." He smiled, leaned back. "I liked Boston, thought about settling there, but the prospects weren't good. I talked with some whalers and hide and tallow men on the waterfront." He grinned. "I was a sailor myself a while back, and I know these places. All these men strongly advised me to think about California. That was a few years ago. I had my family with me this time and still hadn't decided on where to settle. I finally decided on California, and here I am. I bought the mission property in summer of '46 and been here ever since. I like it.

"California has prospects, especially now that it will soon be part of the United States. Yeah, I know all about the war. Everybody who stops here, from north or south, has something to say about the war. It's over, you know. All that's left in the change is formality. I'm William Reed, by the way." He extended a hand.

Jess took the hand and shook. "Jess Winslow."

The men looked up when the young woman set a glass of aguardiente before Reed. Jess slowly lowered the fork to his plate. He was stunned. *My, you are a pretty little thing!* She smiled, revealing small dimples. Her black eyes seemed to sparkle, and he had an overwhelming impulse to touch a soft brown cheek.

"Another?" she said to Jess and pointed at his cup and glass. His trance was broken. He shook his head, said nothing. She turned abruptly toward the men at the fireplace who called and waved her to come. She walked toward the group, glanced back over her shoulder and smiled again at Jess.

Jess watched her go, his fork held motionless above his plate.

Reed laughed. "Yeah, she's a sweetie. Been with us since we bought the place. I swear every fella comes in here tries to make a play for her." He smiled and leaned forward, looking at the six at the fireplace. He spoke softly. "Watch this. See the fella in the serape on her right? See that loose arm. He's going to try to touch her butt."

As they watched, the man slowly reached an arm behind her. She stepped aside, held up the tray as if preparing to strike him with it. She shook a finger in his face and said something sharply to him. He recoiled, laughed with the others at the table.

"Whatever he said, they thought it was funny," said Reed. "She didn't. If he had touched her, she would have knocked him out of his chair with that tray. I've had to step in on occasion, but for the most part, she doesn't need my help. She can take care of herself."

Reed stood. "I'll stop my blabbing and let you finish your meal." He went to stand behind the bar and watched Jess until he had cleaned his plate and finished half his glass of aguardiente.

Jess shook his head, looking at the glass. *Wow. That firewater is…fiery.*

Reed walked to the table. "Done?" He pointed at the glass. Jess nodded. "Now, I'll show you to your room." Jess stood, and they went to the door.

Outside, they walked under the covered porch. "I've had your horse tended to. She's in the corral behind the building, saddle, and bridle in the shed next to the corral. You'll find it."

They stopped at a door. Reed opened the door and pushed it inside. "This was a priest's room, closest to the sanctuary. It was simple then and simple now. Let me know if you need anything. Come back for a drink before bed. Like to talk some more with you. Don't get many Americans, though I expect we'll see more of the like soon." He smiled, backed out, and closed the door.

The priest's room was sparse. A single wood-framed bed, a small dresser of the same style. A cross and candle holder with a short candle were on the desk, also a bowl of water at the end. Hanging on the wall above the desk, a small wooden crucifix with Jesus nailed on the cross, adorned with a crown of thorns and bleeding side. Four pegs on the wall supposedly for hanging vestments and pants, and shirts and coats.

Jess set his bundle on the foot of the bed. He exhaled heavily, sat on the bed, and lay back, his arms crossed over his chest. He stared at the ceiling.

Quo vadis. His sixth-grade teacher, his last school year, said it often. *Quo vadis.* The teacher said it was the most profound saying in any language. Where are you going? What now? Where do you go from here? He wished his sixth-grade teacher, or anyone, could answer that question for him at this moment. He had no idea where he was going. He only knew he was running from a life he hadn't chosen and did not wish to continue.

He dozed. After an hour that seemed only minutes, he woke with a start and sat up abruptly. *Agardentee. Hmm.* He took a few coins from the bundle and dropped the bundle on the bed. He thought about it a bit, picked up the bundle, carried it under an arm and walked to the cantina.

Reed stood behind the bar, talking with two men who lounged there, holding their glasses on the bar top. He saw Jess come through the door. Waving, he hurried to the open kitchen door. "Lorenzo!" he shouted.

A gray-haired man came out immediately, wiping his hands with a cloth. Reed said something to him, and something to the two men standing at the bar. Reed poured two glasses of aguardiente and picked them up. The two men frowned, exchanged a comment with Reed, who gestured toward Jess. The two men looked around and saw Jess. One smiled, raised his glass to him.

Reed gestured with a glass toward a table against the wall. The six scruffy characters still sat at their table before the fireplace. Or they had left and returned while Jess was sleeping. Their conversation was loud, they laughed and cursed each other and others, named and unnamed, continually. They conversed in English, but also some Spanish.

Reed set the glasses on the table, sat down and exhaled heavily. "Would you like something to eat with your drink?"

"No, I'm okay."

Reed smiled awkwardly and his speech suggested that he had not been idle since Jess saw him earlier. He had been depleting his aguardiente supply. Reed leaned over the table, intent on learning everything about Jess and telling everything about himself.

"I'm happy to serve an American, Jess," Reed said, smiling. "I expect more Americans to be coming my way now that the war is over. That bunch at the fireplace are mostly Americans, come down from the gold placers in the foothills of the Sierra Nevada north of here. Gold was discovered earlier this year, and Californians of all stripes are headin' for the diggings. Sailors are deserting ships and farmers leaving their fields. Immigrants coming over the Sierra from back east that had planned to farm or go into commerce are instead going to the gold streams. They'll likely be disappointed. Gold discoveries happen occasionally in California, and they end as quickly as they begin.

"It used to be that we would see only a few travelers here, but now we see lots more. My place is on the only road to speak of between north and south. The old Spaniards got it right. They built a string of missions from San Diego to San Francisco, one day's ride between missions. Each mission got the local Indians to live at the mission and work there." He took a liberal swallow of aguardiente. "Let me put it another way. They forced the local Indians to live and work at the mission and punished any who didn't fall in line. Now that the missions are no longer places of worship and the Indians not required to live and work there, the Indians are not doing well. They sorta forgot the old ways when they were attached to the missions."

Reed took another swallow, leaned back, swung his arm around to encompass the cantina. "What do you think of my place? This was where they held worship, you know. I'm told the paintings on the walls were done by Indians under a master Spanish artist. Some Californios who have been up and down the trail tell me these paintings are the best they have seen at any mission."

"Pretty," said Jess. "I'm impressed. Would have been a nice place for believers to worship."

"Well, I don't know whether the Indians were true believers, but they had no choice. For them, it was 'believe and obey' or watch out." He snorted.

Jess sipped from his glass, squinted. "How is it an Englishman bought a mission and runs a hotel and cantina in it?"

He laughed. "Hah! That's a question I get all the time. And after a few drinks they also ask where did I get the money to buy this big place? And they say are you one of those rich English lords we hear about?" He sniffed, took a generous swallow of fire-water, squinted. "No, my friend, I say, Governor Pico almost gave it to me. The mission closed down in '34 and had been settin' idle and decaying since then. I bought it in '46, gave him the little money I had and got to work. I didn't have much cash then, you see, but I do now." He leaned toward Jess. "I got gold! What do yah think about that?" He drained his glass, leaned back in his chair, grinning close-mouthed.

The six at the fireplace huddled together, but it was Reed that held their attention. At Reed's boisterous mention of gold, they had been struck silent. Now, they talked softly among themselves, but stole sideways glances at Reed and Jess.

Jess frowned. He didn't know what he thought about it. He had not heard about gold in California before his conversation with Larkin. On the other hand, according to Reed, the men at the fireplace table knew about gold in California. They had worked in the diggings up north. That they left the diggings could be evidence they had not found enough to keep them there. But it was common knowledge that some miners were successful. Maybe Reed was one of those. The instant Reed mentioned gold, Jess saw over Reed's shoulder that the six stopped their chatter instantly and listened, leaning over their table, eyes downcast, glancing furtively at each other.

"When I tell this story," Reed said, "people always say, 'where'd you get gold, Reed. There ain't no gold 'round here.' I say, sure 'nough there ain't." He squinted, tapped the side of his nose with a finger.

Jess frowned, started to question Reed, but Reed stood abruptly when Lorenzo, standing at the bar, called him. Reed pointed at Lorenzo and went to him. The two walked through the door to the kitchen.

Jess decided that he had endured enough of Reed's tales and his aguardiente for the evening. He pushed his half-full glass away, rose and walked toward the door, then stopped. The young woman had just come through the kitchen door and went to stand behind the bar. She saw him and smiled, just a hint of a smile. He was paralyzed, wondering whether he dared go to her, to speak to her. Then a customer called. Her smile vanished, and she went toward the customer's table. Jess watched her only a moment, then walked to the door.

———

JESS SAT AT A TABLE, his bundle on the floor beside the chair, his empty plate on the table. He had slept late and decided on an early lunch before setting out. He sipped his coffee, studying the vaulted ceiling and colorful painted walls. *What a beautiful place to worship. I suppose a believer could see a hint of heaven in such a place.*

The young woman came through the kitchen door, carrying two plates. She smiled at him as she passed and placed the plates on a table where two vaqueros sat. She glanced aside at him as she went back to stand behind the bar.

Jess held up his coffee cup. She poured into a cup at the bar and brought it to him. "Thank you," he said. "Uh, can you sit?"

She frowned, looked around. She saw Reed who had just come through the kitchen door. She pointed at the chair. Reed nodded, waved to Jess. She pulled the chair out slowly and sat.

"I'm Jess Winslow."

"I'm Sallie."

"Sallie." That's not Spanish, is it?

"No. And I not Spanish. Or Mexican. I was baptized Maria Jesusa, right here when this was still a mission. I do not like this name and do not answer to it. I answer only to the name of my people. My Salinan name is Sallie."

"I don't know the Salinan. They live around here?"

"We have lived here since the beginning. When the Spanish and Mexicans came, they made the Salinan people live and work at mission. The priests said we must learn Spanish and stop speaking our language. Many refused and were punished. That was long, long ago."

"You speak good English."

"I have worked for Mr. Reed since he bought mission. His wife, Cybil, is good woman. She wanted me to speak good English, so she taught me and talked with me every day. I taught her some of my language too. I don't know much. Nobody knows much Salinan. I so sad that most of our people know little of the Salinan language today. The language is disappearing."

"It's good that you try to keep your native language, as well as your English."

"I speak Spanish also, and I can talk with two other Indian peoples in their languages." She cocked her head, smiling. "How many languages do you speak?"

He smiled. "I think you know the answer to that question. I speak only English. Most Americans, and English too, I suppose, speak only English. How about Reed?"

"He knows a little Spanish, not a word of Sali-nan." She looked aside. Reed, standing behind the bar, nodded to her. "I think I go back to work now." She stood, stepped aside and pushed the chair back under the table. "Goodbye, Jess Winslow." She walked to the kitchen door.

———

JESS STOOD at the hitching rail, tying a bundle to the cantle. The bundle contained his shirt sack wrapped in the blanket he bought from Reed. He looked up, squinting. The sun was almost overhead. He regretted he had wasted the morning, then remembered the conversation with Sallie.

As if in response, she stepped through the door, turned and looked straight at him. He paused, uncertain, pondering. Then the six men who sat last evening at the fireplace strode down the porch, commenting and laughing as they passed her. She took a step backward to avoid them, looked once more at Jess and went back through the door. The men walked off the porch toward the corral.

Jess stood beside the mare, holding reins and staring at the saddle, motionless a long moment. *Quo vadis?* He mounted and rode at a slow walk on the road in front of the mission. He went across a flat plain of lush short green grass, pulled his coat collar up against the brisk cold breeze. He didn't see Sallie who had come out again and watched him turn north.

He had covered hardly a hundred yards to a line of scattered oaks when he stopped. Quo Vadis. *Stop it!* He looked back at the mission. There was no one about except a couple of men who rode slowly on the road in front of the building.

He dismounted, tied the reins to a sapling. Sitting on a large, downed tree limb, he stared at the grassy flat. What to do? Where to go? He had to move farther from the landing in case the captain had sent men searching for him. Perhaps he would go to Monterey to find a ship he could sign on. Or visit Larkin to see what opportunity he might offer. Perhaps continue to San Francisco where he might find a ship or some other prospect. Or turn south to Santa Barbara or Los Angeles or San Diego? *Should be prospects there.*

He shook his head, knowing he was evading what he really needed to settle. What to do about Sallie. He untied the mare's reins and led her into the copse to a small stagnant pool. After the horse drank her fill, he led her back to the edge of the line of trees where he had a view of the mission. Standing there, pondering, he removed the hobbles from saddlebags and hobbled the horse in a sunny spot on a patch of green grass.

He sat on the log until sunset became dusk. Removing the blanket from the cantle, he spread it beside the log, lay down and pulled the blanket over him.

Chapter Three

"JESS! Jess! Help me! Oh, help me."

Jess bolted upright. In the dim first light of morning, he saw Sallie running, stumbling toward him. He stood in time to catch her as she collapsed at his feet. He knelt and held her as she sobbed convulsively. He stood slowly, pulled her to her feet and walked to the log, almost dragging her. They sat on the log, and she leaned against him.

"Tell me what's wrong," Jess said softly.

She swallowed, wiped her face with her scarf. Jess relaxed his hold on her, but she still leaned on him.

"Slowly now, tell me what's happened," said Jess.

She choked back a sob, wiped her eyes with a hand. "The men, the men who sat at the fireplace, they left yesterday when you did. You saw them leave?"

"Yes."

"They came back last night, this morning, before the sun came up. It was still almost dark. I had just come to kitchen. I always come in before anybody else, just before daylight, to get ready for breakfast. I heard front door smash open. It is always locked, but it's an old lock, and they broke it and came in. I ran to a cupboard and hid behind it.

"They went all over the building, into bedrooms and stables and toilets and everyplace. They caught people. They shouted 'where is the gold, where is the gold?' in English and Spanish. The people said, 'I don't know, I don't know.' The men got more and more angry, and they killed them, Jess, they killed them," she said softly, sobbing, rocking back and forth. "They killed them with axes and hammers. They kill everybody in the mission. I was afraid they would find me. I was crying, trying to be quiet but I could not stop crying."

"I'm so sorry, Sallie. They couldn't have missed hearing Reed talking about his gold."

"Yes, they heard him say he had gold, and they came back to get it. When they couldn't find it, they went crazy." She wiped her eyes, inhaled deeply, leaned on Jess. "They kill everybody," she said softly.

"I'm so sorry." He held her close. "You saw them leave?"

"Yes, they gone. I heard them ride away. I did not come out from hiding place until I heard nothing else. Then I came out and saw what they had done. Jess, there are dead people all over. They are all dead." She collapsed against his chest and sobbed, shaking, rocking back and forth.

"Stay there." He stood, tossed his bag on the blanket and rolled it up. Fetching the bridle, he hefted the saddle and went to the horse. He bridled and saddled the horse and tied the blanket behind the cantle. Removing the hobbles, he pushed them into the saddlebag.

He took her hand and helped her stand. "We're going down. Can you do this?"

She sniffed, wiped her cheek and nodded. Mounting, he pulled her up behind him. He kicked the horse into a lope toward the mission.

———

"Oh, my God in Heaven." Jess stood with Sallie in what once was the sanctuary, a place of worship. Now it was an abattoir. Bloodied bodies were strewn about the dining room, the kitchen, hallways, the patio outside the kitchen. Opening a door to a bedroom, Jess pushed Sallie back, refusing to let her see inside. There on the bedroom floor lay the bodies of Reed, his wife and unborn child and their young son. Reed's head was split open. The axe, covered in blood, lay at his side. His wife's throat was slit.

Jess counted ten bodies in the building. He tried to convince Sallie to stay on the porch while he surveyed the carnage, but she insisted that she must see. These were her people, she said, her Salinan people and the English and Mexican people she considered dear friends.

They rode to Chulam, a village less than a mile from the mission, where she said relatives and friends of the slain lived. Sallie told them what happened. The people were aghast at the news. They said they would pray for the souls of the dead, and they would avenge them with swift justice.

At a village gathering that same evening, a small party of six volunteered to gather the dead and bury them. This group was led by Petronillo Rios who lived in a nearby adobe.

"Rios was a partner to Reed," Sallie said. "He bought things Reed needed for the hotel and saloon. He was rarely inside the building except during deliveries. He lucky not to be there yesterday."

A larger party, a posse of thirty-seven, was formed to apprehend the killers. Standing at the back of the gathering, Jess told Sallie he would join the posse, but only if she would wait for him. She said she would stay with a distant cousin who lived in Chulam, but only if he promised to return to her. They looked into each other's eyes. He took her face in both hands and lightly kissed her lips. She put her arms around his neck and held him.

"You come back to me," she said softly. He kissed her again.

Kin and friends, Sallie among them, waved to the posse members when they set out at a lope. Esteban, who had been elected to lead the group, called a halt after a ride of only a few miles to ask a solitary walker if he had seen the fugitives. Yes, he said he saw a group who matched the description. They went that way, he said, pointing south on the road.

―――――

THE POSSE CONTINUED on the road for four days, asking horsemen and walkers for information. Most had nothing to tell them, but some said they had seen a party of horsemen that were probably the bunch they were chasing. They pointed southward. The posse stopped nights at inns or camped in secluded groves.

In the foothills above Santa Barbara, a walker said he saw a group only an hour ago that seemed to be the party described. The men were headed toward the beach, he said. The posse kicked their horses to a gallop.

"There they are!" shouted Esteban.

He pointed toward the culprits, sitting at the edge of the beach. Their horses were tethered to the branches of nearby pines.

Posse members drew pistols and rifles and galloped toward the men, firing at them. The six jumped up and ran in all directions. One bandit was hit and fell. Another ran toward the surf where he was hit and fell into a wave. Others stopped running and raised their hands.

At Esteban's instruction, the men who surrendered were tethered and sent off under guard to authorities in Santa Barbara. Jess did not understand Esteban's instructions in Spanish to the guard. The instruction was translated later by a posse member. "He said they might have trouble finding an authority. Would they be Californio? Americano? Esteban said they were not to turn them over to any authority unless they promised to execute the men. If the authority would not promise, the guard was to take the men away and shoot them."

Jess answered with one of the few Spanish expressions he had learned: "Bien." Good.

The posse mounted and rode up into the foothills, bound for San Miguel. The bodies of the bandits were left where they fell. Before the posse left the beach, crows already were pecking at the carcasses.

———

POSSE MEMBERS DISPERSED on the outskirts of Chulam. Jess rode to the adobe where he had said goodbye to Sallie. She had seen other members of the posse ride by, and she now stood in front. He reined up and dismounted. She came to him and put her arms around his neck. He took her cheeks in his hands and kissed her.

"Is it finished?" she said.

"Yes, all finished. You'll hear all about it, but not from me. All conversation was in Spanish. You're going to have to teach me Spanish, you know, maybe some of your Salinan language."

She frowned. "I don't understand." She looked down. "I'm so confused."

He raised her chin, looked into her eyes. "I hope you're going with me."

Her eyes opened wide. A tear rolled down a cheek. "I have no one. Everybody here says the cantina and hotel will close. I don't know what I will do."

"Then I will tell you. You are going with me. Is that okay? Will you do that?"

She hesitated. "Are you sure? Yes, I will go. I want to be with you."

He took her in his arms and held her. She put

her arms around his waist and rested her head on his shoulder, her eyes closed.

She released him, looked into his eyes a moment. "I will get some things from my room at the hotel. There is no one there now. I will ask Mr. Rios if it's okay for me to go inside." She pursed her lips, looked aside. "Stay here. I will go to Mr. Rios now."

She walked down the road to a cluster of adobes. Jess sat on the low adobe wall, his head hanging, pondering this new stage of his life, an altogether promising stage.

She was gone only a few minutes. "He said none of the doors are locked. Everything of any value has been taken out, and there is nothing for anyone to steal. He hoped my things had not been taken by someone." She took his hand and led him toward the hotel building.

They walked down the covered porch to her small room at the end. The door was open. Inside, she went to the chest holding her things. The top was open, and the contents were in a jumble. Nothing seemed to be missing, she said. He watched her as she chose a few pieces of clothing and personal items, combs, a small crucifix on a chain. Wiping tears from a cheek, she pushed the things into a small cloth bag. She took his hand, and they went to the door and outside. Looking back inside, she bowed her head and leaned on his chest.

"This was my home. I was born in Chulam and christened at the mission and worshipped here. I was taught here. I worked here. I have known no other place." She put her arms around his waist and sobbed.

"Sallie," he said softly, "we will find another place, a place that you will make your own. I promise."

She sniffed, wiped her eyes and nose with a sleeve, looked up. "Okay, you promise." They walked down the arched walkway. When they reached the cantina door, she stopped, looked down, frowning. She took his sleeve, looked up at him. "There's something. Come inside."

They went through the door, and she closed it. There was no one in the room. Tables and chairs were overturned and thrown about. They raised a table upright, each picked up a chair, and they sat.

She clasped her hands on the table, inhaled deeply, looked up at him. "Remember when Mr. Reed said he had gold?" Jess frowned, nodded. "The bad men heard him say it, and they came back for it. When they couldn't find it, they killed everybody."

He waited.

"Jess, Mr. Reed did have gold, a lot of gold." Jess straightened, frowning. "Listen. Just after I started working for him, there was a story passed around that gold had been found years ago in San Feliciano Canyon, not far from here. That was when the missions were still under the friars. Mr. Reed decided to investigate the story and found an old man in Chulam who had been part of a group that had found gold in that canyon.

"The old man told Mr. Reed the story. He said that the men who found the gold reported to the San Miguel friar and gave him the gold. The friar was not interested. He told the men not to talk about the gold because it would cause a gold rush, and that would not be good for the work of the mission. The men were good Christians who always obeyed the instructions of the friars, or they were afraid of them. Anyway, they obeyed. The gold was forgotten. I don't know what happened to that gold.

"Mr. Reed wondered whether there was still gold at San Feliciano Canyon. He decided to send men down there. I asked him to let me go with them. He said it was men's work, but I kept on him, and he agreed. We found gold, Jess. We found flakes and nuggets. I found more gold than any man." She smiled smugly. "I stayed only two months, but the men stayed and worked there almost a year. They took lots of gold, sacks and sacks. They gave the gold to Mr. Reed who paid them with goods. He told us to say nothing about the gold to anybody, and we didn't."

"What happened to the gold?"

"We buried it."

His eyes opened wide. "You buried this gold? Where? You know where it is buried?"

"Yes. I helped Mr. Reed bury it."

"And it was never dug up?

"No. Mr. Reed would have told me."

Jess leaned back, studying his hands on the table, frowning, his brain churning. After a long moment, he looked at her. "Did Reed have family?"

"He told me he and his wife had no family, in the United States or England. He said that's why they left England."

"Then the gold belongs to…"

"Nobody. Maybe it belongs to us."

———

BRIGHT MOONLIGHT ILLUMINATED the yard beside what had been the sanctuary. Tying their horses behind a storage shed, Sallie grasped Jess's sleeve and pulled him to a corner where a storeroom joined the sanctuary. He carried a shovel Sallie had taken from a hotel shed.

She pointed. "Right here at the corner, right up against the wall."

He looked around and confirmed that no one was in sight. He bent forward and pushed the shovel slowly and noiselessly into the dry soil. He removed shovel after shovel of loose soil, grunting with the effort.

After he had opened a hole two feet deep, he straightened, flexed his back. "You're sure this is the place?"

"Yes. Dig."

"Yes, ma'am, you say so." He pushed the shovel again and again into the ground, removing soil, deepening the hole. He straightened, puffing, rubbed his back. "It's knee deep. Are you sure about this?"

"Yes, dig."

He frowned, rubbed his back, bent and pushed the shovel into the hole. After a moment, he paused, looked up at her. He pushed the shovel firmly, then bounced it gently. The metallic thump was unmistakable. Now he dug with a renewed purpose. He soon had cleared the soil around a metal box about one and a half feet square. Bending, he rocked the box until it was free. On his knees and leaning down, he lifted the heavy box from the hole, grunting, and lowered it to the mound of loose soil.

He tried to lift the top, but it would not budge. He examined the top, found no lock. He stood and used the shovel to pry the top open. And there it was. He dropped to his knees and took from the box a small canvas bag. Untying the cord, he dumped a dozen or so small gold nuggets into his palm. He looked up at Sallie. He replaced the nuggets and opened another bag. He looked inside, stuck in a finger.

"Dust," he said. He replaced the bag, stood up, still looking at the box. "Must be a couple dozen bags." He looked at her, frowning, pondering. He looked around, squinting into the darkness, suddenly conscious of what had transpired here. "We need to be on our way."

She looked at the box. "I don't feel good about taking it all. I think…I want to give some to Mr. Rios. Let him do with it whatever he wants."

He frowned. "Hmm. Okay, that's a good idea. How about a third of the bags?"

"Yes, that's good."

"Go to the kitchen. Find a strong bag, and we'll put Rios's share in it. Also see if you can find some cords to tie up the box so I can attach it to my saddlebags." She hurried toward the kitchen back door.

By the time he had refilled the hole, she was back. He went to a knee beside the box, took out the bags of dust and nuggets for Rios. She placed them into the large bag and tied the top. Meanwhile, he wrapped cords around the box and tied them securely. Hefting the box and sack, they went to their horses. He stopped, thought better about how to transport the gold and untied the cords around the box. Removing the sacks one at a time, he pushed them into both sides of his large saddle bags, filling the bags. He patted the horse's rump.

"Sorry, little pard, this is going to add some weight, but can't help it."

The mare shifted and snorted. He looked around, saw a pile of rubbish under a tree. He pushed bottles and decayed boards aside, dropped the metal box into the debris and covered it with trash. He kicked together some debris and leaves and scattered them over the hole where he had removed the box.

He went to Sallie and helped tie her bag behind the cantle. They had just that afternoon bought the mare and tack for her, Jess silently thanking the ship's captain for his contribution. They mounted and rode by moonlight a short distance to Rios's adobe. While Jess held her reins, Sallie removed the bags from her saddle and went to Rios's door. She stacked the gold sacks at the base of a prickly pear cactus beside the door. Hurrying back to her horse, she mounted and nodded to Jess. They walked their horses to the mission road and turned north.

"Hope nobody steals the gold," said Jess.

"They would not dare. I left a note: 'Mr. Rios, Mr. Reed left this for you.' That's all they will know. They will be pleased, but also surprised. I can almost hear them saying: 'where did this come from?'"

He smiled, shook his head. "Oh, yeah? Who else called them Mr. Rios and Mr. Reed?"

———

"GLAD YOU THOUGHT to get lunch from the kitchen," Jess said. They sat on a log at the edge of a meadow of green grass, glistening from an overnight sprinkle, just off the road. Their hobbled horses grazed nearby. The sun in a clear blue sky warmed them on this mild winter day.

"We'll reach San Antonio de Padua before dark," she said. "They have rooms and a cantina, just like San Miguel. I hope you still have some coins or we'll be sleeping outside." She frowned, looked up at him. "Uh, Jess, are we going to be sleeping together?"

He smiled. "Yes, ma'am, we'll likely be sleeping together…unless you have any objections. Cheaper that way than renting two beds." He leaned against her, kissed her cheek.

"Some people may not like it if they know we are sleeping together, and we're not married."

He frowned. "Really? Hmm. Well, if the subject comes up, I'll just say that you're my slave. I think there are slaves in California, aren't there? I knew a slave aboard ship."

She shook her head. "No, you cannot say I am your slave. Anyway, if people see us together, they will know I am not your slave. They will know I know more than you. They will hear you asking me questions, and they will hear me answering. They will know I know more than you." She looked up at him, a smile playing about her lips.

He looked into her eyes. "My, my, what am I gettin' myself into?"

———

"TELL me about San Antonio de Padua," he said. They rode at a walk on the lightly-traveled road.

She looked ahead. "We'll be there soon. I visit San Antonio de Padua twice, once as a girl and once two years ago. It was spring, and the valley was covered with wildflowers. It was so pretty. I told you the padres forced the Indians to live and work at the missions. The people at San Antonio de Padua were Salinan and Yokuts. They plowed fields, worked in shops, cooked food and did weaving. When the government closed the missions, the Indian people were on their own, but most had forgotten how to live by themselves, and they suffered. Some have little farms now, but most of the mission land went to the big rancheros. Since the San Miguel mission closed, the number of Salinan people has gone down. Same at San Antonio de Padua, I think.

"Jess, the Salinan people know nothing of their past. Some of the really old people can remember stories told by their grandparents, but even those people have little memory of the Salinan tribe. We weren't even called Salinan. We were called Mission Indians or neophytes. Most Salinan people today speak no Salinan, only Spanish. They don't have Salinan names. Soon there will be no Salinan culture or language. There will soon be no Salinan tribe, only poor people with no ties to the past, no beliefs."

"But you have a Salinan name?"

"I talked with many old people, and some thought they knew some names, but they weren't sure. I made up my name. I knew no one called Sallie. I made it up. I wanted to know the past before the Spanish and Mexicans made my people come and live and work in the missions and believe in their God. Everything the Salinan people believed in the old days the fathers called superstition. They said the people had to believe what Christian fathers believed. I have heard only faint hints of what Salinan people believed before Spanish and Mexicans came. I *want* to know, Jess, but where can I learn about my tribe when the oldest people know nothing of their past?

"Jess, when government in Mexico decided to end the missions, they decided to ask the Indian people at the missions to decide whether they wanted to receive mission land and become landowners or stay at the missions with their padre.

"I heard what happened at San Miguel. The government man had all the Salinan people come to the mission and listen to him. He talked about the advantages of freedom, working on their own with no one telling them what to do. The people said they had nothing to work with and the land was poor. They said they would not know what to do. Where would they live? Many people lived inside at the mission. There were adobe houses for them behind the mission. Maybe you didn't see them. They are beginning to fall down now. Nobody lives there.

"The government man at San Miguel finally said he was finished talking. He gathered all the people together one day. He said for all who wanted to stay with the padre to move to his left and those who chose freedom and become landowners to move to his right. Jess, almost everybody went to his left. The few who went to his right, when they saw all the others on his left, went to his left. So all the people at San Miguel said they wanted to stay with the padre. That's how much they had lost their way.

"But it didn't matter. The government finally decided not to give them a choice. They sold most mission lands to rancheros, or gave the lands to them, and the Indian people got nothing. They still worked at the mission on the little lands the mission still owned. Soon there was no padre at the mission, and the government put an administrator in charge who was not a good man. He whipped Indians who he said were not working and some who tried to run away."

Jess didn't know what to say. How could he respond to this sad story of the decline of a culture and people? He had heard similar stories of the end of a way of life among Kentucky tribes. He had never thought much about it, assuming it was an inevitable result of the defeat and assimilation of native people everywhere. *Progress*, he thought.

"Sallie, pull up here. Gotta find a bush."

He reined off the road and walked his horse into an oak copse. She reined up, dismounted and tied her reins to a low limb of a large oak.

He did his business, untied the reins and led the horse from the woods. He stopped abruptly when he saw three men standing before Sallie, two holding knives pointed at her. Two of the men were oldsters, the third younger. All were scruffy, their clothes ragged and dirty, their matted hair that had not seen soap or comb in months. He guessed they were Indians, and more frightened than belligerent.

"What's this!" Jess said. The men straightened at Jess's outburst, but recovered. The oldster with a knife thrust it toward Sallie.

She turned to Jess. "They say they want money."

Jess simply stared.

The speaker pointed his knife toward Jess. "Tu… tu pareces americano. Tienes dinero. Suéltalo!"

"What did he say?" Jess said.

"He said you look like an Americano, and you have money. He said to give it to them."

Jess hesitated, glaring at the men. "He did, did he?" He turned to Sallie, frowning. "Tell him I have money and I'll give it to him."

She stiffened. "Jess! You must not! We can fight them."

He fought the impulse to smile. *My little wildcat.* He walked to his horse, put a hand on the saddlebag.

"Jess, don't!"

He untied the cord on a bag and opened it. Reaching into the bag, he turned back slowly to face the men. He held the Colt at his chest, walked a few steps toward the men, lowered the pistol to level on them.

The three were aghast. They dropped the knives and one of the oldsters fell to his knees. "No, señor, no," said the man on his knees. "No somos malos. Es que tenemos hambre."

"Jess, he said they are not bad people. He said they are hungry."

Jess pondered, looking from the men to Sallie. He lowered the Colt, pushed the other hand into a pants pocket, fumbled a bit, and pulled out two coins. He gave her the coins and pointed to the oldster on his knees. The man's eyes opened wide in surprise. He took the coins and stared at them, open-mouthed. He stood with some difficulty and showed the coins to the others who stared at the coins, jaws hanging. They looked up at Jess, then Sallie, wide-eyed.

"Gracias, señor, señorita, muchas gracias," one of the men said. They backed away and began walking on the side of the road northward. One of the men turned, bowed repeatedly as he walked.

Jess and Sallie watched them a moment. "I didn't know whether to shoot 'em or feel sorry for 'em," said Jess.

"You did the right thing. That's what happened to so many Indian people after the missions closed. They had no land and no place, and no one to tell them what to do. They became beggars."

————

SAN ANTONIO DE PADUA. They sat their horses before the building that had once been a mission, the setting sun behind a line of oaks casting slivers of light on the long, arched adobe porch. They dismounted and tied reins to the hitching rail. Sallie said something in Spanish to a man who walked on a path from the main mission building. He replied, pointing toward an entry through a wall topped with a bell tower and cross. The main building behind the wall was topped by another cross.

"He said they have food and rooms for travelers. He said go to that door," she said, pointing. Jess untied his saddlebag and rolled blanket. She untied her bag from the cantle and threw it over a shoulder.

They went under the archway and through the door into a cantina. Sallie hailed a woman who was clearing dishes and spoke to her. The woman straightened, flexed her back and beckoned. She led them through a door to a hallway where she said something to a man who sat at a table, smoking and staring at the opposite wall. Sallie spoke to him. He nodded, stood slowly and without a word ambled slowly down the hall to a doorway. Opening the door, he invited them in with an outstretched arm. He spoke briefly in Spanish to Sallie and sauntered back toward his table.

The room was furnished with a double bed, a chest against a wall, a table against another wall, and two chairs. All were of rough construction. And that was all. No ornamentation of any sort. The room obviously was meant for travelers and had not seen residents for many years.

A thick wool blanket covered the mattress. He looked at her. "Finally, we're going to be warm." Since leaving San Miguel, they had slept on the ground on horse blankets, fully clothed, rolled up in the single blanket he bought from Reed, shivering, clinging to each other for warmth on the cold nights.

He put his arms around her and pulled her close. "Finally."

———

THE SALOON REVEALED some little evidence of its location within what had been a functioning mission just fifteen years before. Windows appeared more appropriate for a church than a saloon, and there were still some faded lines and color on walls that suggested paintings that had disappeared with time and neglect. The high-ceilinged saloon occupied the end space of what had been the sanctuary.

Men in the dress of the country, vaqueros probably, sat at two tables. Sallie and Jess at a corner table had some little privacy and a good view of the room. Jess took his last bite of beef, laid the fork on the empty plate, picked up his half-full wine glass and sipped. He set the glass on the table, stared at her.

"What?" she said.

"Most Indian women I have seen wear their hair long. Yours hardly reaches your shoulders."

She looked past him to the room, sighed. "Salinan women who accepted their place in the mission way of life wore their hair long. Any woman who was not happy with the way of life in the mission wore her hair short. I was the only woman in our mission to wear short hair. Same in the village. After the missions closed, it stayed the same. I don't know where the custom came from."

They sat silent as he sipped his wine, and she looked past him to the room. "These missions are a great mystery to me," said Jess. "They seem like something from another age, another country."

"That's what they are," she said. "The Spanish believed that all people should be Christian. They believed that anybody who was not Christian was like an animal. They felt they were here to bring Indians to the church and baptize them so they would be whole, they would be saved. If Indians did not want to be saved and resisted, the Spaniards forced them to do whatever the friars said.

"They built a bunch of missions up the coast, from San Diego to Yerba Buena. It's called San Francisco now. We can probably stay at a mission building every night till we reach where we are going." She frowned, touched his hand, and looked intently at him. "Where are we going?"

He took her hand and looked past her to the sanctuary. "Wondered when you were going to ask," he said. "Not sure where we're going to end up, but I'm thinking we'll go to Monterey for now. Met a couple of people there a while back who might be able to help us decide what to do." He took her other hand. "Does that sound okay? Do you know Monterey?"

"Travelers at San Miguel sometimes mentioned it, but I don't know anything about it."

"Monterey is the capital of California. At least, until the Americans decide where to put their capital. There will likely be some changes since I was there last month. All of California, everywhere, is going to change. The change is going to be permanent. When the United States takes over territory, there's no going back. We'll have to decide how we're going to fit into this new country, this new American country."

He squeezed her hands. "We'll find a place, sweetheart. If we don't like what we find, we'll move on. There's a lot of country in California. And beyond California."

She frowned.

"What's wrong?" he said.

"You said 'sweetheart'. What is 'sweetheart'?"

He smiled, looked at her a long moment, looked at the ceiling, then back to her. "Hmm. A sweetheart is somebody you care a lot about, somebody you love. I called you 'sweetheart' because I care a lot about you. I love you, Sallie. It's been a short time, but I know." He moved his chair to sit closer to her. He looked around the room, confirmed no one was looking, and kissed her on a cheek.

He bent toward her, spoke softly. "And right now, I want to go to our room and crawl into that bed under the covers with you. Sweetheart." He stood and took her hand. She smiled, stood and walked with him toward the hall door.

Chapter Four

"I never saw that flag," said Sallie. They stood in the road before Larkin's house in Monterey.

"You'll see it everywhere soon. It's the flag of the United States." As they studied the house, a man stepped from the front door to the porch. He looked at the couple in the road and waved. Jess recognized Larkin and returned the wave. He took Sallie's arm and walked to the porch.

"Come in, come in," said Larkin. "Jess, isn't it? I'm happy to see you again." Larkin spoke to Jess but looked at Sallie. "And this is?"

"This is Sallie," said Jess. "She saved my life. She has lived in California forever, and she saved my life."

"Then I want to hear this story." He pushed the door open, invited them inside with an outstretched arm. "Come in, come in, I'll introduce you to good Monterey aguardiente."

As they walked in, Larkin saw a woman in the street

hurrying toward him. "Wait," said Larkin. He smiled at the woman who stopped before him, puffing. Jess and Sallie stopped just inside and watched the couple.

Larkin smiled at the woman. "Good morning, Señora Black. I haven't seen that worthless husband of yours lately. Is he still at sea?"

She caught her breath. "Yes, Señor Larkin. I wanted to tell you. God willing, he will be home on Thursday."

"Good! Tell him I will trade him a glass of my best aguardiente for Sandwich Island news."

"He will be pleased to see you, Señor Larkin. But only one glass, please! He likes his aguardiente too much." She smiled. "Goodbye, Señor Larkin."

Larkin smiled. "I promise, Señora." He stepped inside, nodded at Jess and Sallie. "Cheap price to pay for news from the islands."

———

JESS AND SALLIE sat with Larkin in straight wooden chairs at a low table at the side of the house. They looked out over a garden of shrubs and flowers. Larkin sipped his aguardiente and identified some of the plantings. Manzanita, bush mallow, grove clover. He waved his glass at the garden. "They are local plants, but I haven't the foggiest guess at most of their names. If you happen to be in the area come spring, they will be in blossom. Very pretty."

"You could have called them by any name, and I wouldn't have known the difference. Nice garden." Jess raised his glass and emptied it. "Nice, this

Monterey aguardiente too. I could come to like it, as you predicted."

At Larkin's question, Jess recounted all that had happened to him since their last meeting. Larkin asked many questions about the ship, the captain and crew and the circumstances of his leaving the ship. He listened closely to Jess's account of the San Miguel mission massacre. He had heard about the affair but was grateful for this eyewitness account.

"Young lady, you are fortunate to survive. You did exactly what you should have done. It is appalling that you had to witness this. In my official capacity, I may ask to speak with you further about the incident."

Larkin refilled their glasses, and they talked about Monterey and California and what lay ahead for the province. In addition to listening to Jess's and Sallie's tales, Larkin told something of his own past and business and political interests. He had been in California since the 1830s, happily acclimated and enjoyed success in commerce and logging. His trade with the Sandwich Islands was brisk and profitable. He married an American woman he met aboard ship and never became a Mexican citizen.

He remained American in citizenship and belief in American superiority. He had always advocated and believed that California was destined to become American and, in fact, was President Polk's secret agent during the war. He chuckled and said that it was best not to talk about this relationship with the president. He was the American consul to California and would happily relinquish the post when California became American in fact.

"Actually, you must know that the war is over," said Larkin. "The Treaty of Guadalupe Hidalgo officially ended the war, but the transition is moving slowly. Nevertheless, understand that since the signing of the treaty last year, California is American territory. Mark the date of the signing, February 2, 1848."

They talked about the local population, the Hispanic Californians and the Americans, most of whom seemed to have blended and assimilated with no difficulty.

"We ran across some ragged Californians, maybe Indians," said Jess, "on the trail that were in bad condition, but the people in Monterey all seem to be comfortable and well dressed. I'm impressed."

Larkin chuckled. "Middle-class Californios will dress like grandees, even if it means they will have nothing to eat."

"The American flag," said Jess, "did any locals object to you flying it?"

Larkin stared at the garden a moment before answering. "They knew I was Consul. No one objected until the war began, especially when it spread north from Mexico to California. Of course, no one objects now but for the few who will be hurt in some way with the loss of ties with Mexico.

"Did the war show up in Monterey?"

"Only briefly and not very seriously. With the war behind us, we are on the verge of a burst of activity around here. Californios are fine people, but they don't have much interest or competence in commerce. When the Americans are in full control of the economy and government, things will change. And..." He leaned toward Jess and gestured with his glass. "And California will soon become a state in the United States of America." He leaned back, smiling. "Mark my word! The opportunities in an American California are going to be absolutely enormous! Especially for those of us on the ground right now, right here!" He pointed at the ground.

Jess pondered, staring into the yard. He turned back to Larkin. "Sounds promising. I suppose your business will benefit from all this."

"Oh, yes, it will indeed, on a number of fronts. Now, that brings up a question that I have been pondering since we began our conversation. You said you had no ties in California. How about working for me? My import operation will expand, from both the east coast and the Sandwich Islands, my timber business will grow, and other prospects as well.

"There's one particular opportunity that is going to be very promising. For the last couple of years, a trickle of immigrants has been coming to California from the United States. This trickle has increased of late since the discovery of gold last year in the foothills of the mountains east and north of here. We'll talk about that. With the establishment of an American California, this trickle will become a deluge. I'm sure of it.

"Some, like yourself, will come by sea, but I suspect most will come overland. It's cheaper and usually faster than by ship from the east coast. Most will enter California over a pass that leads directly to a settlement in the central valley. Sutter's Fort, it's called. It was founded by John Sutter, a Swiss émigré, in the early '40s.

"Sutter had a thriving establishment supplying the early immigration of Americans into California. Since the gold discovery, he has been overwhelmed by the influx of gold-seekers who range from honest men who want to improve themselves with the gold they are sure they will find to the basest sort of men who will do anything to advance their own fortune. The fort has changed from an enterprise based on agriculture and handicrafts to the meanest sort of business. Sutter has pretty much lost control as he rents space to people who have taken advantage of him. He's a drunkard and a philanderer. He has Indian mistresses." He looked at Sallie. "Sorry, Sallie." He turned back to Jess. "Sutter's just about turned over his establishment to his son, August, who is in the process of selling bits and pieces of the property to try to pay his father's debts.

"Now the picture becomes sticky. Sutter and some others laid out a town they called Sutterville. This pleased old Sutter. And they began selling lots. August, his son, had a different idea. Sutterville is a distance from the fort, so he and others laid out a town on the river closer to the fort. They called it Sacramento after the river. Lots were surveyed and are selling. Sutter's ego took a hit, but the sales have begun to pay off an enormous debt he had accumulated. He owed everybody, even the Russians! He bought their Fort Ross on the northern California coast and still owed for it. That's another story I'll tell you someday. I'm getting off track here.

"The point is this. Hundreds, more likely thousands, of people will be coming to California this year and years following. Some will arrive by sea, but most will come over the Sierra looking for some way to get rich, mostly by gold mining. These people will need equipment and supplies of all sorts. That's where we come in.

"I've been to the diggings, Jess. After I talked with some miners who had come to Monterey with sacks of dust, I went to the mountains to have a look for myself. I visited a camp where a dozen men were making an average of fifty dollars a day. That's fifty dollars a *day!* Unbelievable. I talked with a couple of fellas who said they breakfasted a few days before I arrived on sardines, bread and butter and cheese and two bottles of ale, and they paid forty-three dollars! You wouldn't pay that much for that breakfast at the fanciest place in San Francisco!

"All this is to say that my first impressions of the gold discovery have changed. Since I'm going to convince you to work for me, I should tell you where I stand on the subject. When I first heard about the work in the diggings, I figured the gold would last a few months. Now, based on what I have seen personally, I am convinced gold will be taken in great quantities from the California placers for years. I am so convinced that I have written to the Secretary of State in Washington to confirm the stories of the gold discovery and workings in the placers. I included in my dispatch examples of gold dust and nuggets." Larkin leaned forward in his chair and spoke slowly, earnestly. "Gold mania has spread across the continent, indeed around the world. I have done some investing personally in the placers with some cohorts I trust. I'm watching those operations closely."

He leaned back. "Now, back to my offer. If you will agree to work for me, I will send you to Sutter's to assess what the immigration can mean for me. Sutter and others have stores that will sell to the overlanders, but they're likely to be overwhelmed. Sutter has no business sense. Don't tell him I said so." He chuckled. "Actually, by the time you reach the fort, Sutter may not be a contender.

"You can help me decide whether I should investigate supplying the newcomers. If so, how? Should I open a store at the fort, or between the fort and the mountains? Should I open a store or two *in* the diggings? Should I buy up land in the area suitable for farming and resell the land to the immigrants? Should I have you point immigrants to Monterey, with promises of my helping them settle in? You would be my eyes and ears east of Sutter's, where all the newcomers over this pass likely will visit." He leaned back, picked up his glass. "What do you say?"

Jess had listened with growing interest. *Why not indeed?* He knew no one. He had no prospects. He and Sallie didn't even have a place to sleep this very night.

"Sounds most promising, Mr. Larkin, if you're willing to take a chance on me. I have no skills that this job might require, but I'll work hard. I've been told I'm a fast learner."

Larkin clapped him on a knee. "You appear to have a large measure of common sense, my boy, and that's what counts most since there is no precedent for what I'm asking of you." Larkin emptied his glass, set the glass on the table and straightened. "Now. I don't suppose you have arranged lodging in the town for yourself and your lady."

"No, sir."

"Then you'll stay here. I'll have Calixtro—he works for me—set you up in the storeroom in the barn out back. It should do until you leave for Sutter's in a few days. You'll eat with us in the house. My wife will be happy to have new people at the table to dilute my ravings. Does all this suit you?"

"Yes, sir. Sounds like an interesting prospect, for you and for us."

"Good! I'll get Calixtro." He started to walk away.

"Uh, Mr. Larkin," said Jess, "I wonder if you can advise me on something." Larkin stopped, waited. "We have come into possession of some gold dust. Could you tell me where I can exchange the dust for coin?"

Larkin frowned. "Gold dust. If you don't mind my asking, where did you get gold dust? I don't think you have been to the diggings east of Sutter's."

"Sallie here, before I knew her, and some friends from her village heard about gold being taken at San Feliciano Canyon, not too far from where she lived. She and the friends went to the canyon to have a look. They worked the stream for a time and took some dust, not a whole lot, but enough for each to carry some away. Sallie here was the best gold miner of the lot and took more than anybody else."

Sallie smiled, ducked her head and bumped against his arm.

"You're lucky to have such an accomplished, um, companion," Larkin said. He smiled, leaned back in his chair. "I'll take care of the dust for you. I know a man who deals in this sort of thing. We haven't seen much dust here, but that seems to be changing. By the way, don't talk about the dust with anybody locally. You might attract more attention than you want. Now, wait here for me. I'll find Calixtro and come back in a few minutes." Larkin walked beside the porch and around the corner.

Jess turned quickly to Sallie. "What do you think? This is happening so fast."

"If you trust him, I trust him." She frowned. "You're going to change all the gold?"

"Ah. Hmm. Good question. Maybe we should change only a part. I trust Larkin, but maybe we shouldn't let anybody, including Larkin, know how much we have. I'll exchange enough to pay expenses till my pay from him begins. We'll keep the nuggets and most of the flakes for now. Sound okay?"

She nodded.

Larkin walked from the back of the house and came to them. "Calixtro will check the room, and he'll take care of your horses. Come back to the garden in a couple of hours. We'll have a drink before supper." He stepped up onto the porch, went to the door of the store and inside.

Jess took Sallie's arm, and they walked to the barn. A smiling Calixtro stood at the door of the storeroom. He spoke to them in Spanish, and Sallie thanked him.

They walked inside, Jess closed the door and took Sallie in his arms. "You've listened to me for a couple of hours talking about plans and prospects. Now what do you think? Am I doing the right thing? You must know by now I would not do anything you don't want to do. I would not go anywhere or do anything unless you were with me."

She leaned up and kissed him. "I do what you want to do, as long as you say that. Sweetheart." She giggled.

———

THEY SPENT the next two days as Larkin's guests. Larkin and Jess talked at length about Jess's appointment. He would carry a letter of introduction addressed to Sutter, or in his absence to his son or whoever seemed to be in authority at the establishment. He would apply for employment with that person. He would not reveal that he was acting for Larkin. Maybe later, but not now. Sutter, if he's still in control, will suspect the connection, Larkin said, since he is a calculating sort, especially when he learns that you have come from Monterey, and this is the kind of scheme he would employ if it were to his advantage.

Larkin had arranged with a casual acquaintance, a Monterey merchant, to exchange Jess's gold dust for coin. The merchant had seen a little dust recently, but he was as intrigued as Larkin had been when Jess told him about it.

"He asked too many questions," Larkin said, "but I told him nothing. We haven't seen much gold in any form around Monterey until recently. I suspect we'll see more when the diggings east of Sutter are in full swing."

———

JESS AND SALLIE rode on the well-traveled road from Monterey toward distant Sutter's Fort, or whatever had replaced it, in the interior valley. Jess often consulted a sketch map of the route Larkin gave him. The consul had assured him there would be people on the road that could help with directions.

Jess held the lead of the donkey Larkin gave them to carry their goods. They had spent the last day in Monterey buying clothes, two good blankets, and a basket for the donkey. Larkin loaded them with more than enough food supplies to last until they reached the fort. Believing that all people and animals deserved a proper name, Jess called the donkey "Peso". Peso because Larkin said that horses and donkeys were so plentiful in California that most were worth no more than a peso or two.

The road lay on the banks of the Sacramento River which they would follow all the way to the fort. It was wide with a languid flow. Thick stands of tule reeds, willow, pipevine and wild grapes grew at the waterline. Colorful butterflies hovered about and alighted on the pipevine. Scattered stands of oak, cottonwood and box elder grew on the banks and along the edges of the adjacent meadows.

The wide river glistened in the bright, warming sun, the surface undisturbed. Early in their journey, they saw only an occasional small boat with a single sail. Later, they saw larger craft carrying passengers sailing in both directions. Boxes of goods were stacked in the center of the boats. Passengers waved, and Jess and Sallie responded.

Sallie and Jess camped in woods just off the trail and occasionally found rooms at inns, including a night on the grounds of the old mission at Santa Clara. They asked the priests about accommodation and were told that travelers were welcome to worship here, but food and rooms were not available. In conversation, Jess and Sallie were surprised to learn that Santa Clara, unlike all the other missions, was never abandoned by the church after secularization. It continued to function as a parish church to the present day.

A priest invited them to come see the sanctuary. Sallie looked at Jess who told her to go ahead, and he would watch the animals. She was gone a half hour, bowed to the priest when she came out and went to Jess, wiping her cheeks with a sleeve.

After a particularly cold uncomfortable night in a clearing near the mission, they rode early in unseasonal warm sunshine, planning to stop for breakfast at the earliest opportunity, hopefully an inn of some sort.

Only a couple of hours from Santa Clara, they were surprised when two men stepped from behind roadside brush into the middle of the trail. They were scruffy, unshaven, their clothes well-worn, just short of ragged.

The younger man held a pistol pointed at the riders. The older man's face was troubled. He stood a bit behind his companion, alternately looking at Jess and Sallie and at his partner.

"Orillense del camino, para allá, y bájense de los caballos," said the younger man, motioning with the pistol. He pointed to a small clearing in the roadside brush.

Sallie frowned. She appeared more annoyed than frightened. "He said to ride over there and get off our horses," she said, pointing to the clearing.

Jess sat still, looking hard at the men, then reined his horse slowly to the clearing, Sallie following. They dismounted, and he tied their reins to a manzanita limb. He ran his hand over the red chocolatey surface of the limb. He always found the smooth bark soothing, even at this moment. Jess tied the donkey's lead to his saddle horn. They stood beside their horses, facing the bandits, waiting.

"Dame su dinero y su oro," said the young man, waving the pistol.

Sallie looked abruptly at Jess, wide-eyed. "He said to give him money and our gold."

Jess stared at the men. "Somebody's been talking."

"Ahora mismo! No hablen!" He pointed the pistol at Jess. His hand wavered. "Ahora!"

Jess saw the man's nervousness. Hesitating a moment, he turned slowly to his horse. He unbuckled the flap of the saddlebags, his back to the bandit. He reached slowly into the bag, pulled out the Colt, holding it before him so the bandit could not see the gun. He turned slowly, brought the pistol down quickly, leveled on the bandit.

The man jerked backward, wide-eyed, raised the gun to point at Jess, his hand shaking. Jess fired, blowing him backward, his gun flying into the air over his head.

The old man, wide-eyed, stretched his arms high. "No dispares! No llevo arma."

"The other man doesn't have a gun, Jess!" said Sallie.

"Good for him," Jess said softly. He lowered the pistol. "Tell him we're going to ride away, and I'm keeping an eye on him till we're out of sight. If he makes any funny move, I'll kill 'im. Tell him."

She spoke to the man who nodded rapidly, backing away, arms stretched high.

Jess and Sallie untied reins and mounted. Removing the donkey's lead from the horn, Jess moved into the road, and Sallie followed. Jess watched the old bandit who lowered his arms, looking down at his dead friend.

"Poor man," said Sallie. "He probably had nothing to do with planning all this."

Jess looked back at the unsuccessful bandit, still standing over his dead comrade. "Let's hope that an American California is kinder to his sort than Mexican California."

———

JESS AND SALLIE sat on their horses, looking across a grassy meadow at Sutter's Fort. The compound was both formidable and welcoming. A thick high wall of adobe bricks surrounded the inner courtyard. Tall bastions at the northwest and southeast corners, towering above the walls, held cannons that were meant to protect gates in the walls. The walls were pierced at intervals by gun loopholes.

The fort with its strong defensive features was built in more perilous times. Now walkers and riders moved in both directions through the wide-open gates. Jess and Sallie rode to the main entrance, dismounted at a hitching rail outside the gate and tied reins. Jess shouldered his saddlebags, and they went inside.

They wandered among the slipshod venues of what had been Sutter's Fort. Except it was no longer a fort. Whether it was Sutter's was questionable. It was a hodgepodge of shops, a bowling alley, a boarding house, two saloons, and a billiard parlor. There were hints of a bordello out back of one of the saloons. In idle conversation with shoppers and shop owners, they learned that Sam Brannon, the entrepreneur who had announced the gold discovery in the streets of San Francisco, operated a thriving store selling anything the immigrants needed, from shoes and shirts to mining equipment of all sorts.

They strolled back to the hitching rail where the horses and donkey were tied. Jess untied Peso's lead rope. "Pretty much as Larkin described," he said, "though I suspect it's worse than he thinks. Seems to be some time since he's heard anything firsthand about the place."

"Pretty little thang you got there."

Jess and Sallie jumped at the voice and turned to see two smiling men who had walked up unnoticed. In their late forties to early fifties, they were well-shaven and well dressed in clean working clothes and broad-brimmed hats.

Jess held Peso's lead. He cocked his head, smiled, looking at the donkey. "Yeah, she's a pretty girl, hard worker too, never complains."

The man was not amused. "I thank you know what I meant. Where'd you get 'er?"

Jess slowly tied the donkey's lead to his saddle horn. He turned back to face the men, sober faced. "If you refer to the lady, I didn't 'get' her anywhere, as you say."

"I'll buy 'er. How much you want for her? Does she speak any English?"

Jess frowned, turned to Sallie. "Hablas inglés?" Do you speak English? It was one of the few Spanish phrases he had learned from a ship's crewman who said it could come in handy when one wanted to buy grog or a woman's company.

Sallie could not completely avoid a hint of a smile. Then, sober faced, she turned to the prospective buyer. "Claro que hablo inglés, mejor qui tú. También hablo español y varios dialectos nativos. Me imagino que eres un americano típico, que hablas solo inglés, y ni el buen inglés. Como respondes a eso, tonito? Yes, I speak English."

Jess smiled. "Then you heard this fella say he wants to buy you."

She stared at the man, then softened, smiled. She touched Jess's arm. "He can't sell me. He doesn't own me." She leaned forward, pointing at Jess. "I own *him*! I sell him to you. He's a good worker. How much you pay?" She leaned forward, unsmiling. Jess failed to suppress a smile.

The speaker's pard laughed out loud. "She gotcha, Fred!"

Fred looked hard at him, then turned to her. He smiled thinly. "So she did." He nodded to her, then turned to Jess. "Hadn't seen you folks about. You headin' to the diggins? I'm Fred, by the way. This here's Benny." He motioned to his companion with a nod.

"Hadn't thought much about that," Jess said. "Mostly we came to have a look at Sutter's Fort, or what's left of it. Looks to be in a sad state. I heard that it once was a grand place."

Fred looked back toward the fort, sighed, sadly it seemed. "That it was. It's these fellas coming from San Francisco and over the mountains that's ruined it. Or maybe it's Sutter hisself that's ruined it. He's tried to make money from the influx, but he's just not doin' it right. He's too busy havin' a good time. He's a drunkard and don't know most of the time what he's doin', 'cept when he's with his Indian whores. Benny and me are from San Francisco and been comin' up for years, shippin' goods both ways, and we've seen the place go from grand to ruin."

"You've not been to the diggings?" said Jess.

"Oh yeah, we were up there long enough to decide it wasn't for us," said Benny. "We took a little dust, but not enough to convince us it was the life we wanted. Actually, our business on the river has took off, and it's certain without breakin' our backs at a stream in the mountains and hopin'.

"More promising than what those fellas are facing at the moment." He pointed at a scattering of tents in the meadow east of the fort. "Those are miners who came here for the winter. They'll be heading back soon as the snow in the foothills melts.

Some will strike it rich, but I don't envy 'em. I'd rather sleep in a warm bed with a warm woman than tough it out on the ground in a tent." He smiled at Sallie. She stared blankly at him.

"That's the signal for us to head out, Benny." Fred turned to Jess. "We're off for the Bay at first light tomorrow with a load of foodstuffs and goods. I tell yuh, anyone who wants to settle in this area, they should get a farm. As people come in to work the placers or settle in the valley, they gotta eat, and farming is a sure bet to make a good living here. I feel for the poor devils who think they're gonna get rich at the diggings. A few will get rich, some will make expenses, but most will get nothin' more'n stiff joints and disappointment.

"If you folks ever want to take a break and visit San Francisco, you're welcome to sail with us. Ask anybody at the wharf, and they'll know where to find us, Benny and Fred. That's the Sacramento wharf, by the way, not Sutterville. That burg is already just a neighborhood of Sacramento." He pointed at Sallie. "If you want to get away from this fella, pretty lady, come to the wharf without him, and I'll take you aboard."

He leaned toward Jess with an open hand at his mouth, pretending to hide his comment, and looking at Sallie: "I still want to buy her."

Sallie smiled, took Jess's arm. "If I get tired of him, I look for you." Fred touched his cap and nodded. He and Benny walked briskly in the direction of the river.

Jess watched them go. "Nice fellas," he said. "By

the way, what did you say to him when he asked if you speak English?"

She smiled, ducked her head. "I just say I speak better English than he does, and I tell him I speak other languages. I ask him how many languages he speak. And I called him a 'tonito'." She laughed out loud.

"What's a tonito?"

She frowned, looked up. "Uh, stupid, no, silly, something like that."

He put an arm around her shoulders. "You got the last word, whatever it means."

They watched the two men walk around the fort and toward the town. "Now what, sweetheart? I'll report back to Larkin, but there seems to be no one in charge at the fort, and I just don't see any way I could work for him in this situation. That means I'm out of a job before I begin."

They walked slowly toward the fort complex. She pointed at the scattering of tents just beyond the fort.

"Look," she said, "some of the men seem to be packing up. That must mean the weather in mountains is warming and now they can go back to streams. If we're not staying here, we could go to mountains, and I'll show you how to find gold."

"Hmm. That might work. We could give it a try. If we find gold, we'll stay a while, but since we don't depend on it—we already have our gold—we can leave any time. I can add this to my report to Larkin. Okay, we'll do it. As long as I have my little sweetheart with me, I don't care where I am." He reached around her back and under her arm, groping.

She shrieked and jumped aside. "Don't do that! People will see."

He stepped off and held out a hand to her. "C'mon, we need to do some shopping."

Chapter Five

JESS AND SALLIE went into what had been Sutter's Fort. Now it was a cluster of enterprises offering a wide variety of goods and services. One store displayed an extensive selection of clothing, shoes, blankets, saddles, and bridles, a great variety of foods and mining equipment.

Jess and Sallie wandered among the shops, stopping to examine the goods. Jess bought boots for Sallie and himself. He selected a new shirt and pants, more substantial than the sole outfit he had worn since jumping ship. Sallie also selected a shirt and, to his surprise, held up a pair of pants at her front to check the length.

"You want men's pants?" he said.

"Yes." She looked at him, her face blank. "Why not?"

He had no response, so bought them. "Don't be surprised if you're mistaken for a man."

"If somebody thinks I am a man, I know how to show I'm a woman." She smiled.

He looked sternly at her, pointed a finger in her face. "Don't." He leaned down, kissed her.

They made their last stop at a small establishment just outside the fort's walls. The proprietor stood in front of his ramshackle shop, holding a shallow metal pan in each hand. "Don't head for the mountains without a pan. It's the miner's friend, best tool for taking gold. I'm Joseph Wadleigh, and I have everything you need for the placers!"

Sallie stared at the pans, frowning. Wadleigh brightened at her interest and explained how to use the pan.

"You scoop up some sand and water from the streambed. Swirl the mix around like this." He moved the pan in a circular, swirling motion. "Push the sand around and look carefully for color. Gold is heavier than sand and will sink to the bottom."

She leaned over, staring intently at the pan, nodding as he spoke. She turned to Jess, wide-eyed. "Oh, how I could have used this when we were looking for gold. Buy two."

Jess paid for the pans and pushed them into his pack.

"I can tell who's in charge here," said Wadleigh, grinning. "It stands to reason since it was women who first discovered gold in the foothills. Yeah! Not old Marshall. The women were part of an immigrant train that crossed the Sierra. While doing laundry in a stream, they found gold, a full year before Marshall made his discovery."

"Who's Marshall?" said Jess.

"Ah, you don't know James Marshall. You'll get to know about him if you stick around here long enough. He discovered gold on the south fork of the American River where he was building a sawmill for old Sutter. That was some months ago. People don't know about the women's discovery because they and their husbands never did follow up and go back to work their discovery. Too bad for them.

"Ever'body now gives Marshall the credit for the discovery because ever'body talked about it. One fellow who knew about it, Sam Brannan—you'll learn about him soon enough—even went to San Francisco, walked up and down the streets, yelling 'gold on the American River' while waving a bottle of gold flakes." Wadleigh chuckled. "Old Brannon knew what he was doing. He owned stores that sold goods to miners. He was no dummy.

"Anyway, all that's to say you made a good buy here, folks," said Wadleigh. "You'll be happy with the pans. Take my word for it. Time was when miners used all sorts of stuff to look for flakes. Early on, some eager fellas used a bedsheet!" He guffawed. "Then they switched to wooden bowls and Indian baskets, better but not as good as the pans you just bought." Wadleigh pocketed the coins. "You headin' up to the placers now?"

"Yeah, well, we're going up for a look," said Jess. "Any suggestions? We're new to the country. Someplace that'll make us rich real quick."

Wadleigh snorted. "If I knew for sure where that place is, I'd pack up here and hightail it for the mountains myself. But I ain't unhappy. I'm doin' okay, minin' th' miners. As for your question. Mining country is pretty much in two sections, northern mines and southern mines. I don't know much about the southern mines. They're provisioned out of Stockton at the head of the San Joaquin River. That's a new town, nice little town, I'm told, named after Commodore Stockton, a U.S. navy officer in the war with Mexico. I hear Stocktonians are really miffed that the Commodore never visited the town." He snorted and slapped a knee.

"Anyway, you won't likely go there either. You're close to the northern mines, and that's where you should go. In fact, I can make a suggestion. A customer and friend of mine is leaving tomorrow for his claim. Maybe he could help. Dave Clark's his name. He's camped at the edge of that line of trees." He pointed at a cluster of small tents. "He told me he'll be breaking camp at first light tomorrow. If you're interested, you need to talk with him today. He's a nice fella. Ask anybody over there. Somebody will know him.

"Wherever you go, it's up there." He pointed eastward. "That's the Sierra Nevada." The gray cloud layer that had shrouded the mountain range all morning had just lifted. They stared at the dark foothills, the series of ranges above gradually lightening, the towering snowy peaks at the top, glistening in the bright sunshine, the now cloudless blue sky above.

"I never get tired of the view," Wadleigh said.

"Pretty," said Sallie.

"Hope it's as pretty close up," Jess said.

He thanked Wadleigh, and he and Sallie went to the hitching rail where they fetched their horses and Peso. They walked the horses toward the three or four dozen scattered tents. Men seemed to be busy packing up, not yet taking down tents. Most stopped what they were doing to watch the two newcomers. They focused mostly on Sallie rather than her escort. Jess stopped and spoke to a couple of men. They shook heads, still staring at Sallie. They walked on and Jess talked with a man who nodded and pointed at a tent under a huge oak at the edge of the encampment.

They went to the tent indicated. Jess spoke to the man who had just dumped an armload of kindling beside the fire pit. "Dave Clark?" said Jess.

The man straightened, flexed his back. He was in his mid-thirties, rough dressed, but clean. His abundant longish hair almost reached his shoulders. "Yep." Jess introduced himself and Sallie and told about his conversation with Wadleigh.

"Sure, be glad to have the company," Clark said, looking Sallie up and down. "I'm leaving early, at first light. If you're not set up somewhere else, camp here for the night so we'll be sure each other is up early. We can have an early supper and talk."

Jess thanked him, and he and Sallie walked their animals to a patch of grass near Clark's tent. He removed saddles and hobbled the horses and donkey. Dropping saddles and saddlebags near Clark's fire pit, he walked about under the trees, collecting bits of dry limbs. He dropped the kindling at the fire circle.

Clark squatted at the fire, stirring beans in a pan. Chunks of bread were heaped in a bowl beside the fire. A coffee pot lay on coals at the edge of the fire. "Slim pickins' this evening so I don't have much to clean up. I'll give you a better feed in the mountains."

Dave spooned out beans into bowls and saucers, topped with chunks of bread and coffee poured into two cups. Sallie waved off the offer of coffee. "Well, that's convenient since I have only two cups. I don't often have more than a single visitor. By the way, there's a little store a short walk from my claim, so you'll be able to pick up a few things there. I notice you don't have much. I need to add to my cupboard as well."

"Quite right," said Jess. "We really appreciate what you're doing for us." He noticed that, while Dave talked with him, he mostly looked at Sallie. "I'm sorry I haven't introduced Sallie here."

She smiled.

After a moment, Dave spoke to Sallie. "Me imagino que hablas español y sospecho que vives aqui en California por más tiempo que todos los demás por aqui. Y supongo que este amigo tuyo no habla español?"

She glanced aside at Jess, nodded. Jess's slight smile was part questioning, part annoyance.

"Bien. Si hay algo que no queremos que entienda, hablamos español." He smiled.

She looked at Jess, whose smile had turned to a frown. "We just say funny things," she said.

"Okay," Jess said. "I like funny things too."

"Sorry, pard," said Dave, busy collecting dishes. "It's a two-day ride to the diggings. We'll reach the river early enough on the second day to settle in. We'll go to my claim, and I'll suggest a couple of spots nearby where you can take your choice. Do you have a tent?"

"No." He said it sharply, wondering whether this fellow was worth his friendship.

"You'll need a tent." Dave pointed down the way at the edge of the encampment. "See the tent down there with the blue rag hanging on a guy rope?" Jess nodded. "Tommy down there is not going back to the diggings. I wager he would be happy to sell his tent cheap. If you like, I'll talk with him."

Jess softened, relaxed. "Yes, please. Thanks. Haven't even thought about needing a place to live in. Shows how ignorant I am in all this."

"Everybody who comes to the diggings for the first time is new and ignorant about what comes next. We'll reach the diggings a bit early in the season for a good reason. News of this gold discovery has reached the east coast by now, and it's spreading all over the world, I'm told. I'm betting there is going to be a big rush to the diggings this year from the east coast and from everywhere else. I think the diggings are going to get real crowded real fast. So we need to be sure our claims are so well defined that nobody can move in on us. Sound reasonable?"

"It does indeed," Jess said. "On the other hand, I'm not sure we are going to be there long enough to be concerned about all this. We'll see."

Dave smiled. "Yeah, we'll see what you have to say after you have collected a sack of dust and nuggets." He stacked the supper dishes in a pan and went to his tent.

———

THE RIDE from Sutter's early on was on a well-traveled road on a flat plain along the course of the American River. The weather was mild, but as they began to climb into the foothills, they saw thin patches of new snow on bushes and tree branches. Mid-afternoon of the second day, they arrived in what locals hopefully called "gold country." Here the trail branched to run along streams and tributaries of streams.

"We'll see a bit more snow here than on the plain," Dave said. "We're lucky though. Locals tell me this is the mildest winter they've had in years. Still gonna be cold though."

They rode on a narrow trail that lay through woods above the stream bank where an occasional solitary miner or two or three miners stood on sandy banks or in the shallows working the stream with small knives and pans. Most miners turned to watch the passing riders. A few waved or nodded.

One yelled, "Hey, Dave!"

Dave soon turned off the trail on a path that led down the bank toward the stream. He bent forward to ride under a low oak branch and pulled up beside a small log cabin. He reined up and dismounted. "Leave the animals here. I want to show you the stream." Sallie and Jess dismounted and tied reins to a hitching pole. Jess tied Peso's lead to the pole.

Jess was surprised to see the cabin. It was small, log-sided, a solid chimney of rocks and plaster or cement. The roof of planks was topped with soil and weeds and a light dusting of snow. Jess frowned, looked at Dave.

"You build that?"

"I did indeed. Well, I had help from a couple of fellas downstream who had built their own cabin. They began ignorant but ended experienced builders. They were happy to hone their skills by helping build mine. When you're ready to build yours, we'll all pitch in."

"Thanks," said Jess, "we won't need a cabin since we may not be here long. The tent will do nicely for us." He looked toward the stream.

"Let's go down," said Dave.

They walked down to a narrow flat sand beach alongside the glistening stream. Just above the claim, the stream coursed over a gentle, sloping rocky bed, then spread to a twenty-foot width. Across the stream, a light crust of ice lay along the bank overhang where there was little flow. A thin layer of snow still covered the ground under the bare branches of pines and oaks across the stream.

A sign on a stake in the sand at the waterline proclaimed: "This is the claim of Dave Clark." A miner's shovel lay on the sand behind the sign.

Dave turned to Jess and Sallie. "I might have appeared calm when we turned off the trail to the claim, but inside I was shaking. I half expected to see a dozen men working the claim. I figured I might have to shoot somebody or find a new claim." He looked around. "The stream isn't normally this wide or the current this fast. The snow melt has widened it and increased the flow. That sign there was five feet from the water when I left after the first good snow late November.

"I was exaggerating, of course, when I said I expected claim jumpers. I was just nervous. That's the first time I have left the claim for more than a couple of days. It's been pretty calm in the diggings. For the most part, folks respect other people's claims, probably because they have good claims of their own and don't need to bother other people. I've even left sacks of dust in the cabin, and they weren't bothered. Wouldn't do that today. Too many strangers expected to show up with the approach of spring. Not counting you, of course. Nobody's going to worry about you two." He smiled.

Jess looked blankly at him.

"Anticipating some problems with the appearance of a lot of new people, there's been some talk about setting up some sort of organization to settle disagreements and claim jumping, but nothing has come of it yet. It'll happen one day. For now, a miner just has to show that he's working a claim. If he has to go away, like for the winter or to a store or a doctor, he just leaves something to show evidence of the claim. The cabin and the shovel and the sign say this is my place. Either nobody wanted my claim, or they honored my claim. Whatever the case, I'm lucky."

"Looks like a good spot," said Jess. "I take it you've been successful here?"

"Yep, it's been productive. This whole stretch of the stream, about a mile or so in each direction, has been surprisingly productive. Now, let's think about locating you. There's an attractive spot about a hundred yards upstream that you might consider. If it's not claimed now, that is. It was clear when I left in November.

"Let's go up and check it out." He walked to the door of his cabin. "I need to dump some things first. Come in and have a look." He unlocked the door, pushed it open and stepped inside. "Whew, smells stale."

Jess and Sallie followed him inside. Jess was surprised to see a neat board floor.

Dave noticed. "Yeah, most folks hereabouts are satisfied with a hard-packed dirt floor. Not me."

Jess and Sallie looked around. A faded white curtain hung over the single window. Dishes were stacked in open shelves lined with white paper. Pillows and folded blankets lay on the sturdy double bed. Two chairs were pushed under a table covered with a flower sack tablecloth. Thick dust lay on every flat surface.

"I'm impressed," said Jess. "Didn't expect such comfort in gold country. Did you make the furniture?"

"I did. Everything you see in here I made, including the fireplace. Well, I made everything with a lot of help. Folks in the diggings arrived with all the talents they owned in the States, and most are quick to offer help. You'll find the same when we build your cabin. Most people arriving in the diggings expect to find hard cases up here, working to get rich and daring anybody to interfere. It's not like that, at least for the most part. Most of them are good men."

He smiled, looked at Sallie. "I say 'men' because

almost everybody here is a man. The few women hereabouts are what miners call 'greasers and squaws', and you'll know why they are here. Sorry, but these men haven't seen white women for months, even years."

Sallie frowned, looked at Jess. "Later," he said.

They went outside, and Dave closed and latched the door. He pointed at the pole corral beside the cabin. "If you settle on a place not too far away, you can plan to leave your animals in the corral there until you build your own."

The three mounted and rode up the trail less than a half mile to the spot Dave mentioned. It lay on a gently sloping frontage, a narrow sand beach and a grassy flat above where horses and the donkey could be kept if they decided to keep the animals here, also where the tent could be set up. The trail behind the tent site ran through oak woods. Across the stream, a row of oaks lined the banks.

The stream at the upper end of the claim flowed over a rocky ledge that lay across the flow. Below the ledge, the stream spread and the flow slowed.

Sallie stood on the beach, looking about. She took Jess's arm. "I love it," she said.

The spot showed no evidence of use or claim. They quickly erected the tent Jess bought from the failed miner, and Jess lay the shovel he bought at the fort on the sandy beach near waterline.

Dave looked around. "Looks good. You have a claim. Now let's head back to my place for some supper and coffee."

———

AFTER A LIGHT SUPPER at Dave's claim, they sat at the firepit, leaning against a downed log and holding coffee cups. Sallie declined Dave's offer again, saying coffee tastes like warm mud. Dave smiled, held up his cup to her. "You gotta stop drinking warm mud, Sallie." He smiled.

Dave and Jess sipped their coffee in the twilight, staring into the low flames and embers of the dying fire.

"So you were a sailor before landing in California?" said Dave.

"Well, sort of. I was a Kentucky cowboy farmer who got shanghaied in Boston. Really dumb. How 'bout you? You haven't been a gold miner your whole life."

Dave laughed. "No, no. I've been a gold miner for about four months. I was a doctor in my other life. Can you believe that? My marriage went bust, and I went from my home in Richmond to Boston to get away. I was so low and so drunk I signed on to a ship a week before it was set to sail. Sound familiar?" He smiled, pointed at Jess. "Didn't even know where it was going when I signed. The captain was as desperate as me. Dumb.

"Heard about the gold when we docked in San Francisco early last fall and jumped ship, just like you. I heard about the gold at dinner on the day we docked and left the next morning after breakfast. I went to a livery where I heard I could get a horse and found five shipmates already there. We kept a lookout for the captain and ship's officers. They probably would have shot us on sight. Except the first mate. He was also at the livery." Dave laughed, sobered and shook his head.

"Not exactly what happened to me," said Jess, "but the result was the same. We got away."

Dave looked at Sallie. "And you, Sallie?"

She took Jess's arm, leaned against him. "He saved my life." Dave waited, but she said no more. When it appeared Dave was going to speak, Jess held up a hand, palm outward, ending the conversation. Dave nodded, stared at the dying fire.

Dave took a stick from the stack of kindling beside the fire pit and stirred the dying embers. "If you like," he said, "you can come down in the morning, and I'll show you how I hunt for gold. If we're lucky, I'll show you a few flakes."

"We'll be here," said Jess. "I'll watch Sallie as well. She's experienced, took a good quantity of flakes and nuggets from a stream down south near her home. She's anxious to try the pans we bought at the fort. She'd never seen gold pans before." He stood, took Sallie's outstretched hand and helped her stand. "She also wants to show me up." He pulled a face.

"I'll watch her as well," said Dave, "I'm still learning." Jess said goodbye with a wave as they walked to the brushy path behind camp.

On the trail to their claim, Sallie stopped. "What mean 'show me up?'"

He took her arm and moved ahead. "I'll explain. Maybe." She punched him on an arm.

———

JESS CRAWLED BAREFOOT from the tent, stood and stretched. He looked up into the leafy canopy of large oaks that stretched over the stream. He looked down and was surprised to see Sallie, squatting in the shallows, wearing her new pants, rolled up to the knees.

She leaned forward, swirling a pan. She stopped, reached into the pan, moved the soil around, then swirled again. He walked quietly down the sandy beach to stop behind her. He bent down and kissed her neck.

She jumped up, twisted around, smiled and kissed him. "Look!" she said. She pulled a small glass bottle from a pocket and showed it to him.

His jaw dropped. In the bottom of the bottle, a pinch of golden flakes. She shook the bottle and showed him again. He saw the small pea-size nugget.

"Oh, my, my, I'll get my pan." He ran to the tent and fetched the other pan. He came back, barefoot, and stepped into the cold shallows. He recoiled, stepped back on the sandy beach, shivering. He watched her a good minute, then, standing on sand at the waterline, commenced the panning routine. On the second attempt, he saw a single gold flake, sparkling in the morning sunlight.

"Sallie, I got a flake!"

She smiled and took the bottle from her pocket. He carefully pinched the flake from the soil in his pan, dropped it into the bottle and returned to his pan.

"Wait! Here's another." In removing the first

flake, he had disturbed the soil in the pan and uncovered a second flake. He carefully lifted it and dropped it into the bottle.

They continued to work this spot, moving only a foot or two to the side, she in the shallows and he on the bank. They took flakes in almost every pan.

"Ah! Sallie, look!" he exclaimed when he found a tiny nugget and showed it to her.

After a couple of hours, he straightened, bent backward, flexing his back. "That's enough for now. That's hard work, and *cold* work. Let's take a break."

She stepped from the shallows to the sand beach. Only then did they see the two men who stood on the path beside their tent.

The men took a few steps toward them. They were middle-aged, dressed rough in soiled clothing, scraggly unkempt beards, long wild hair. Their faces were hard.

"You're trespassing," said one of the men. "This is our claim."

Jess pondered, frowning. "You fellows have probably been in the diggings long enough to know the unwritten law that you show ownership by leaving some evidence on the site. There was nothing on the site that showed ownership. Look around and you'll see the evidence that this claim is now owned. By us."

The men mumbled softly to each other. "That don't hold water," said the speaker. "You need to clear off. And I'll take the bottle you been puttin' the flakes in. And any other color you been takin' from our claim."

Jess didn't move. He simply stared. Then he looked at Sallie. "I'll need to go to the tent to get it." She looked aside, stifling a smile. He walked past the men to the tent. He rummaged around the clutter on the floor, stood and turned toward the intruders. He held the Colt loosely at his side.

"This conversation is over, fellas. Leave quietly. If I see you again around here, I'll let my six-shooter friend here do the talking. Are we done here?" He brought the Colt up slowly to point in their direction.

The men's faces fell. Grim-faced, they turned and shuffled toward the trail, disappearing into the brush, disturbing the dusting of snow on bushes.

———

JESS AND SALLIE continued to work their claim, moving along both banks in both directions until they came up against another claim. They made peaceful contact with other miners along the stream who were content to remain within the shadowy boundaries of their own claims. The miners were universally surprised and enticed by the pretty pants-wearing female miner. When encountering other miners, Sallie waved, spoke and smiled. Jess warned her to remember that most of the miners had not seen or touched a woman in months. She was a delectable novelty. She shrugged and said she could take care of herself. Maybe so, he responded, but he now wore the Colt on his hip every day.

With the passage of days, the cold winds of

winter began to give way to brisk mornings and soft balmy afternoons. Jess and Sallie occasionally walked north and south on the trail, enjoying the woods and meadows and looking at the claims along the trail. A few of the claims had rough log cabins, but most had tents of various sizes and quality.

They saw a number of brush houses. Dave had described these as temporary structures, suitable mostly in the warmer months. Some were simple huts of brush thrown together. Others were more substantial. Four uprights were connected with cross pieces, topped with leafy branches that were tightly interwoven. Three sides were filled with a tight basketwork of brush. Some of these brush houses were abandoned. Others were still in use, judging from the usual camp equipment in the yard.

Still farther on the trail, they stopped to study a particular brush house. It was a tight structure that enclosed a tent, with an opening at the tent entrance. It showed evidence of long use and was still occupied.

"Maybe that will do for us," said Jess. "We'll keep this in mind."

———

THEY WORKED their stream every morning and afternoon, taking a couple of hours off at noon. Jess usually built a fire to warm up from the cold stream and enjoy a casual lunch and a rest, leaning against the log at the fire. On this day, after a satisfying lunch and a restorative lie-down beside the fire, he scooted over, kissed Sallie and began to explore her body.

She raised her head, looked around and pushed his hand away. "Jess, somebody might see you from trail."

"You don't like it?"

She put a hand on his cheek. "I like it, you know I like it. But in tent, not out here and not now. We need to get back to stream."

He kissed her lips. "We can get back to the stream after." He stood and offered a hand to help her up. She smiled and took the hand. He pulled her up, and she dusted off her pants.

"Jess!"

Sallie and Jess jumped at the shout. They saw Dave and a stranger stumbling down the path to their tent.

"Dave," said Jess, "what's up?"

Dave stopped, bent to put hands on knees, gasping. After a moment, catching his breath, he straightened. "There's hell to pay up the trail. They need help."

"Who needs help? What's happened?" Dave was still breathing hard. "Come over here and sit down," Jess said. They walked to the downed log and sat.

Dave exhaled heavily. He gestured toward his companion. "This here's a friend, Homer. He's just come down from north of here. Tell 'em, Homer."

"A bunch of miners 'bout a mile up north are raising hell with Indians," Homer said. "They've rounded up nearly a hundred Indians and say they're gonna kill all of 'em!"

"Why?" said Sallie, "what have they done?"

"Nothin'," Homer said. "It's confusing. Mostly it's a bunch of Oregonians who have a grudge against Indians in general. They hate all Indians because Indians killed some white people last year in Oregon. It was called the Cayuse War.

"When the bunch came down a few months ago to go to the diggings, they abused any Indians they came up against. Seems they raped some local Nisenan women. Sorry, missy. Nisenan men then killed five Oregonians. This really set 'em off. They organized and invited any other Indian haters to join to kill Indians, any Indians. They soon killed four Indians who couldn't have had anything to do with killing the Oregonians. Local Indians retaliated by burning the woods in the mountains above the diggings, threatening the camps along the river.

"The Oregonians decided to kill all Indians in the area. The miners went on a rampage. They slaughtered twenty peaceful Indians and rounded up nearly a hundred more. The angriest men wanted to kill the bunch, but others suggested they just kill the leaders. They're holding them near Coloma and talking about it. That's where it stands right now."

Jess looked at Sallie, took her hand. He looked at Dave. "Are we going to Coloma?"

"Yes. Homer and I are riding up now," said Dave.

"All right," Jess said. He stood.

"Can I go?" said Sallie.

"These men are Indian haters," said Dave. "They're out of their minds." She stared at him a moment, then looked aside.

While Dave and Homer walked up the trail, Jess

and Sallie went to the patch of grass where their three animals were hobbled. She stood aside as he saddled and bridled his horse.

"I'm afraid," she said.

"Stay here," Jess said. "There's no problem around here, but let's play it safe. Stay in the tent, out of sight. Don't come out."

"I mean, I'm afraid for you."

He went to her, leading his horse. He put a hand to her cheek and kissed her. "Both of us need to be careful."

————

DAVE, Homer, and Jess rode into the outskirts of Coloma near the site of the discovery of gold by James Marshall last year. Just off the road they saw the rope enclosure where some captive Indians were held by rifle-wielding miners. They reined up at a gathering of a couple of dozen men in the road, some who were shouting angrily and shaking fists.

The three dismounted and tied reins to a hitching rail. They stood well behind the mob, watching. Jess recognized Marshall from an encounter a couple of weeks ago when he and Sallie had met him by chance at a store a couple of miles from their claim.

On that occasion, after Jess introduced Sallie, the conversation turned to the question of Indians in the mines. Marshall confirmed what Jess suspected, that the animosity toward Indians in the mines was more than simply racial hatred; it was also due to the cheap labor the Indians provided their masters or employers.

Marshall recognized Jess and walked to him, seemingly relieved for a brief respite from the angry mob. "Jess, if I remember correctly."

Jess nodded. He introduced Dave and Homer.

"I suppose you know of the affair here," Marshall said.

Jess nodded again.

"The men don't trust me. They know that I care about the rights of Indians, and they won't listen to reason. I told them I would ask Mr. Sutter to help out here. Everybody in the diggings knows Sutter or knows about him. The more moderate leaders in the mob persuaded the others to release all of the Indians except the seven there who were thought to be the leaders." He pointed. "They said they would wait for Sutter's reply. I sent an urgent dispatch yesterday to Mr. Sutter. Maybe the men here will listen to him. I expect a reply at any moment."

He studied the gathering of captives surrounded by the angry Oregonians. "Most of the miners there are half drunk. They're enjoying this too much." He shook his head. "Hope Sutter comes through."

As if on cue, a rider galloped into the camp. He reined up when he saw Marshall and jumped off, leading the horse. "Sutter's not havin' it. He said he was threatened by both Indians and miners last winter when he tried to help settle disputes. He said he couldn't help. If you ask me, I think he was scared."

"So where are we now?" said Jess. They looked toward the enclosure where the leaders of the mob still held the seven suspected Indian leaders. Out of earshot, all watched the rider and Marshall, waiting.

Marshall walked slowly toward the Oregonians and the Indian captives. "Boys," said Marshall, "I hope we can work this out. Mr. Sutter declines to get involved. He said nobody seems to pay any attention to him anymore. He said when he tried to help work out some problems last winter, nobody would listen to him. He said both miners and Indians threatened him."

Jess huddled with Dave and Homer. "This could turn real ugly," said Jess softly.

"We're a bit outnumbered," Homer said, frowning and looking about nervously.

Some miners shouted that they should shoot the Indians immediately. More moderate leaders, also more sober, suggested they hold a meeting, a trial of sorts, to decide what to do now. Some few called for an end to violence and a reprieve for the captive Indians.

The angry drunken opposition shouted defiance. "Kill 'em now!" yelled one, "they're guilty!"

"Guilty of what?" said Jess. "What are these seven charged with? What evidence do you have they are guilty?"

Suddenly all shouting ended as everyone looked abruptly at Jess. After a long moment of silence, a miner stepped slowly toward Jess. His face was hard. "Charged? Evidence? Who th' hell are you?"

"I'm a miner," Jess said.

"You like Indians?" he said softly. "You got Indians workin' for you?"

Jess squared himself, tense. "I have no Indians working for me."

"He's got a Indian woman," shouted a miner from the back of the mob. "I saw her with him at th' store."

The miner leaned into Jess's face. "Well, that changes things, don't it." He stepped back slowly and pulled his coat away from his hip.

"Look out!" shouted a voice from the mob. "They're runnin'!"

All turned to see the captive Indians bolting, running frantically toward a line of trees. Immediately miners drew pistols and raised rifles and opened fire at the fleeing Indians. Two fell before they were halfway to the trees. Another was hit and collapsed to his knees. He tried to stand but was hit again and fell. As Indians ran into the woods, miners continued firing blindly.

Jess drew his pistol at the first shot and was bringing it up when arms from behind encircled his chest tightly, holding his pistol arm at his side.

"Don't do it, Jess. They'll kill us all."

Jess slumped, and Dave released him.

"Sorry, pard. We couldn't change anything. They'd kill us for sure. They may yet." He took Jess by an arm, pulling him away. "C'mon, we need to get out of here before they come back. They'll be so crazed with killing they'll likely want to get us as well."

They hurried to their horses, watching the miners who were disappearing into the grove of trees, still shooting. The three mounted and kicked the horses to a gallop on the road away from

Coloma. "Good luck, Mr. Marshall!" shouted Jess. Marshall looked at him, waved and turned back to watch the melee in the woods.

They heard later that all seven Indians, the supposed leaders, were killed. The Coloma affair was not forgotten or regretted by the instigators. It would stimulate a routine slaughter of Indians in central California that lasted well past the gold rush era.

Chapter Six

SALLIE AND JESS sat on the grass at their fire circle, staring into the glowing embers, backs against the log. She leaned against his shoulder as they sipped from coffee cups. Sallie finally had learned to tolerate coffee as long as it was hot and watered down. But, she told him, it still tasted like flavored mud, and she preferred warm water.

"Look at the lights," she said, pointing at the line of trees across the stream.

The setting sun cast slivers of light through the oaks behind the tent onto the canopy of the woods across the stream where the beams danced with the movement of the leaves in the breeze.

"It so peaceful here," she said. "I could stay here."

"Hmm. It's peaceful today, this evening. It may not always be so for us."

She snuggled against his shoulder. "Why do white people hate Indian people so much. Why do they want kill us? Just because we are Indian?"

He put an arm around her shoulders, pondered. "Mostly it's because whites want Indian lands. But it's not that simple. Spaniards came to California and took the land from the tribes. They gave no thought to Indians having rights to the land. To them, Indians were part of the land, like wild animals. Mexico made war on Spain and took California from them. Mexico built missions and said the missions would take care of Indian people, but the care amounted to slavery. The United States wanted California, so it made war on Mexico and took it. Most Americans believe the same as Spaniards and Mexicans. Indians are part of nature; they have no rights to the land. In an American California so far, Indians have not fared well."

She turned to him, frowning. "What means 'not fared well'?" They have killed us or made us slaves!"

He pulled her to him. "It just means that Indians have been treated badly. California almost surely will become a state soon. I hope leaders in the new state will be kindlier toward Indians and will protect them."

"Do you think they will protect Indians?"

He leaned against her, rested his cheek on her head.

"Do you?"

He looked into the languid stream. "No."

"Then what should my people do, kill whites?"

He looked up at the canopy, now darkening as the sun slipped below the horizon. "No, that would solve nothing, and you know that."

She looked at her feet, looked at the dark forest across the stream. "Maybe I will stop being Sallie.

Maybe I should be Maria Jesusa." She looked up at him. "Or Mary? Who am I, Jess?"

He took her cheeks in his hands. "You are Sallie, my Salinan sweetheart, and I'll fight any man who denies that."

She leaned up and kissed him, held his arm with both hands and rested against his shoulder.

They stared into the low flames, quiet. They looked up abruptly, startled at the haunting hoot of an owl. Sallie tensed, searched the canopy across the stream for the bird. "An old Yokuts woman told me one time that owls live in the spirit world and can see into the future, and they protect the home and the family." She looked at him. "Have you heard that?"

He shook his head. "No. I hope it's true. I like owls."

Seeing nothing in the darkness but the silhouette of the line of trees against the brighter sky, they looked back to the fire.

"Do you miss your mother and father?" she said.

He stared at the dancing flames. "Yes, I miss them. I'll see them again, don't know when."

She snuggled against his shoulder. "I want see my mother and father. I will see them in Heaven, and I will see all the old people of my tribe. I will ask them many questions about our people, things I have wanted to know for so long, but nobody remembered anything. The padres said we should forget the old ways."

"I understand, and that's too bad."

She looked up at him. "Do you believe we will

see the old people in Heaven? Do you believe in Heaven?"

He paused, frowning. "When I was growing up, I suppose I believed what my parents believed, and they believed in Heaven and Hell."

"Not now?"

"I don't think about it."

They lapsed into silence. He stood, picked up some kindling from the wood pile and placed each piece gently on the embers. Low flames erupted from the dry wood. He sat down, and she took his arm.

"I remember one time a man came to the mission hotel, an American," Sallie said. "An Indian woman was with him. He said she was his wife. She was Miwok, from the mountains. I don't remember how we started talking about life after death, but she said her people believe when they die, they go to a good place beyond the sunset called El-o-win. They would see all the people who had died before them and gone there. It sounded just like Heaven."

"Hmm. I suppose people who have a good life want it to continue. On the other hand, I had a friend, a black slave, who was the strongest believer in Heaven I ever knew. He said he could not be happy in this life, and he would know happiness only in Heaven where he had no master but God who loves him."

Jess looked at her, smiled. "I know this fellow pretty well. I said if God loves you, why did He let you live such a miserable life in slavery? He said that's blasphemy, and I shouldn't say it. Do you know 'blasphemy'?"

"Yes. The padres talked about it a lot."

He reached an arm around her shoulders and pulled her to him. "Well, right now, life is good. We're not going to worry about anything, except maybe, do we have coffee for tomorrow morning?"

She punched him on an arm.

———

JESS HAD PLANNED at the outset to stay in the diggings a few days out of curiosity, a few weeks at most. But he and Sallie were taking so much dust and nuggets that he could not bring himself to call it quits. Soon, perhaps, but not yet.

As expected, Sallie took more gold from the stream than he, though they usually worked with their pans side by side. They both marveled that they continued day after day to find gold from their small stretch of water. Jess guessed that flakes and nuggets were continually washed from the rocky ledge across the stream on the upstream border of their claim.

Today they worked silently, squatting barefoot in the shallows. Jess worked the edge of the deepest stretch of the stream, just below the ledge, Sallie about thirty feet downstream. Each had a small bottle in a pocket to hold the flakes gathered. They always compared the bottles each evening at day's end. Sallie's take invariably was more than his. They estimated that they took about an ounce and a half each day, more than the ounce per day that seemed to be common in the diggings.

"Still raking it in, I see."

Jess and Sallie had not heard Dave walking down the path from the trail behind their camp. They both stood and stepped from the stream to the sandy bank.

"Not sure raking is what we're doing, but we're still finding color," said Jess. "And freezing!" He shuddered, stamping in the sand to restore circulation. "Amazing spot you found for us." He rubbed his back while Sallie bent backward, flexing her back.

"Did you know that a sore back is the miner's worst complaint?" Dave said. "Course you did." He looked across the stream where the evening sun's golden rays colored the canopy. "Time to quit for the day. Come down to my camp. I'll feed you some supper and show you something I just bought. Okay?"

"Okay with me," said Sallie, "don't know about my partner here."

"Uh, don't encourage him, Sallie. I'll make supper for just you and me, and we'll get along just fine." He grinned.

Jess glared, smiled. "Guess I shouldn't be surprised that even my miner pard is horny like every other man in the diggings who's eyed my mate here. You watch out for her, old friend, she's fierce." Jess reached around Sallie's shoulders and hugged. She put an arm around his waist, smiling.

"We'll be down in a few minutes," said Jess. Dave raised a hand in acknowledgement and walked up the path to the trail. Jess took Sallie's pan, and they went to the tent.

Inside the tent, he dropped the pans in a corner,

whipped around and grabbed her with both hands. "All this talk of horny and Sallie's charms has made me a little, well, horny." He put his arms around her waist, kissed her and slowly moved his hands down her back, smiling and kissing her lips, cheek, and neck.

"Not now, you horny man. I'm hungry for Dave's supper. You can be horny after supper back here." She pushed his hands away, kissed his cheek, and went to the tent opening. "You better come too, or I'll have supper by myself with horny Dave."

They went out, and Jess secured the tent flap. Walking down the trail toward Dave's claim, Sallie turned to Jess, frowning.

"Jess, I understand what horny means, and I know what a horn is, like a cow horn, but what is the word, 'horny'?"

Jess frowned. "Hmm. Well, uh…when a man gets excited about a woman, he sort of acts like a big bull with big, uh…horns."

She frowned. "I still don't understand. But… okay." She took his arm.

They walked off the trail and down the path to Dave's camp. He looked up from the fire where he kneeled over a skillet of chunks of potatoes and fish. A sliced bread loaf lay on a plate near the fire.

"Come on down!" said Dave, "right on time." He pointed to a log near the fire where they sat on the ground, leaning against the log. He spooned helpings of fish and potatoes on plates, passed the plates to them and pointed to the bread slices.

"For drinks, I have a treat. Coffee later, but first, look at this!" He held up an opened bottle. "Zinfandel! My favorite. Did you know there are a bunch of wineries in the foothills? I sure didn't know." He poured wine into two glasses, handed a glass to Jess. He held up the bottle. "Sallie?"

She frowned, wrinkled her nose.

He smiled. "That's what I thought." He set the bottle down.

While eating, they talked of weather and the fine balmy days of spring, the growing numbers of miners in the diggings, the coarseness of the newcomers, the fear of crowding along the streams.

"It'll all work out," said Dave. "It won't be long before we'll have some official or voluntary unofficial bodies that will work for a system of order and peace in the diggings. With all the newcomers who seem to be less friendly and more aggressive, we need some organization to keep the peace."

Dave set his empty plate on the ground beside the fire and stood. "Enough of that! Are you done? I want to show you something."

Jess and Sallie stood. She took his plate and put the two plates with Dave's at the fire.

They followed him to the bottom of his claim where a wooden contraption lay on the sand near the waterline. Dave put a hand on it and beamed.

"What's this?" said Jess.

"Jess, I'm surprised that neither of us has run across a rocker. There's a bunch of 'em up stream. I'd heard of 'em but never saw one."

Jess and Sallie saw a boxy contraption that looked like it had been built of scrap wood pieces. They looked up at Dave, frowning.

Dave smiled. "Looks a little like a baby's cradle, doesn't it? I'll show you how it works."

He pushed a shovel into the sandy bottom in the shallows. He dumped the sand into a box on the top of the rocker that had a rawhide sieve bottom with half-inch holes. He picked up a bucket, scooped it full of water from the stream and poured it on top of the soil.

"You pour on water, and you rock the cradle with these handles, like you would rock a baby's cradle. The soil washes down through the sieve. Remember when you use a pan, gold is heavier than sand, so the flakes go to the bottom of the pan? The sand washes away, leaving the flakes. Same here. The soil washes away down the slide while the gold collects behind these three cleats along the bottom." Dave reached into the box at the bottom, moved the bit of soil that had been trapped at a cleat, and carefully pinched at the cleat. "Look," he said and showed them a gold flake.

Jess and Sallie had closely watched Dave.

"Looks interesting," said Jess.

Sallie picked up the pan she had placed under the bottom end of the rocker when Dave first began the demonstration. The pan was filled with the water and soil that had drained from the rocker. She swirled the soil, moving the solution with her fingers, pushing soil over the rim. She moved the remaining sediment in the pan and carefully pinched at the bottom. She dropped the pinch into her palm.

"Look," she said. She showed them three flakes.

Dave smiled. "Yeah, I thought that's what you planned when you dropped that pan under the drain. Sure enough, the rocker will miss a few flakes, but you can process a hundred times more soil with the rocker than you can by hand. Sure is easier on the back as well."

"Might give it a try," Jess said, "if I can find one. Where'd you get it?"

Dave looked at the stream. "Bought it from an old boy I met at the store. He said he was finished with it, finished with mining, in fact. Said he had taken enough gold to retire from working for a living. He said now he'll go back home and put his rocking chair on the front porch where he'll sit with his coffee each evening, pet his dog and watch the sunset. Sounded good to me. Maybe his contraption will do it for me as well."

———

DAVE STOOD in front of Jess and Sallie's tent, waiting. He wore his heavy coat, scarf wrapped around his neck, his rifle strap over his shoulder. Jess bent and stepped from the tent opening. Sallie followed. They were similarly dressed for the cold.

Sallie frowned when she saw the rifle. "I don't like kill animals."

Dave smiled. "In that case, I promise not to offer you any deer meat. Or bear meat, or whatever we take today. I'm getting tired of beans and potatoes without meat since the local beef supply ran out." He shifted the rifle strap. "Ready? It's going to be cold upcountry, and we'll see some snow."

With Dave leading, they walked up the path to the trail and turned north. After but two miles or so, they walked into a camp where Dave had arranged to be rowed across the stream in the miner's boat.

Two miners at the stream bank set their pans aside and stood.

"Ready for the hunt, I see," said Clarence.

Dave shook hands with the miners, introduced Jess and Sallie. Jess rolled his eyes as the men studied Sallie longer than the introduction required.

"Yep," Dave said. "If all goes well, I'll leave a haunch of venison with you this afternoon."

"Sounds good. Now let's get you across." Clarence held the side of the small boat as his passengers boarded. He stepped into the stern, picked up an oar and used it to push away from the bank. "Somebody get the oar there in front, and we're off."

Dave picked up the oar at his feet and stroked while Clarence rowed from the stern, using his oar as a rudder between strokes.

They crossed the narrow stream in short order, crunching through the thin ice at the bank. The miner guided the boat until it was broadside against the bank. "Step out carefully there, folks."

Dave grabbed a bush and held it while Jess and Sallie stepped onto the bank. He followed, gripping the rifle strap with his other hand. "Thanks, Clarence. Should be back late afternoon."

"Just give me a shout. You'll likely see me gittin' rich at streamside." He waved.

Dave led the way on a faint trail that lay under stands of pine and cedar, brushing against thick bushes, disturbing the fine dusting of snow. A few snowflakes swirled about in the light breeze.

After they had trudged up the trail a half hour, the clear skies at the stream below gave way to a dark overcast and light blowing snow. Sallie pulled her coat collar tight about her neck and retied the scarf around her head.

"I don't see animals, just birds." She looked up through branches of a huge sugar pine at a Steller's Jay, its blue feathers fluffed for warmth, and a nearby flicker and a goldfinch, appearing twice their size in their fluffed-up feathers.

"Hold on!" said Jess. "Hear that?"

They stopped, searching, listening, motionless.

"I didn't hear anything," said Dave. "What did you hear?"

"Be quiet," said Sallie, softly. "I hear. It not animal. It sound like person."

Jess and Dave turned abruptly to Sallie.

"Where?" Jess said, softly. "Point."

She pointed off the trail, down a slope of heavy bushes. "I hear again." She left the trail and pushed through thick bushes, disturbing the dusting of snow on the branches. Jess and Dave followed.

The down slope became a shallow ravine.

"There he is!" said Sallie.

They slid down the slope, grabbing bushes and digging boots into the wet slope, until they reached the man who was stretched out at the bottom of the ravine. A rifle lay beside him. He was dressed for cold, but his red face suggested he had suffered from long exposure. Dave kneeled beside him.

"Is he alive?" said Jess.

"He has a pulse, weak, but alive. We need to get him down. Help me." Jess and Sallie knelt and helped bundle the man tighter. Dave tied his scarf about his head.

"I'm going to carry him. Jess, take my arm and steady me. Sallie, take his rifle and mine. Everybody ready?" Dave pulled the man to a sitting position, picked him up in his arms and stood.

"Hold on, pard, we've got you." Jess gripped Dave's arm and steadied him as they climbed the slope, gripping bushes for support.

Sallie wrinkled her nose as she picked up the two rifles and climbed up the slope behind them.

———

JESS AND DAVE knelt beside the injured man who sat at the miners' fire, sipping hot coffee. He clenched his eyes in pain, rocking back and forth. Sallie stood aside, watching.

"Hurts…leg."

"It's broken," said Dave. "I've braced it the best I can, but you need to be in the hospital. We've got a wagon coming, should be here shortly. I'm taking you to a hospital in Sacramento. Clarence here will watch your claim."

The man turned his head to see Clarence. "Hey, old friend," he said. "Didn't see you." He grimaced in pain.

Don't worry about anything, Rob," said Clarence, "we'll take care of everything at the claim."

The wagon driver arrived and announced that he was ready to go immediately. They bundled Rob up, carried him up the path to the trail. Lifting him to the wagon bed, they covered him with blankets. Clarence put a small bag beside him and wished him good luck at the hospital.

Dave held back with Jess and Sallie. "I'm going with him. Don't know what I can do on the way, but we'll see. I should be back in a few days."

"Don't worry about the claim," Jess said. "We'll watch it."

Sallie kissed Dave's cheek. "You a saint. God will reward you." Dave smiled, a hint of a smile. He patted Jess on a shoulder and hurried up the path to the wagon.

When they were gone, Clarence laid a hand on Jess's back. "You folks probably saved the old boy's life. Not much of a life. He's had a bad turn lately. He's a pretty good miner, but he don't know how to handle his takings. Ever' time he accumulated a bottle of flakes, he gambled it away. Right now, he's broke. It's the main reason he was up huntin'. He thought he could sell deer meat to the camps. Now this. He's got no money to pay the cost of doctoring him."

He inhaled deeply, pondered. "Well, we'll take up a collection to help him. Same sort of thing happened last month to a miner up the way who couldn't pay doctor's bills. They took up a collection from miles around to pay his bills. People who didn't even know the man chipped in. Most miners are pretty good fellas."

"Keep us in mind," said Jess. "We'll donate. You're a good man, too, Clarence. Rob's fortunate to have you for a friend."

"You know, it's things like this that make people

stop and think about what's important," Clarence said. "I'll bet everybody 'round here has been touched in some way by somebody else's suffering. Johnny down the stream from me told me what happened when he was on his way home from Nevada City couple of weeks ago. He stopped for the night at a cabin that doubled as a café and a place to spend the night. He and a few others were sittin' before the fire, smokin' and shooting th' breeze. One of the fellas smiled and chatted a bit, but mostly listened.

"Then the landlady called everybody to come to the next room for supper. They got up and followed her. All but the quiet fella. Johnny thought he might not have heard the landlady, so he went back to the front room to get him. He wasn't there. Johnny went outside and there he was. The fella was leaning against the cabin wall, staring into the woods. Johnny told him to come to supper. The fella just looked down. Johnny told him to come to supper, and he would treat him. When the fella tried to thank him and say no, Johnny said 'you'd do the same for me. Now come on.' He came with him. I think most fellas in the mines would've done the same."

———

DAVE RETURNED FOUR DAYS LATER. He visited Jess and Sallie at their camp on the evening of his return. After supper, they sat at the fire circle, sipping coffee and watching the dancing flames. Dave reported that Rob's break had been taken care of, and he was recuperating at the hospital. He might have to get used to a slight limp, but he was okay. Jess told him about the conversation with Clarence and his plan to take up a collection for his impoverished friend.

Dave nodded. "That's good. It's good to know we're a community."

"On that point," said Jess, "have you noticed the difference in the miners who recently arrived and those who have been in the placers for a time? It's a bit surprising. The men who recently arrived seem a bit coarse, a bit grasping, impatient, mostly intolerant, hard to get along with. Maybe it's to be expected. They came for a reason, and they're anxious to get on with it.

"On the other hand, the men who have been here a while are calm, tolerant, friendly for the most part, quicker to smile than the newcomers. Course, there are exceptions, and we've seen some of those bad apples, but for the most part, long time miners are pretty good fellas."

"True enough." Dave sipped his coffee. "But even some of those good fellas get a little worked up when they see your companion there." He smiled, gestured with his cup toward Sallie.

Jess smiled, threw an arm around Sallie's shoulders and pulled her roughly to him. "Yeah, Maybe I should keep her in the tent, but can't do that. She's too good at collecting gold."

Days became weeks as the work on their little claim became a most satisfying routine. The new morning sun on this day sent thin shafts of light through the line of oaks across the stream, etching dancing patches of light and shadow on the woods behind the tent, the trees beginning to sprout green buds and new needles.

Sallie squatted in the shallows, trousers rolled up to her knees, swirling her pan as water and soil poured in a thin stream over the rim. Pinching at the bottom of the pan, she reached back to the sandy beach with her other hand and retrieved the glass bottle. She dropped two flakes into the bottle. Replacing the bottle on the sand, she dipped the pan into the gentle flow, bringing up soil and water.

"Are you ready for a rocker?" Sallie turned and saw Jess coming, barefoot, hair tousled, buttoning his shirt, hitching sagging pants. He bent and kissed the top of her head.

"That rocker seems too much like work," she said. "I like pan."

"I'm going up to the store, meeting Dave up there." He tucked shirttails in pants, buttoned the pants and closed the belt. "We need flour, and I'm going to look for fresh vegetables and fruit. I heard an old boy on the trail last evening say they had eggs. Haven't tasted eggs in a month of Sundays. Probably cost a fortune."

She stood, picked up her shoes from the bank. "I'm going with you. I've already taken an ounce, I think. I was up when you were still asleep, mumbling and moving around like you had a woman under the covers. I started to wake you up and ask her name, but you would have pulled me down, and I wanted to go to work." She leaned up, kissed him and walked up the bank. She beckoned. "C'mon. Let's go."

He watched her stride toward the tent. *My, my, you're always in charge, aren't you?*

————

Jess and Sallie walked off the trail to the store. The neat two-room freshly painted frame building was hardly four months old. Dry limbs and trunks of trees that were removed from the building site still lay at the perimeter of the space that was cleared for the construction.

They waved to Dave who stood on the store's porch and climbed the short stair to the front door. They went inside, stopped in the middle of the store and looked around, mesmerized. The large room was crammed with foodstuffs, fresh and packaged, and tools of all sorts, anything the miner could conceivably need, and many things he didn't know he needed. Goods filled shelves and covered most of the floor space. Tools hung from ceiling hooks, endangering anyone of more than average height.

Three miners wandered about the store, looking over the offerings. One, taller than the others, moved his head side to side as he strolled among the stacks of goods on the floor. One of the men straightened when he saw Sallie. He nudged the tall miner and nodded toward Sallie.

"What do you need?" Sallie said to Jess. He

pondered, looking at the ceiling array. She leaned toward him, "sweetheart," she said softly.

He turned to her, sober faced. "I'm still looking. I'll tell you what I need most when we get back to camp. Honey."

She smiled, took his arm.

"No Indians here!"

Jess and Sallie turned abruptly to see the tall miner glaring at them. Jess looked down, closed his eyes. He opened them and looked up at the miner, said nothing. Then, softly: "I beg your pardon?"

"I b'lieve you heard me. No Indians in this store." His face was hard.

Jess looked around. The man's pards stood mute behind him. The store clerk watched, fearfully, it seemed.

Jess looked back at the miner. "You own this store?" said Jess.

"We want no Indians in the diggins', anywhere!"

Jess was becoming impatient. "Are you blind, man? There are Indians all over the diggings."

"Yeah, and I don't like it." He leaned toward Sallie, his face hard. "Now get outta here!"

The miner suddenly straightened, looked down at the pistol barrel that was pushed hard into his gut. His face fell as he inhaled sharply.

"Now you're going to walk out that door without another word," said Jess, "or I'm gonna put a new hole in you that will hurt. Understand?"

The miner's eyes were wide open, his jaw hanging. He nodded and took a step backward, then spun around and walked hurriedly toward the door, his two friends following, glancing back at Jess.

Jess inhaled deeply, exhaled. "Dave, is it my imagination, or is the world populated mostly with imbeciles? At least, I seem to be meeting up with a large contingent lately."

Dave smiled. "Well, as long as you consort with an imbecile-attractor, you'll have to deal with it." He looked aside at Sallie, pulled a face.

Sallie looked back and forth between Dave and Jess, apparently confused. "What?" she said.

Jess smiled. "I'll explain later." He pushed the Colt into its holster. "Let's get what we need and be on our way."

He walked among the shelves and sacks, selecting goods and putting them into the sack he carried. Passing a window, he stopped, looked outside and saw two men standing in the yard in front of the store, looking in the direction of the porch. One was the tall man he confronted in the store. Jess went to the clerk who stood behind a counter.

"You have eggs?"

———

DAVE AND SALLIE went through the front door to the porch. They stopped when they saw the two men watching them. Dave nodded to Sallie, and they went down the stairs and walked toward the trail.

"Stop right there," said the tall man. He brushed his coattail aside, rested his hand on the grip of the pistol in its holster. His face was hard. "I told you inside..." He stopped, frowning. "Wait a minute. You're not—"

"No, he's not." The two men whipped around to see Jess, his Colt leveled on them. Jess had left the store by the back door and walked among trees until he was behind the two miners. "Now both of you toss your guns into the brush back there." He pointed. The tall man drew his pistol slowly, turned and tossed it into the brush about five feet away.

"And you?" Jess said to the other man.

"I ain't got a gun. I didn't know what he had in mind. I don't own a gun."

Jess pondered, the Colt still leveled on the tall man. "Dave, what should I do with this trouble-maker? Twice in less than an hour I've had to deal with him threatening us."

Dave frowned. "Well, Jess, I think you oughta shoot him dead right now, and you won't have to deal with him again."

Jess turned serious. He spread his feet, braced himself, leveled on the tall man's chest and cocked the hammer.

The tall man shuddered. "Don't do that, boss. I ain't a bad man. I just get upset sometimes and don't act right." He shook, saliva dribbling from his mouth. "I won't do this no more. Look, I'm movin' my claim. I'm movin' up north, goin' tomorrow. You won't see me again."

"What do you think, Dave?"

"I don't know," said Dave. "Sallie?"

She stared at the tall man. "I believe him. He doesn't look like a bad man. Let him go."

The tall man nodded, swayed back and forth, still shaking. "Thank you, ma'am, thank you." He took a couple of steps backward, looked at Jess. "Can we go now?"

Jess slowly lowered the Colt. "Yeah. You said you're moving up north tomorrow. If I see you again, it means you're a liar and can't be trusted."

The tall miner continued to back up, pulling his pard with a hold on his sleeve. "You won't see me. I'll be gone."

They turned and the tall man hurried toward the brush where he had tossed his pistol.

"Leave it," said Jess. "You can get it after we're gone. One more thing. I'm going to tell everyone I see about you so you're going to be famous. One more reason you should move north."

The tall man nodded and strode, almost running, toward the trail with his friend scurrying after him.

When the men had disappeared up the trail, Dave turned to Jess. "You keep your eyes open, Jess," said Dave. "I hope you've scared him off, but you might have put a target on your back. A lot of people round here agree with him on the question of Indians in the mines." He looked at Sallie, smiling. "Especially pretty Indian women. Sorry, Sallie."

"Don't be sorry," she said. "I'm getting used to that kind of talk from men who have their brains between their legs."

"Whoa!" said Dave, grinning.

She frowned, looked at Jess, back to Dave. "Well, that's what Jess said. Is it bad?"

Jess took Sallie by an arm. "C'mon, let's be on our way before that imbecile comes back with a bunch of like-minded friends." They walked briskly to the trail, and Dave followed.

"You know you two are going to be more famous in the diggings than the miner you just chastised, don't you?"

"Yeah, I s'pose so," said Jess.

She looked at him, surprised. "You don't think he is going to leave and go up north?" she said.

Jess thought a minute, eyes on the trail. "Maybe, maybe not. Probably depends on his wounded pride and how much whiskey he's been drinking. And whether his friends get as worked up as he's likely to be when he tells them about the store affair."

"On the other hand," said Dave, "he might be so embarrassed about the store affair that he won't talk about it."

When they reached the path to their camp, they waved to Dave who continued walking on the trail. Inside their tent, they deposited their bags in a corner.

He started to leave the tent, but she grabbed his sleeve. "In store, you call me 'honey'. I thought honey was sweet stuff bees make."

He smiled, took her cheeks in his hands, kissed her lips. "That's what it is, but you can call someone 'honey' if you think they are really sweet like bee honey. I think you are sweet like bee honey, and I'm about to eat you up!" He began slowly unbuttoning her shirt as she threw her arms around his neck.

Chapter Seven

SALLIE AND JESS stood at the back of the sanctuary in the new church. The frame building had been completed but two months ago. The twenty benches were occupied by a dozen men, all Californio but two white Americans, all dressed in their best clean clothes. The church was Methodist, but the liberal minister was happy to rent the space to a Sacramento priest for a monthly early Sunday morning service.

The priest, wearing a long black gown, spoke in heavily accented English to his charges. On occasion, he would lapse into Spanish but reverted quickly to English. When he saw Sallie and Jess enter and stand at the back, he beckoned them to come forward and sit with the others. Sallie turned to Jess, and he motioned for her to go to the front. She walked to the fourth bench and sat at the aisle, behind all the other communicants.

Jess removed his hat, sat in the aisle seat of the last bench.

During the service, Sallie knelt and crossed herself appropriately with the others. When the priest called for attendees to come forward for communion, she followed the others to the front, knelt and received the bread and wine.

When the service was finished, the others, all men, filed out, nodding while staring at her. She lowered her head as they passed. When she was about to leave, the priest motioned to her to stay. He walked to her.

He spoke to her in English. "I was surprised, and happy, to see you here."

She replied in Spanish. "Me sorprendío saber que iba a haber una misa católica por aqui."

His eyes opened wide. "You speak Spanish!"

"It is my native language."

"You are not from around here, I think."

She glanced to the back and saw Jess still sitting on the bench, watching, his look a question. She turned to the priest and told about her beginnings, her upbringing at the mission. She said nothing of Jess. "I was baptized Maria Jesusa. I choose to call myself Sallie to identify with my Salinan people."

"Ah, yes, I know something of the missions, before my time, of course. I hope your people have done well since their, what shall I say, their emancipation."

"My people have not done well. Mexico and the church did nothing for them, just pushed them away."

He lowered his head, clasped his hands at his chest, seemingly at a loss for words. He raised his head. "Um, and your...companion?" He nodded toward Jess.

She raised her chin, knowing what was coming. "He saved my life. I love him."

"I take it you are not married?" She closed her eyes, bowed her head. "I can marry you," he said. "Living together unmarried, even when you love each other, is living in sin."

She inhaled deeply, looked at Jess, and back to the priest. "Thank you for letting me come to your church today." She bowed slightly and walked to Jess. He stood, nodded to the priest and they went out.

Outside, Jess put on his hat as Sallie took his arm, and they walked silently to their horses. Jess had noticed that Sallie's face darkened at the close of her conversation with the priest as they both looked at him. He suspected that it had something to do with him. He would talk with her, later.

———

As THE DAYS grew warmer and longer, Jess and Sallie marveled that they continued to take flakes from their claim. They worked both sides of the flow to the upstream and downstream extremities of the claim. Jess sometimes waded up to his thighs to dig with his knife into the rocky ledge that crossed the stream at the top of their claim. Once he loosened a nugget as big as a small marble, on a few other occasions, nuggets the size of a pea. On other instances, he was sure he saw flakes loosened by the knife disappear in the flow. *No problem. Sallie or I will see them again in our pans.*

He concluded something he had been pondering for some time. The rocky ledge must be loaded with gold. It must have trapped flakes for eons and now releases the flakes in the flow. *That accounts for the larger take of flakes after a rain.* He had pried a few nuggets from the ledge with his knife, so he figured if he dug deeper, he surely would find more and possibly larger nuggets.

If his supposition were true, then they could likely stay on this claim indefinitely. He had heard tales from other miners about leaving a worked-out claim and going prospecting. On occasion, about once weekly, on the trail or at the store or at any sort of gathering, Jess and Sallie would hear excited tales of a gold discovery on a stretch of water that fell outside anyone's claim. They often got caught up in the excitement and rushed with a passel of miners to the site. They worked, almost shoulder to shoulder, on both stream sides of the reported discovery. The group usually took few flakes and quickly decided that they had been flummoxed or the person spreading the news of a discovery was overly enthusiastic after finding a few flakes.

When Jess and Sallie joined the throng at a supposed new bonanza, he always looked around to confirm that the person spreading the news was present. If he were not, he called Sallie and they hurried back to their camp to see whether they had been robbed.

Jess was never overly concerned. When leaving their claim for any reason, he carried the canvas bag that contained the jars of gold they had collected. They had nothing else of value in the camp that could not easily be replaced. However, their store of gold was increasing to the point that the hoard was becoming difficult to transport. Maybe they would have to bury it somewhere on the claim, a chancy solution since he had heard reports of claim jumpers digging everywhere on a rich claim for a buried hoard.

On this latest occasion, they hurried back to their claim and found that nothing had been disturbed. He built up a fire, made coffee and offered her a cup. He knew she didn't like coffee, but he offered it out of habit. Sometimes, she would opt for warm water, but not today. She waved him off and went to the stream. Removing her shoes, she squatted in the shallows and dipped her pan in the water. He smiled, leaned against the down log and sipped the coffee.

Jess was always concerned at any gathering of miners in close proximity with the attention they paid to Sallie. Clad in a baggy shirt and rolled up pants, she was still the only woman within miles, and a young, pretty woman at that. He had pondered on more than one occasion how much less complicated his life would be if he and Sallie lived on a farm, miles from any rutting male.

He sipped his coffee and shook his head, knowing that he could never be satisfied with such a sedentary, isolated existence after enjoying the excitement of the search for gold. He accepted the reality that henceforth, his life would be defined by two necessities, earning a living and protecting

Sallie. *Oh, how I love that woman. It hurts to wonder where I would be, in mind and body, without her.*

"Get to work! You're not going to find any gold in that coffee cup!" She squatted in the stream, looking back at him over her shoulder.

"Yes, ma'am."

Removing his shoes, he rolled up his pant legs and struggled up. He threw the dregs into the fire and set the cup on the ground. Picking up his pan, he walked down and squatted in the water behind Sallie. He set the pan on the sand behind him and put his arms around her chest. Resting his head on her shoulder, he kissed her neck and squeezed.

"I know what you want, Jess Winslow, but in daytime, we look for gold. Work now."

He smiled, kissed her neck again, and moved over beside her. Picking up his pan, he dug into the sandy bottom. They worked silently until the setting sun cast slivers of light through the trees behind the tent that danced on the canopy across the stream. They carried pans and bottles of flakes to the tent and made a light supper, leaning against the log, watching the flames turn to embers in the gathering gloom.

They started when shots rang out from the claim immediately upstream. They jumped up, Jess ran to the tent and came out carrying his pistol. He ran to the line of brush at the ledge, pushed branches aside. "Okay?" he shouted.

The two miners at the camp stood outside their tent, holding pistols. One man bent, peering into the tent through the opening. The other miner stood beside him, looking at Jess, grinning.

"Damn rats," he shouted. "People above us had an infestation. Must be our time. We'll send 'em your way." He chuckled.

———

Jess had been away from his Kentucky home well over a year now, and he wondered whether his mother and father still thought of him. Likely they thought him long dead. They last saw him when he waved goodbye on that morning when he set out for an excursion to Boston simply to have a look. Did they receive the letter he posted at Juan Fernandez or the one posted on the first visit to Monterey? He posted another on the second visit to Monterey and mentioned that they could write to him at Larkin's address. Larkin said he would hold letters for him or forward them as soon as Jess could give him an address. *And what would that be? The Diggings, Sierra Nevada, California?*

That problem was now solved. The owner of the store nearby, the store where he had the confrontation with the Indian-hater, announced to all his patrons that he had made arrangements with the post office in Coloma, just recently opened, to handle their letters, sending and receiving, at the store. Jess now could contact Larkin to ask him to forward any letters he might have received, and he would write again to his folks, telling them all that had transpired since he wrote from Chile and Monterey. He hoped to receive letters, but he figured that there was still not enough time elapsed for his letters to be delivered to Kentucky and a reply from there to reach California.

He chuckled when he conjured up a picture of them reading his letters. After recovering from the shock of hearing from him, confirming that he was still alive, what would they think of his tale? The impressment in Boston, the long voyage to California, his escape from the ship, and his transformation to gold miner. *Oh, they will be dumbstruck!* He sobered when he recalled how they must have suffered, surely believing long since that he was dead.

And Sallie? What will he say of Sallie? His parents had been more tolerant about Indians than their neighbors, but to say they believed Indians could be good people, deserving of equal treatment by society and law, might be a bit generous. Nevertheless, he would tell them about Sallie, her story, how he met her, and something of his feelings for her. He had said nothing of Sallie in the letter from Monterey, nor in the sole letter he had written from the placers. He determined he would write again soon.

What indeed would he say? That he cared for her as a companion? A sexual companion? He smiled. Or a sweet woman whose company he had grown accustomed to, and now needed. Indeed, while pondering what he would say in the letter, he realized that he could not visualize a future without her. He had known for some time that he loved her.

Jess wrote to Larkin, telling all that had transpired since he left Monterey. He also asked whether he had received any letters for him and, if so, to forward them to him in care of the Coloma post office. Now he would wait.

———

SALLIE USUALLY BATHED at dusk in shallows, wearing her old cantina dress, now worn and tattered, and mostly protected from view from the trail by tall reeds at streamside. On this unusually warm late spring day, she had worked in the sun and had perspired heavily. Soon after entering the stream at her bathing spot, she pulled the dress over her head, shook her hair loose, and tossed the dress on the reeds. Jess sat on the sand nearby, sipping from his coffee cup, watching her. She moved closer to the reeds, smiling, pretended to hide herself with her hands in mock embarrassment, then raised her hands to her cheeks.

Neither saw the two men who crouched behind the tent, peering through the low branches of a pine tree, silently watching Sallie, jaws hanging.

———

AFTER BREAKFAST THE FOLLOWING MORNING, Jess decided to go down to Dave's claim to have another look at his rocker. He was not convinced that he wanted a rocker of his own, but he was still intrigued. Since Sally was even more skeptical than he, perhaps he could ponder a plan in which he would work the rocker, and she would process the flow at the bottom, catching any flakes that the rocker had missed.

He walked to where she worked just below the cross-stream ledge. "Do you want to go?" he said.

She frowned. "No. You go waste time. I work here. I will have five ounces by the time you come back."

He smiled, kissed the top of her head. Walking up the path, he turned downstream on the trail toward Dave's claim.

————

THE SUN WAS high when Jess walked back down the path to his claim, Dave following. Jess had persuaded him to come to his place for lunch and to give his opinion on the best place to set up a rocker. If he decided to get a rocker.

They stopped in front of the tent. Jess looked inside, then at the stream. "Sallie!" he called. *Maybe she's in the bushes downstream*. He walked down to the thicket of bushes and reeds at streamside and called again. No answer. He went back to where she had been working when he left that morning. Her pan lay on the sand at streamside. Upside down. *She never set her pan upside down.*

Then he saw the boot prints he had overlooked. Two sets of boot prints. The sand was disturbed, suggesting a struggle. He looked back to the path and saw boot prints that he suspected were not his or Dave's.

He touched his holster, turned to Dave. "I'm looking for Sallie. She wouldn't leave while I'm away."

"I'm going with you."

They hurried up his path to the trail, turned right, upstream. "We know they didn't go downstream," Jess said. "They would've passed by your place, and we saw no one."

Passing by claims, Jess called to anyone he saw at the stream or on the trail. No one had seen a woman, alone or with others. More than one miner said they would have noticed a woman.

After walking a couple of miles, a miner standing at a rocker scratched his head and said he saw three or four men mid-morning, huddled together hurrying up the trail. And he heard a muffled sound, a sort of whimper. "Could've been a woman, I s'pose, now that you mention it."

Jess mumbled his thanks and quickened his pace, his face hard. He continued to question everyone he saw on the trail or working at the stream. Most shook their heads or said they had seen or heard nothing.

Then a miner working alone dropped his pan at Jess's shouted question and hurried up the path to the trail. He pointed upstream.

"There's a bunch of bad 'uns up there. Noisy and not too serious about minin'. They make a lot of noise and drink all day. They started early today after a ruckus 'bout mid-mornin'. I think they got 'em a squaw. She ain't too happy about it and has been makin' lots of noise, but they shut her up real fast."

Jess ran up the trail, Dave close behind. They stopped at a path leading down to a camp of two tents fronted by a large fire circle. Debris of all sorts, clothing, utensils, sacks, littered the site. Two men stood at streamside, holding bottles, laughing. One upended his bottle and drank.

Jess and Dave hurried down the path, sliding on the wet leaves and roots. The two men at streamside, an oldster and a younger man, saw them. The younger man raised his bottle and shouted, grinning. "Hey, what's up?"

"Where is she?" shouted Jess. He drew his six-shooter.

"Jess, I—" Her shout became a muffled whimper. Jess ran to the tent and saw inside the man holding Sallie with an arm around her shoulders and a hand over her mouth. Jeff brought the pistol grip down hard on the man's head, and he crumpled. Sallie threw her arms around Jess's neck, tears streaming down her cheeks.

"Wait," Jess said quickly.

He stepped outside to see the younger man at streamside holding a pistol, pointing at him. Jess quickly leveled on him and fired. The man was blown backward. He threw his arms up, stumbled sideways, lost the gun, and collapsed on his back. Jess whipped aside, leveled on the oldster who stood empty-handed, his arms stretched high.

"I got no gun," the miner said, trembling.

Jess went to the tent where Sallie stood in front with Dave, gun drawn. Jess went inside, saw the man lying where he had fallen. He bent down, saw bloody scratches on his cheeks and a dark bruise beside an eye.

"Yeah, he's still out," Dave said.

"I don't care if he doesn't wake up, th' bastard."

He put his hands on Sallie's cheeks and kissed her. "You okay?"

"I'm okay. I knew you would come. They didn't do anything to me. I think they wanted to get drunk before they did something."

"Were you trying to rearrange his face?"

"Rearrange? Uh…I was trying to scratch his eyes out."

"My, my, I'll never cross you, my little wildcat."

———

A NUMBER of miners from claims close by had rushed over at the ruckus and Jess's shot to investigate. Loud carousing at any time of the day was not unusual in the diggings, but shots were not common. One of the miners acknowledged he knew nothing about what happened, but he believed that the incident should be investigated to discourage a recurrence. He asked for comment. The dozen or so men looked around.

"I have a suggestion," said a miner. He told about a similar circumstance in the diggings a few miles north. A miner was killed in a drunken knife fight. There was so much confusion on what caused the fight and who was responsible for the death that they decided to hold a hearing. In the absence of organized law and order, they set up a miner's court overseen by one from among them, a Pennsylvania lawyer in his previous life.

"Sounds good," said a bystander. "How do you know so much about all this?"

"I was on the jury."

"Oh!" said another of the group. "What was the jury's decision?"

"Hung jury. We couldn't decide who was responsible. Everybody involved in the fight was drunk, and all the bystanders were drunk, and nobody's testimony was reliable."

"Well, it was a good move, anyway," said a young miner who had listened with interest. "I don't think we'll have the same result here."

"You're surely right there," said a miner who had listened with interest. "I heard about a incident up north that was pretty clear on the outcome, too, but in the other direction. It was in Coloma. A woman—don't recall whether she was Indian or Mexican—stabbed a miner and killed him, right there on the street in full view of a dozen people. They tied her up and right there formed a jury of a dozen men, some who had seen the murder, and tried her, right there on the street. People walking by began to bunch up, watching. They knew what was coming.

"The jury found her guilty and hanged her that same afternoon. They put the noose around her neck, put her on a horse and slapped the horse's rump. Yeah. Hundreds of people watched. When they slapped the horse and the woman swung, everything went quiet, from shock, I s'pose. Then some people cheered before walking away."

Another miner chimed in. "There's bad 'uns all over, but they ain't all bad. I heard about a miserable old man who was caught stealing some stuff from a claim. They gave him some lashes with a rawhide whip, sent him on his way and told him not to come back. But some miners who had watched all this took up a collection from their own pockets and gave it to him. Most people hereabouts are good folks."

———

THE MINER'S court trying Jess's case convened in the same Methodist church that Sallie had attended as worshipper and Jess as spectator. The minister agreed to permit the hearing in the church in the interest of order and justice. The Pennsylvania attorney agreed to come down to officiate, a working holiday he called it. He interviewed a goodly number of miners in the district and secured the participation of six to sit as jurors. He explained that neither he nor the court had any legal authority so the best they could do was to hold the hearing, reach a decision and pass the particulars to authorities in Sacramento.

The six jurors were unanimous in their enthusiasm for the hearing. They agreed that it should be instructive, a short respite from productive work, and a bit of fun.

Since the court had no legal authority, no one could be compelled to attend. The oldster who stood beside his pard when he was shot by Jess, agreed to attend as a witness. Dave enthusiastically agreed to attend and be named a witness. The Pennsylvania lawyer was impressed that Dave offered to show proof that he was a doctor, a Yale graduate, though not practicing at the moment.

Sallie attended as victim and witness. During the

proceedings, she told about her abduction from their claim and her struggle with the miner who tried unsuccessfully to have his way with her in the tent. The miner was not present at the hearing. Dave told what he saw, Jess rushing into the tent and rescuing Sallie, Jess emerging from the tent to face the pistol of the enraged miner and Jess defending himself by shooting the miner.

The oldster, when questioned as a witness, agreed with Dave's description. "That's what happened. He was a bad 'un. I figured something like this was gonna happen someday."

And it was finished. The Pennsylvania lawyer thanked all for their participation. He said he would forward the particulars to the Sacramento Sheriff and leave it to him whether to pursue Sallie's attacker. He included the judgment of the court that Jess was entirely blameless. It was a clear case of self-defense.

———

JESS'S TRIAL to the contrary, lynch law, hanging without trial of any sort, was still the norm in the diggings. Jess had not thought much about the almost total absence of law and authority. Miners for the most part were decent fellows who were the same people who had lived in settled communities back home where law and order and police and courts were part of everyday life. It seemed that the diggings were becoming a community of sorts and the occupants were moving toward a desire for order and respect for authority.

But justice? Jess recalled hearing on his last visit to the store that miners up north had hanged an old black man for theft. No arrest, no trial, just a mob of angry miners and a prejudice they brought with them from their eastern homes.

"No, there was no talk about a trial like when you shot the miner that carried away your woman," said the store owner. "There was some tools and food stolen from a claim, and there was a black man seen on the trail. He didn't have any of the stolen stuff on him, but the mob hadn't seen him before, so they put two and two together and decided that he stole the stuff. They hung him the same day. They left him swingin' all day and all night as a warning to passersby. Next morning, a woman and her boy cut him down and buried him. Seems she said a prayer over the grave, and that didn't set well with the locals."

"Sad," said Jess. "People, even otherwise good people, can be blinded by prejudice sometimes." He pushed his purchases of vegetables into his cloth bag. "Wonder what that old fellow's story is, how he came to be in the diggings alone. I haven't seen any black people in the mines. He might have been the only black man around here."

"I haven't seen any black people around here either," said the clerk, "but I did hear about a black man at a claim a few miles north. Young man, I hear. Don't know his story though." He waited as Jess slowly stowed his purchases in a couple of bags, frowning, preoccupied. "By the way, I'm Barney. I know who you are."

Jess nodded, thanked him. Walking from the

store, he stopped on the porch. He frowned, looking blankly at the pine grove beyond the yard. *A young black man, alone.* He shouldered the bags and strode toward the trail.

———

NEXT MORNING, Jess stood with Dave and Sallie on the store porch. "Now you stay right here till we get back," Jess said to Sallie. "Barney said you could stay here."

She frowned.

"Yeah, I finally got his name. We'll be back today." He kissed her, then followed Dave down the steps.

They walked north on the trail, passing claims, waving to miners who looked up from where they squatted in the shallows, or where they stood beside rockers or long toms. They avoided conversation, asked no questions. Jess did not want to reveal their purpose, fearing an encounter with some who might sympathize with the miners who worked a black person as a chattel.

After walking a couple of hours, they stopped at a path that led down past two tents to a wide sandy beach where half a dozen men worked a long tom. Three stood on each side of the tom, pouring water at the top end, working the soil, picking out flakes. The middle man on the far side was a young black man. Jess walked down the path toward the beach, Dave following.

"Reuben!" Jess called.

He and Dave stopped ten steps from the long tom. Everyone on the tom jerked around, scowling, to see the intruders. Their faces were hard, surprised. All except Reuben whose face lit up.

"Jess!" said Reuben. He stepped back and started walking toward the end of the tom. The miner at the end grabbed his shirt and roughly stopped him.

"Where th' hell you think you're goin'? Git back to work." He turned to Jess, his face hard. "Who th' hell are you?"

Jess ignored him. "Reuben, what's going on? These guys give you a better offer than I did?"

"Hey, you're talking to me, not him!" said the miner. "He's my boy, and you got no claim on him."

Jess glared at him. "You're beginning to bore me, mister. Reuben is not a boy, and you don't own him. He's a free man and a friend. He's going with us."

Two of the miners stepped toward Jess and Dave. They stopped abruptly when they saw two six-shooters leveled on them.

"Reuben, if you have anything you want to take away, get it while these good fellows stand where they are or go back to working that fine-looking tom."

"Right, Jess," said Reuben. He ran to one of the tents, came out a moment later carrying a small bundle and almost ran to Jess.

The miner who had done the talking had not taken his eyes off Jess. "You ain't seen the end of this. 'Jess,' is it?" He smiled thinly.

Jess waited a moment, glaring at the speaker.

Then: "If I even get a glimpse of you around my claim, or anywhere actually, you're in my gun sights. And I'm passing your description around among miners for miles away to watch out for you and to notify me if they see you." He waved the pistol toward him and slipped it into its holster. He put an arm around Reuben's shoulder, and they walked up the path behind Dave. All three glanced repeatedly back at the miners.

As they walked, Reuben told them his story. Leaving the ship in a territory that was about as familiar to him as the surface of the moon, he headed for the only place in California he had visited. He knew only that Monterey was north. He asked travelers along the trail for information. They gaped at this black man, a rarity in the territory, but gave him directions until he arrived in Monterey and visited Talbot Green at Larkin's place.

Talbot pondered and suggested he try the diggings. Talbot set him up with provisions and a shovel, gave him directions and wished him luck on the road and in the diggings.

"When these miners saw me walking on the trail, they stopped me and asked me who was my master. They laughed when I said I was a free man. They put me to work and said they would kill me if I didn't work or tried to run away. I was so surprised to see you. How did you find me?"

"I heard about a young black man in the diggings and figured it might be you. You got to be very careful since there are many southerners around here who have no sympathy for black people. And they likely hate free black people more than slaves."

"How about Reuben staying at my place, Jess?" said Dave. "There's plenty of room in the cabin, and he can help me with the rocker." He turned to Reuben. "If that's okay with you."

"I'll do anything you say," Reuben said, "anything both of you say. You saved my life back there. I wouldn't have put up with it much longer, and they would've killed me for sure."

"Sounds like a good arrangement, Dave," said Jess. "Our claims are only a few minutes apart, Reuben, and we get together regularly."

They turned off the trail and walked toward the store. Sallie stood on the porch, smiling and waving wildly. They climbed the stairs, and Jess introduced Sallie and Reuben.

She nodded to Reuben, her face blank, and turned to Jess. "What happened?" she said.

"I'll tell you later," Jess said. "Let's go in. We need vegetables."

Inside, Jess waved to Barney who returned the wave. Barney looked alternately at Reuben and Sallie. He smiled at Sallie, then looked abruptly at the woman who stood near the back door, scowling at him.

Barney turned back to the room. "Uh, Jess, Dave, this is Annie, my wife." Jess smiled at her, raised a hand in greeting.

She nodded, still frowning, looking at Sallie and Reuben.

"Barney, Annie, this is Reuben," said Jess. "He's

a friend visiting the diggings. He's staying with us. He may come in occasionally to pick up things for us."

The storekeepers, solemn, nodded to Reuben.

Sallie and Jess wandered around the store, looking over the offerings, selecting vegetables and fruits, pushing them into the canvas bags they carried. Dave stood at the window, watching the others. He had already told them he had shopped at the store the previous day.

Barney suddenly brightened, smiling broadly. "Boys, almost forgot. I have letters for both of you."

He reached under the counter, pulled out a box of letters. He leafed through the letters, picked out three. He handed two to Jess and gave Dave a single letter. Dave nodded to him, looked at the envelope and pushed it into a pocket.

Jess thanked Barney and walked to the window. He was not surprised to receive nothing from his folks, still not enough time for his letter to reach them and their reply to come. He opened the envelope from Larkin and read the single sheet. Larkin told of reports that gold mania in the East was spreading, and thousands of hopefuls were either on the trail or making plans to embark soon. He asked if Jess had anything to report. Jess folded the letter slowly and slipped it into the envelope. *What indeed shall I report?*

The other letter was from Fred Biggs. He hadn't known Fred's last name. He didn't give it when he tried to buy Sallie that first day at Sutter's. In the letter, Fred said he had a business proposal for him. He explained that San Francisco authorities, expecting the explosive interest in California real estate lately was just the beginning, were surveying lots around the city and offering them for sale. Lots bought six months ago, Fred said, had tripled in value. He added he was planning to invest and invited Jess to join him in this sure thing.

Jess showed Dave the letter from Fred. Dave read it, frowning. "Who is this fella?" Jess told him about the meeting at Sutter's. "Sounds most interesting," said Dave. "Stands to reason, worth investigating. Sounds like something I could be interested in, but I would invest on my own rather than joining your friend." He tapped the letter on the windowsill, looking through the panes. He turned back to Jess. "I'm going to San Francisco to have a look. How about it? Go with me?" He handed the letter to Jess.

Jess frowned. He was not convinced. The value of San Francisco lots would surely increase as long as gold was taken from the diggings. What if the gold plays out? Inversely, what if the gold harvest increases so much that the value of gold declines? *But why not have a look?* He had enough gold from the mission and the placers to speculate with some of it. Fred had been involved with Sutter and gold prospecting, though as an outsider, from the outset. And he knew San Francisco.

Jess beckoned to Sallie to come to the window. She came over, looked from Dave to Jess. Jess told about the contents of the letter and asked what she thought. She replied that she was ignorant of white man's affairs and his strong wish to make money and own things.

"Oh, Jess. You're never gonna be rich," said Dave, smiling.

Sallie's eyes opened wide, and she looked back and forth between Dave and Jess. "What? I just say I don't understand. I didn't say not to do something."

Jess smiled. "You see, Dave? Sallie will be my anchor. She will prevent me from jumping into something foolish. Would you like to go to San Francisco, sweetheart?" Dave looked sharply at Jess.

She frowned. "San Francisco. Is that a big town, like Monterey?"

"Yes, ma'am," said Dave. "It's a big town, and it's going to get a lot bigger."

"Yes, I would like to see it." She turned to Jess, her eyes wide open. She gripped his arm. "We not going to move to big town, are we?"

He smiled. "No, I would never do that. We're just going to have a look, only a day or two." He turned back to Dave. "I'll write to Fred to ask when he'll be in Sacramento. We'll take his boat and talk with him on the sail to San Francisco. What about our claims? Will they be secure while we're away?"

Dave pondered. "I know people within a mile of our claims, north and south, who should be willing to spend some time on the sites each day we are away, to demonstrate that these are working claims and not available to outsiders. We'll be okay."

"What about Reuben?" Jess said.

"Hmm. Yeah." Dave pondered, rubbing his chin. "I'll be sure to choose fellas to watch our claims who have no problems with black people. I'll tell Reuben to stay in the cabin latched from the inside any time these fellas are not around." Dave shook his head. "Isn't this a sad state of affairs? Reuben is as good as any man in the placers, and better than most, and he may have to hide. Sad."

"Sad indeed," said Jess.

They went to the counter where Jess paid Barney for the vegetables, and Sallie stuffed them back into the canvas bags. Jess thanked him and hefted the bags. He started walking toward the door but stopped and turned back.

"By the way, Barney, how did these letters for us reach you?"

Barney grinned. "I sent the Coloma post office a list of everybody I know in the diggings for miles around."

"Good idea," said Jess. "Much appreciated."

"Pays to be lucky. Did you see the papers there?" He pointed to a stack of newspapers at the end on the counter. "Came in yesterday from Coloma."

Jess and Dave leafed through the stack. One paper was from Philadelphia, others from New York and Washington. Articles on the front page of each reported in excited prose details of the gold discovery, the emigration from the East and early tales from the placers. They leafed through the papers, skimming the articles.

"The diggings are gonna get real crowded real fast," said Barney.

Jess waved his thanks to Barney as they walked to the door. Dave glanced aside at Jess. "Sounds like it may be a good time to find opportunities somewhere outside the diggings."

Sallie took Jess's arm, looked up at him, frowning. "I don't want move to big town."

"We're not going anywhere, sweetheart. In fact, if we decide our claim is going to keep paying, I just might ask Dave to help us build a cabin. What do you say, Dave?"

"I'm ready just as soon as we come back from exploring the big city," Dave said.

Chapter Eight

Two weeks passed before they were able to arrange a sail to San Francisco with Fred and Benny. It was a two-day ride from their claims to Sacramento, and they arranged to stay the travel night at The Big Bear Inn. Opened only a few months ago, the inn featured a small café and rooms for travelers.

Arriving at the inn at dusk, they checked in, put their horses in the corral in back and tack in the shed, and came back in for supper. Inside the café, they saw three tables. A table in the corner was occupied by three men, farmers, ranchers or miners, judging from their rough clothing and sunburned faces. Their plates were empty, glasses almost empty.

Jess, Sallie, and Dave sat down at a table near the kitchen door. The door was open, and they heard a woman's voice inside the kitchen, speaking in Spanish.

A man's voice replied softly, "English, English."

A moment later, the woman came to their table.

She smiled, told what was offered this evening, and they placed their order.

"Gracias," she replied, then scrunched her shoulders, made a face, smiled. "Thank you."

Sallie touched her hand. "No olvide su español, señora. Quizás llegará un día cuando los blancos tendrán que aprender nuestro idioma."

"Si!" The waitress smiled broadly at Sallie, squeezed her hand. She went back through the kitchen door.

Jess leaned toward Sallie, spoke softly. "What did you say?"

"I told her to not lose her Spanish. I said that someday white people will need to learn *our* language."

"Hmm. Nice thought, but...well, not likely."

The woman returned only a few minutes later with the plates. "Aguardiente? Wine?"

Dave ordered wine, aguardiente for Jess. Sallie shook her head. The woman went to the kitchen and returned promptly with the drinks.

During the meal, the three men at the corner table spoke softly to each other, grumbling, glancing at the kitchen door and at the other diners. Their glasses were empty.

Soon the woman came out again and went to the corner table. "Dessert? We have apple pie?"

The man who had been the chief grumbler during the meal leaned back in his chair, spoke loudly. "Send the boss out here. I'm done dealin' with th' greaser."

She stepped back, hand to mouth, then retreated

quickly to the kitchen. Immediately a large man burst through the door, his face livid.

He strode to the corner table. "Who said that?"

The two men turned instinctively toward the man who said it. The owner stepped around the table, grabbed the speaker roughly by the lapels.

"I've had it with you sumbitches." He jerked him upright, dragged him to the door, pushed the door open and threw the grumbler outside to the ground. "Don't come back, or I'll have your ass!"

The owner came back inside, his face contorted with anger. He stepped aside to permit the other two men to sidestep out through the door, eyes downcast and eager to escape.

The owner closed the door. He slumped, looked at the three at their table. "Sorry, folks," he said, as he walked past them toward the kitchen.

"Good man!" Jess called. "Tell her we would like the apple pie, please."

———

Jess, Dave, and Sallie met Fred and Barney at the wharf in Sacramento, exchanged pleasantries, and all set to work loading the boat with foodstuffs bound for the city.

As Fred and Jess hefted a large bundle and swung it to the boat deck, Fred gestured with a nod toward Sallie. "Set a price yet?" Fred smiled. Flexing his back after tossing the bundle to the boat deck, Jess exchanged a glance with Sallie.

She leaned against Jess's back and put her arms around his waist. "I decide not to sell him."

"Well, that's a relief," said Fred. He beckoned to Barney and Dave, who had been loading near the bow. "Are we done? We need to be off."

"Ready!" said Barney.

"Okay," Fred said. He grinned. "But before we go. Look." He pointed at a boat tied a short distance down the wharf. "That, folks, is our new boat. It's about ready. Next time we go to the bay, it will be in the new boat."

They saw the stern of a wide, square-built boat with not a sail in sight.

Dave frowned, looked closely at the boat, then at Fred. "Is that a…steamboat?"

Fred beamed. "It is indeed. A sternwheeler steamboat, not new, but newish, and one of the first steamboats on the Sacramento River. We'll use it on the runs to the bay and to towns upriver, even to towns on streams that flow into the Sacramento. Depth is no problem. That boat has such a flat bottom it will float on a heavy dew!"

"Are we gonna get to see it?" said Jess.

"Yes indeed, but not now. Too late. We gotta get underway. We'll see it when we return. Been dying to show it to you."

They untied lines and tossed them aboard, climbed in and pushed away from the dock. Raising sails, they were underway. Sails filled in the light breeze and the boat moved to midstream, aided by the slight current. Standing near the bow, the three passengers quietly stared at the steamboat as they slowly passed.

Sallie tugged at Jess's sleeve, leaned up and spoke softly. "What is 'sternwheeler steamboat'?"

Jess smiled and pondered. "Oh, my. Well, it is a large boat that is driven by steam instead of wind. And—"

She moved closer to his ear. "Jess. What is 'steam'?"

He frowned. "Um, honey, let me think about this."

He looked at Dave who cocked his head, smiling. Jess pointed at the bench midships along the gunwale. All found seats, and conversation turned to San Francisco real estate.

Jess, Sallie, and Dave stood on the wharf surveying what was the marvel of San Francisco. A sleepy coastal town but two years ago, it now was an emerging metropolis. It was a mélange of old wooden structures and new brick and wooden frame buildings and tents of all sizes. The streets were crowded with men and women, some dressed in Sunday finery, others in drab rough work clothes. All seemed to be busy and hurrying to be somewhere else.

Fred stood on the wharf where he would watch the boat's cargo that was stacked beside the boat. Barney already was off to the town to notify the merchants who had ordered the produce.

"You folks head on out," said Fred. "Just tell the agent what I told you. When they hear you've been talking with old Fred, they'll know you're serious. There they are, right there." He pointed at a shop on the first street facing the bay.

"Thanks, Fred, we're on our way," said Jess. "You said we'll leave tomorrow at 10:00 a.m., right?" Fred nodded. "We'll be here. We should have seen all of San Francisco we want to see by then. Don't leave without us."

Fred waved. "Watch out for the hustlers. They'll recognize you for strangers real fast." In fact, Jess and Dave wore sturdy shirts, pants, and heavy coats, all clean and crumpled, the sort of gear that miners wore in the big city. Sallie wore a stylish, long dress and shoes that Jess had instructed Fred by letter to buy for her in San Francisco. She had changed to the new clothes after all the men had disembarked. She was embarrassed when Jess first saw her in the new outfit, but he said he loved it, not as much as her trousers, but very pretty. He smiled when he said it, and she punched him playfully on his arm.

Jess and Dave returned the wave to Fred. Jess took Sallie's arm and the three walked off the wharf toward the storefront pointed out by Fred. It was a new frame building with large glass windows. The sign on the front door read simply: San Francisco Real Estate.

Jess opened the door, and they went in. A man sitting behind a desk at the far wall looked up from his papers, stood up immediately and, grinning broadly, hurried around the desk to meet them. He was dressed in a black wool suit, black bow tie, and wearing a bowler hat. He motioned to two chairs before the desk. "Come in, come in out of the cold. I'll warm you up with the hottest deals in San Francisco real estate you'll find anywhere. I'm Winston Thurston." He extended a hand, and they shook it. "How can I serve you?"

First off you can serve me best by shutting up. Jess went to a table against a wall and pulled a chair over beside his. He motioned for Sallie to sit. After she sat down, he turned to Thurston. "Fred Biggs said you could sell us some lots that will increase in value so much we'll never have to work again. I'm Jess Winslow, that's Dave Clark, and this is Sallie." He touched her shoulder. Dave nodded to Thurston, and Sallie looked blankly at him. Thurston stared at her a moment, silently. Jess looked at Dave, frowning.

Thurston brightened, looked at Jess and smiled. "Ah, Fred Biggs. I suspect you met Mr. Biggs in San Francisco or Sacramento or in the gold country. Yes, Mr. Biggs bought lots, let's see, about three or four months ago, and they have already *tripled* in value." He turned toward a man who sat at a desk at the wall near the front window. "What do you think, Wally?"

"Well, Mr. Thurston, don't know specifically about Biggs's lots, but all San Francisco lots, including the ones we've sold, have increased in value at least three times, some even more, especially those overlooking the entrance to the bay."

"Ah, yes," said Thurston. "Those are choice lots. I own a few of those myself. I might add that I sold a large block of those lots to Mr. Thomas O. Larkin just a month ago. He said he would come back sometime soon to discuss an additional purchase. Mr. Larkin is the American consul to California, you know, or maybe you don't know. He lives in Monterey."

"In fact, I do know Mr. Larkin. In fact, I work for him." Thurston's eyes opened wide. He cut a quick glance at Wally. "Now," Jess said. "I would like to buy lots near Mr. Larkin's at the same price you sold to him. I'm investing two thousand dollars. I will be talking with Mr. Larkin soon and will tell him about my purchase. If I am pleased with the result of our business today, and if Mr. Larkin encourages me, I'll likely be back to buy more."

Thurston looked nervously at Wally. Wally simply looked blankly at him. Thurston turned back to Jess. "I, uh, don't think we can sell you lots at the price Larkin paid a month ago. The lots have increased in value substantially since then."

"I suspect that's just speculation," said Dave. "I don't suppose you or Larkin or anybody else who owns those choice lots has resold any of those properties lately."

"Well, yes, that's true. Our clients have been so pleased with the prospects they have held onto the lots." He pondered, looking down, frowning. He looked up. "Tell you what. Best estimates are that the bay view lots have increased in value 300% in the last three months. I'll sell you bay lots in the same general location where Mr. Larkin bought, at the price Mr. Larkin paid, plus fifty percent."

Jess and Dave looked at each other. Dave nodded. "Okay," Jess said. "I'll be talking with Mr. Larkin, and I'll check back in with you. Two thousand dollars now, and if I like what happens to these, I'll be back for more."

"And you, sir?" Thurston, smiling broadly, said to Dave.

"Same location, same terms. I'm investing three thousand dollars now. We'll see what happens later."

"How will you be paying for the deeds, gentlemen?" said Thurston, smiling.

"Dust," said Jess. "What's it worth today?"

"Hold on. I check every morning since some purchasers, like yourselves, pay with gold." He opened a drawer, rummaged in papers, selected a sheet, adjusted his spectacles and read from it. "Yes, this morning the rate quoted to me was twenty dollars and sixty-seven cents per ounce."

Jess and Dave exchanged a glance. They dug into packs and handed containers of dust to Thurston. He placed Jess's containers on one end of his desk and Dave's on the other end.

"Right!" said Thurston. "Wally, let's look at the plat map and turn these miners into San Francisco property owners."

"I'm encouraged," said Jess. "I had qualms about spending good money on speculation, sorta like gambling, but it looks good, especially since Mr. Larkin bought into it."

They walked in a neighborhood of shops and saloons and boarding houses. The street at dusk was crowded with pedestrians, shoppers, and drunks, stumbling from saloons, singing, shouting and laughing. They passed a lamplighter who was reaching up with a long pole to light a streetlamp with a burning wick on the end of the pole.

"Agreed," said Dave. "I'm not a gambler. I like sure things, and this seems more sure than hunting for gold." He looked aside at Jess. "Your take on Larkin sealed the deal. If he liked the prospects, I like the prospects. I'd like to meet him someday."

"You shall, next time I see him." Jess had his

arm around Sallie's shoulders, pulled her close. "What do you think about the day's business? The money I invested is more yours than mine."

"I don't know anything about what you call business. I trust you. I don't need money."

Jess smiled. "Oh my, we need to talk. If we grew potatoes and tomatoes and kept chickens, I suppose I could agree we don't need money. But that's not the case, is it? We need money to *buy* those things. And some clothes now and then."

"You need money, I got money and I'm buyin'!"

Jess and Dave and Sallie started at the loud voice behind them. They stopped and turned to see three men close behind. They had not heard them come up. Jess looked over their shoulders to see the saloon they had just passed. The door was still open. The men wore heavy workingmen's clothes, though one sported a wide-brimmed sombrero, and another had a knit cap pulled down over his ears.

The three were so drunk they could hardly stand upright. One almost fell, as he weaved to the left and had to step quickly leftward to steady himself. Another blinked slowly and seemed ready to go to sleep on his feet.

"I said I'm buyin'!" said the third drunk, standing between his pards.

"From the looks of things," said Dave, "you've been buying all evening. You need to buy a place to lie down."

The grinning drunk pointed at Dave. "You are right on there, my man. I need to lie down now, with that pretty little squaw." He weaved, pointing at Sallie. "How much you want? I'll give you a hundred dollars, right now!" He pulled a handful of coins from a pocket, fumbled as he tried to count, dropping coins that clinked on the stone pavement.

Jess shook his head. "If the three of you have a brain among you, be on our way and find a place to lie down and sober up."

"Hey, hey." The drunk braced himself. "Okay, I'll give you *two* hundred dollars. C'mon, squaw, you're comin' with me." He reached for Sallie as she retreated behind Jess.

Jess knocked the drunk's hand down and pushed him away.

The drunk's eyed opened wide. He dropped the coins, brushed his coat aside and fumbled for the pistol in its holster. Jess saw the move and punched the drunk hard in the stomach. He fell backward, stumbled a few steps, and collapsed on his back.

Jess had drawn his pistol before the drunk hit the ground. He held it at his side until he confirmed that the other two were not drawing. "Can you take care of him," Jess said to the downed man's companions, "or shall I call the police?"

The two men appeared to have sobered quickly, at least enough to nod their response to Jess. "We'll take him," said one, slurring softly. They bent and pulled their companion up, walked off slowly, dragging him between them, as he tried to walk, stumbling and dragging, mumbling incoherently.

"That was not how I wanted to end this evening of our first visit to the big city," Jess said.

———

Dave, Jess, and Sallie walked up the steps of the hotel that Fred had recommended. They had enjoyed a nice dinner at a café with a view of the bay. That is, they enjoyed it after avoiding an altercation with the greeter at the door who had looked at Sallie and stepped in front of them.

He was about to speak when Jess sighed, stepped into the man's face, almost nose to nose, and said softly: "Table for three with a view of the bay."

The man had blinked, thought about it only a moment, then turned and showed them to a table for three with a view of the harbor.

At the hotel, Jess went to the desk. "Two rooms for this one night," he said.

The clerk looked over his shoulder at Dave and Sallie who sat on a couch just inside the door.

"Sorry, I don't want to inconvenience you, but we don't take Indians."

Jess clenched his eyes, raised his chin. He opened his eyes, looked at the clerk a long moment. He bent forward and spoke softly, slowly, and deliberately. "My good man, you have just committed an act with international implications. The woman there is not Indian; she is Burmese, a Burmese princess. She just arrived in San Francisco today to join her husband who is a Burmese official, visiting California officials about a trade agreement between the two countries. I am her guardian until she joins her husband, uh, tomorrow. Shall I tell her husband and his American counterpart that this hotel, the Bayview, and its clerk, Mr."—he looked pointedly at the clerk's nametag—"Mr. Andrews, has insulted the princess and her country? Shall I tell them that?"

The clerk's face had fallen during Jess's recitation. "No, uh, no, please. Let me, uh, let me show you to your rooms." He hurried around the desk. "This way, this way." He waved to Sallie. "This way, please, madam." When she and Dave came up to him, the clerk bowed slightly. "This way, princess." He stepped off, chin raised.

Sallie caught Jess's arm, spoke softly. "What?"

Jess put a finger to his lips, smiled. He bent over to whisper in her ear. "Princess."

She pulled back, frowning. Jess took her arm, stepped off after the clerk.

———

SALLIE AND JESS lay facing each other in bed. She wiped a bead of perspiration from his forehead, kissed him lightly. "You call me 'princess'. What is 'princess'?"

He raised up on an elbow, frowned. "Mmm." He pursed his lips. "A princess is a very pretty woman who is an important person in the leadership and government of her people, in this case, the Burmese people."

She leaned over and kissed his lips. "I don't think so. I don't know 'Burmese'. You just say all that so they will let us stay here at hotel."

"Well, whatever it takes to make a point. We're here in a warm bed instead of walking around on the streets in the dark."

"Yes, I'm glad." She pulled back, frowning. "When clerk takes us to rooms, you said something

to him, then put a finger on your lips. What does
that mean, finger on lips?"

"Ah. It means to not say anything right then."

She thought about that a moment, frowning.
"What if important person you talk about is a man,
not a woman. What do you call him?"

"A prince."

"Okay, sweetheart prince." She put her hands on
his cheeks, pulled him to her, kissed him hard and
put her index finger to his lips.

———

"THERE IT IS!" said Sallie.

The boat approached the wharf on the Sacramento riverfront. Dave and Jess, sitting at the bow,
looked up. They had sat at the same spot for virtually the entire trip, talking about San Francisco, its
present condition and its prospects. They had
already asked Fred to send them news as often as
possible. Jess said he planned to write to Larkin to
tell him about his purchase of lots and to ask him for
any thoughts on the future of their separate investments. He promised to tell Fred about Larkin's
response.

As the boat approached the wharf, Sallie,
wearing her trousers and work shirt, collected their
two bags of clothing, including her new dress and
shoes, and made her way to the bow. When the boat
nudged the dock, Fred stepped over the gunwale to
the planking and Benny tossed the bowline to him.

"Okay, folks, come ashore," said Fred as he tied
the boat's line to the dock cleat.

Dave and Jess stepped onto the dock. Jess took the two bags from Sallie and offered her a hand as she stepped up to the dock. Benny followed.

Fred stopped, looked along the dock to the steamboat. "I had wanted to show you the new boat, but we're all gonna be too busy this evening. We'll have a look next time you come down. Sorry about that."

"Just as well," said Jess. "We need to get on the road."

All walked off the dock, Fred and Benny heading for a shack where their contacts stored goods for shipment to the bay.

"I'll keep in touch," Fred said.

"Thanks, Fred. I'll let you know when I hear from Mr. Larkin. I'm thinking we'll be going back to the city before long to buy more lots. We'll see." He and Dave waved.

"Bye, Fred and Benny," Sallie called. They waved to her.

"You two have anything you need to do here before we pick up the horses?" Dave said. "If we get away pretty quick, we'll reach the claims tomorrow. We should be able to stay tonight at the inn."

"Sounds good. Nice to see some conveniences opening up. The livery too. Wonder where people going to the bay left horses before it opened a few months ago."

"I doubt many people were going from the diggings to San Francisco a few months ago."

———

"So help me God, if I ever see the bastard who did this, I'll shoot him dead. I swear I will. I would bet my last horse it was the fella we saw here." Jess shook his head slowly.

They stood before the ashes and a few charred uprights of The Big Bear Inn. "I hope the owners got away. We'll probably hear the news from somebody in the diggings. Somebody will have been this way." He shook his head again. "Why do we have to put up with imbeciles? Imbeciles with guns. Maybe there should be a law that prevents imbeciles from owning guns."

"Good luck with that," said Dave. "That sort of law would require that the law define 'imbecile'." He shook his head. "Never happen."

"So sad," said Sallie. She took Jess's arm. "Where we sleep tonight? Cold." She pulled the scarf up to cover her neck.

Jess put an arm around her, looked around. "I suppose we'll have to find a soft patch of grass. We can cover with your long dress." He smiled.

She looked up but did not respond.

"We'll keep a fire going. What do you think, Dave?"

"Yeah. Looks like a likely place over there under the trees." He pointed to an opening in a small grove of oaks behind the remains of the inn. "Patch of grass there as well. You have hobbles?"

"Yep, always carry 'em in the saddlebags, just in case. If you'll take care of the horses, Sallie and I will get wood for the fire. We'll need a good pile. We'll keep the fire going all night."

While Dave hobbled the horses, Sallie and Jess

collected kindling and dry limbs which they broke into short lengths. Jess cleared a space under the trees for a firepit, filled it with kindling and lit the fire.

Dave came over and rubbed his hands over the crackling fire. "Tighten your belts, folks. I'll give you a good feed soon as we reach my claim tomorrow."

———

THE THREE RIDERS rode down the path to Dave's claim. There was no one at the stream or in the yard. They reined up before the cabin.

"Reuben! Are you in there?" shouted Dave.

There was a moment of silence, then the door flew open, and a smiling Reuben stood in the doorway. "I'm glad to see you!" said Reuben. "Everything go okay?"

"Yeah. Where's Charley? Dick?"

"Charley was last with me. Somebody came in yesterday and told him about some trouble up north. I didn't hear it all, but it seems a bunch of men was chasing some people from the diggings. Charley thought he should go up to see what was goin' on. I went inside and locked the door."

"Good idea. Now build up that fire, and I'll get an early supper for some hungry people."

With Reuben's help, Dave put together what could only be called a feast of beans, potatoes, beef, and cornbread in record time, plus wine during dinner for himself and Jess, and coffee afterward for all but Sallie. Supper and conversation finished, Jess and Sallie offered to help with cleanup, but Dave sent them on their way to check their claim before they lost the sun.

Jess put the horses in Dave's corral and tack in the shed, then shouldered their clothing bag for the short walk to their claim. They found the site empty, but embers glowed in the firepit, evidence that whoever watched the claim that day was only recently gone.

Jess built up the fire, and Sallie came to sit with him. They sat there, staring into the flames. They talked about San Francisco and town lots, The Big Bear Inn and Reuben's story.

They talked about the value of gold, a frequent topic of conversation, though it was mostly Jess that did the talking. "Sallie," he said, "if Thurston is not blowing smoke about the value of gold, we're making over a hundred dollars every day! That's seven hundred dollars a week and three thousand dollars a month! One of these days, we need to talk about what we're going to do with all that money."

"You buy San Francisco lots."

"Yeah, well, beyond that. That's an investment, but it has nothing to do with what we want to do or where we want to live after we leave the diggings."

They studied the flames, quiet, then: "I don't want live in big city," she said.

"I know, sweetheart, I don't either."

They looked up at the darkening sky where small stars were popping out, sparkling, the skies beginning to fill with bright orbs.

"You said something about Thurston 'blowing smoke'. I thought that was what people do when they smoke pipes."

"Ah. 'Blowing smoke' means not telling the truth."

"Oh." Sallie snuggled against his shoulder. She went quiet until he thought she might be asleep. After a long moment, she began to talk about her childhood, what little she remembered. "What will happen to my people in American California?"

Jess shook his head slowly, stirred the fire with a short bough and dropped it on the flames. Jess put an arm around her shoulders and pulled her close. She rested her head on his chest and sobbed.

Chapter Nine

JESS STOOD knee deep in cold water at the rocky ledge that ran completely across the stream at the head of their claim. He had speculated many times that the reason their claim continued to provide color was that flakes and nuggets washed from the ledge. He had planned as many times to harvest the gold from the ledge with a knife or pick.

But not today. They needed provisions, and he needed to go to Barney's store up the way. He left the water and went to where Sallie squatted in water hardly ankle deep. "C'mon, we need to go to the store."

She continued swirling the sand in her pan. "I'll stay here. I already got half an ounce while you stand up there."

"No, you're going with me. I'm not leaving you alone anymore, not as long as there's men in the diggings who are more interested in you than in gold dust. We'll be quick."

She stood. "Okay, but only if you buy me hot

chocolate. Last time we were there, Barney say he was going to start selling Mexican hot chocolate. I like it. He said he was going to sell hot coffee too, so you can have coffee."

She gave him the small bottle she had been putting gold flakes in and went to the tent to put on shoes and get their coats. Jess went to the tent and came out with a short-handled shovel. He walked to a stand of shrubs and brambles near the ledge at the top of their claim. The thicket was so dense the downside was hidden from the trail above.

He looked around a full minute. Seeing no one, he quickly stooped and, pushing the lowest branches aside, he raked leaves away with his hands, then stood and pushed the shovel into the wet soil. He continued until he had opened a narrow hole eighteen inches deep. He knelt, reached into the hole and brushed the soil off the top of an almost filled canvas bag. Pulling the bag out, he opened it and dropped the bottle inside. He tied the bag and placed it back in the hole. Looking around nervously, he quickly filled the hole, pushed leaves over the soil until the spot was indistinguishable from any other spot on the claim. He stood and looked up at the trail, upstream, downstream. He saw no one except Sallie standing at the tent opening, watching him.

He walked to the stream, dropped the shovel on the sandy beach. "Okay, we're off." He took her hand, and they walked up the path. "I don't like leaving the gold on the claim, even buried like that, but we've too much now to carry. I really need to take the lot to a bank in Sacramento."

————

"WHAT HAVE WE HERE?" Jess said, frowning.

He and Sallie stood at the bottom of the stair at the store, looking up to the porch where two small square tables stood with two chairs pushed under each table. They climbed the stair and went inside.

"Barney," said Jess, "what's with the tables outside?"

Barney smiled. "That's my newest offering. Little cold to be outside today, but anyone interested can sit inside, over there, to drink their coffee and chocolate." He pointed to a bench in the corner. Display boxes had been pushed into the aisle to make room for the bench.

"Glad you're offering hot drinks. Sallie told me," said Jess.

"Yep! Customers have asked why don't I offer hot coffee, and Sallie here asked if I could sometimes offer Mexican hot chocolate. So that's what I'm doin'! What'll you have?"

Sallie beamed. "We will have hot chocolate and coffee!" She looked at Jess.

Jess smiled and nodded.

"We also got Mexican cakes, brought up from the city! One each?"

"Yes!" Sallie said, ignoring Jess's frown.

"You folks sit down over there on the bench, and I'll bring it to you, soon's Annie has it ready."

Sallie sat on the bench while Jess and Barney wandered about the store, Jess selecting vegetables and fruits which he dropped into his bag, and other items, flour, sugar, coffee, salt and seasoning which Barney would have to sack for him.

Annie shortly came over with a tray. She called to Barney who hurried over. He removed two bags from a small table and pushed the table over beside the bench.

"There," Annie said, smiling. "You're our first customer for the chocolate. Hope you like it. A San Francisco supplier is trying to introduce chocolate and cakes and other drinks and things in the placers."

Jess went to the bench, sat and put his sack on the floor at his feet. "Thanks, Annie, Barney. This is a pleasant surprise."

"Yes," said Sallie. "Thank you."

"Couple of my regular customers asked me to serve alcohol drinks," said Barney. "It's a fact that some stores up north double as bars, but I don't want to get into that. Too risky. Invariably there'll be a ruckus. I don't need that. I'll stick with chocolate and coffee. Gotta keep up with the times and sell what my favorite customers want." He smiled. "Well, not everything that my customers want. Remember when you asked me a while back if I sold clothes, Sallie?" She nodded. "Course, I said I don't sell clothes, and I still don't. But come back here, let me show you something." He beckoned, and they followed him to a side door.

He opened the door and pointed across the yard at the beginnings of a cabin. The walls were up, and rafters in place. "That's a new store that's gonna sell clothes. Some Jews that operate a clothes store in Nevada City wanted to get closer to the market here and will open in a week or so. You probably know that Jews operate all the clothes stores anywhere in or near the diggings. There're single-minded people. You won't see a Jew working a gold pan or a rocker. There are lots of Jews in the mines, but not mining. They just sell clothes. Strange people."

"That's good," said Sallie. "I will buy some clothes from them. Mine look like rags." She leaned toward him. "And Barney, I don't put people inside different boxes."

Barney frowned while Jess and Sallie returned to their table, sat and sipped their drinks. Jess looked into her eyes. "Sallie, I put you inside a special box." She patted his hand, squeezed it.

Each selected a cake and nibbled. Sallie took a swallow of chocolate, pondered. She leaned toward Jess, spoke softly. "I think it need something, more cinnamon, maybe more sugar. But it's good. I like the cake too. We had these sometimes at mission café." Her face clouded, remembering, and she leaned against Jess's shoulder.

"Uh, Jess."

Jess looked up. They had not seen Barney walk over.

"Remember when we talked about black men in the mines," said Barney, "and I said I had not seen any. Since you were interested, I been asking around. It seems there's a good number of black men up north. Some are working with masters, and some are free, working with the white men who freed them after reaching the mines. Word is that they are pretty good workers and collect gold just like the white workers beside them. The cafes and bars let 'em come in with no problems, figuring their money is as good as anybody's. In fact, those cafes and bars are real happy to hire the Blacks since no self-respecting white man wants to wait tables when there's gold to be had at the streams.

"Also, I heard from some miners who've been in San Francisco and Monterey that politicians who figure that California is about to become a state are writing a constitution that will outlaw slavery. So all these black people are gonna be free, if they ain't already."

"Hadn't heard that," said Jess, "good news all around."

"Right, enjoy your chocolate." He smiled, started to walk away, stopped and turned back. "By the way, I finally got me some gold scales, so you can pay from now on with dust, if you want. Going rate at the moment is twenty dollars to the ounce, but that changes occasionally, I'm told."

"Good news," said Jess. "Hope you have a good safe."

"Well, I have a safe, but from what I hear, there's been no robberies of stores and hotels or taverns. Even the messengers who take a couple hundred pounds of dust to Sacramento from time to time have never been robbed, so I hear." He chuckled. "I sure wouldn't chance it."

"We'll hope the roads stay safe," said Jess to Barney who waved over his shoulder. Jess took the last swallow from his cup. "We'll finish up here, sweetheart, and be on our way." He said it to Sallie, but he was listening to the anxious conversation between a man who had just come in and went straight to Barney. Jess recognized Eddie, who worked a claim just below Dave's.

Jess stood and walked to the counter. "What's goin' on, Eddie?"

"Hey, Jess," Eddie said. "You know the claim a mile or so below mine that's worked by some Californians? Half a dozen miners I don't know are down there breaking up the Californians' stuff and telling 'em to leave the diggings. I thought Barney should know in case the troublemakers come by here."

"They can't do that," Sallie said.

"Oh, but they can, Sallie. They been wavin' their pistols around and threatening the Californians. Dave said he would go down with me to see if we can do something. I came up to see if I can get somebody else to go with us."

"I'll go," said Jess.

He paid Barney and took the sack Barney handed him. Going to their table, he absentmindedly picked up the empty cup, set it down and dropped what was left of his cake in the sack.

He and Sallie walked quickly, almost running, down the stair to the trail. "Sallie, you stay with Reuben in Dave's cabin with the door locked. We won't be long."

"Why can't I go with you?"

"Sallie, these men ain't rational," said Eddie. "They're not chasing these guys because they're competition. They're chasin' 'em because they're Californians. Like you."

Jess, Dave, and Eddie walked into the Californians'
camp to see them stuffing belongings into bags
beside the remains of their tent, now ripped and
lying in shreds. Shovels, pans and parts of a cradle
were strewn about the sand at streamside. Six
miners stood between the ruined tent and the
stream. They stared at the three newcomers, seemingly wondering whether they came to join the fun
or to challenge them. Three held pistols at their
sides.

"What's going on?" said Jess.

"You know damn well what's goin' on. We're
chasing the outsiders from the diggings."

"Outsiders?" said Dave. "Why are they
outsiders? They've probably lived in California all
their lives. How long you been here? A year? Three
months?"

"It don't matter," said another miner. "These are
American diggings. There's no place for Mex'cans."

"These men aren't Mexicans," said Jess.
"They're Californians. Since the war is over, actually, they're Americans."

"You know damn well what I'm gittin' at. Now
shove off, or you're in as much trouble as them."
Two more miners drew pistols and held them at
their sides.

Jess, Dave, and Eddie looked at each other. "It's
done," said Dave, softly. "Nothin' we can do here
but get shot."

They looked up the path toward the trail where
the Californians had stopped to watch what
happened below. Now they hefted their bundles and

walked up the incline. They disappeared in the heavy brush.

Jess, Dave, and Eddy walked off the site toward the trail. They ignored a couple of whoops from below, followed by laughter and a gunshot.

"We all know that lot is not typical of the good people that make up the mining population here," Jess said, "but it's people like them that seem to forecast the future."

"Yeah," said Eddie. "On that point, in our hurry to get down here, I didn't mention something I heard just yesterday. Somewhere north, up around Nevada City, I think, they did the same thing with a bunch of Frenchies. Ran 'em off, said there was no place in the placers for a bunch of foreigners. Don't know where they was from, maybe Canada. I doubt the people that ran 'em off asked."

Jess walked with head down. *What would these people do with Sallie? Born in California. Lived all her life in California. Born to a people who had lived in California since the beginning. To those imbeciles, she has no place here. I must watch her closely and, by god, I'll shoot dead anybody who threatens her.*

———

JESS AND SALLIE walked on the trail that lay on the bank above the streamside claims. He wore a small backpack. He had talked with the Jews who were building the clothing store near Barney's place, and they confirmed it would be about two weeks before they opened for business. They referred him to a store operated by friends about five miles north. He and Sally decided to take a day off to walk up and have a look. Sally was delighted though she had already calculated how much money they would lose by their absence from the claim.

As they walked, they looked down the bank to the miners working in the shallows with pans or standing beside rockers. At one claim, half a dozen men worked busily at a long tom. They stopped a moment to watch, just long enough for Sallie to shake her head, push him ahead on the trail and exclaim that she did not want them to get a long tom.

"No fun," she said, looking down at the footing on a rocky stretch of trail.

They trudged on in silence, stopping occasionally to listen to birdsong and search for the singer. They left the trail at high noon to sit in the shade of a huge oak just off the trail. Beyond lay a broad meadow of wildflowers, white Mariposa lilies, magenta-colored fireweed, red and pink paintbrush.

"Pretty," said Sallie.

He looked up, nodded, opening the sack that held their lunch. He stopped, pondered, looking toward the meadow. "Mmm. Now if we owned this meadow...I can see a little ranch house over there in that grove." He pointed. "A little fenced vegetable garden beside the house, a few fruit trees behind the house. And a herd of fat cows on this meadow."

"Nice. But put your cows behind the house. I don't want them stepping on my flowers."

After a leisurely lunch, he dusted his hands and lunged for her. She lay on her back, and he kissed her face and neck, her lips. He lightly touched a nipple through her shirt.

She turned her head to look toward the trail. "Don't do that. Somebody coming."

Jess saw the walker. He sat up, then stood, waving to him. "We're looking for a clothes store somewhere up ahead. Are we close?"

The walker stopped, stared a moment before answering. "Yeah, not too far, 'bout a half hour or so. You'll know you're getting' close when you hear the Chinaman chatter. You cain't miss it. The store is just a few minutes past the Chinaman claim."

"Many thanks," said Jess, waving.

The walker returned the wave and started off, looking back over his shoulder at them.

Jess put papers and cloths inside the pack, and they set off on the trail. Sallie put an arm around his waist, and they walked silently, passing the occasional miner at the stream or on the trail. He nodded to the strangers, or waved or greeted them. Mostly the walk was quiet, interrupted only by the whisper of a light breeze in the oak canopy.

That is, until they neared the "Chinaman" claim. Before they saw any Chinese, they heard a chatter that grew in intensity as they moved closer. Then they saw the camp below on the stream bank. A cluster of large tents lay around a ramshackle cabin and a shed constructed of boughs and planks.

Jess guessed that the claim was populated by more than fifty men, most busily working a huge long tom. A half dozen more squatted in the shallows, panning. The miners saw Jess and Sallie, and many stopped what they were doing to stare silently at them. Then they turned back to their work and the chatter commenced.

All but one. One miner, an oldster, closest to the trail, continued to stare. Then he waved and beckoned them to come down. Jess and Sallie looked at each other. Sallie nodded, and they went down the path.

At the bottom, the miner nodded sharply, smiling. "Come, eat." He pointed toward a cluster of men who bent over steaming pots on a smoldering fire. Jess looked at Sallie who smiled at the miner.

"Qing, xie xie," said Sallie.

Both Jess and the miner gaped.

"You speak Chinese!" said the miner.

She grinned. "That's all I know, 'qing, xie xie,' just 'please, thank you.'"

"That is more than anybody around here knows who is not Chinese. Nobody else is interested in anything Chinese." He beckoned again, and they walked to the cooking fire. He spoke rapidly to the cooks, and they dished out two bowls of rice, beans, and some sort of shredded meat. The miner picked up chopsticks and pushed them into a pocket. He took the two filled bowls from a cook and carried them to Jess and Sallie, pointing to a log where they could sit. He gave them the bowls and the chopsticks from his pocket.

"Xie xie," said Sallie.

The miner smiled, waved as he walked back to the cooks, joining the other workers who had left the long tom to stand at the fire circle, waiting for their bowls, chattering loudly, animatedly, laughing and gesturing. The miner who had spoken to Sallie and

Jess pointed at them, and the others waiting to be served turned and looked.

Jess and Sallie sat on the log, holding the bowls in their laps. Jess frowned at her. "Sallie, you surprise me every time you open your mouth. Where in hell did you learn Chinese?"

She grinned. "Chinese man come to mission hotel, and we talk. He taught me some Chinese words, and I taught him some Spanish words. He was from a Sandwich Island ship that came to Monterey. He said he had heard of missions and wanted to see some. He visited missions at Carmel and San Antonio de Padua and my mission hotel. He was nice man. He also show me how to use chopsticks." She laughed, pointing at Jess's chopsticks which he held awkwardly, one stick in each hand. She showed him the proper one-handed technique.

They ate slowly, watching the miners who ate quickly and returned to the long tom and stream. They chatted as they worked, pouring soil and water on the tom, working the soil and extracting gold flakes.

The man who had invited them to eat with them walked over and collected their empty bowls and chopsticks.

"That was good," said Sallie. "Xie xie."

He smiled, bowed.

"Your men are very busy at the tom," said Jess. "Have you been successful here?"

The miner pondered, looked aside. "We not very successful. We have lots of men, work hard, not much gold." He bowed slightly again, walked toward the cooking fire.

"Very wise man," Jess said.

"What do you mean, 'very wise'?"

"Did you notice how busy the men were at the long tom? They were raking it in. He's smart to downplay it. If the word got around that they were taking lots of gold from this claim, we know what would happen, don't we?"

"They would be run off?"

"Oh, yes, and a few killed if they resisted. They're not white Americans."

She leaned against his shoulder. "Oh, Jess. Isn't there any place where all people like each other, where they don't hate people not like them?"

He reached around her shoulders and held her. "Sweetheart, if we can decide where that place is, we're going there." They looked around the Chinese camp, the cooks washing dishes, miners working furiously at the log tom, all chattering busily.

"I know one place," she said, "but I don't want go there now."

He frowned. "Why not? Where is this place?"

"Heaven."

He smiled, a hint of a smile. "Yeah, let's put that journey off for a while." He stood, offered her a hand and pulled her up. The oldster who invited them down saw them moving and waved. Jess and Sallie returned the wave.

"Good luck, old man," said Jess softly. He hefted his pack, and they walked up the path to the trail.

————

SALLIE AND JESS strolled about the clothing store. It was twice as big as Barney's store and filled to the ceiling and wall to wall with clothing, hanging and stacked on shelves. A dozen men wandered in the aisles, picking up items, holding them up to estimate fit, asking the clerks about prices, even trying to bargain. Clerks smiled and pointed to the price tags.

Jess selected a shirt, pants, socks and a pair of boots. Sallie was overwhelmed with the variety and quantity of things. She went to Jess and tugged on his sleeve.

"Help me find things. I like everything, but you have to see me wear them, so help me."

He smiled, helped her narrow down the selection until she decided.

Jess took the stack of clothes to the counter where the smiling clerk waited. Sallie walked to the window where she looked at dresses that hung on a rack. Jess deposited his stack on the counter and watched as the clerk tallied the cost.

"Our first time here," Jess said. "I like your store. There's a clothing store going in a few miles south that is near our claim. I understand it's part of your operation."

The clerk looked up, smiling. "Ah, yes! That's my cousin's store. We also have another store a few miles north of here that is operated by my uncle."

"Business must be good. The local miners must be pleased with your stores. You get along okay with them? No, uh, problems?"

The clerk stopped the tallying, frowned. "If you mean, do the miners resent Jews in the placers, yes, we get along with them. As long as we stay in our stores and sell clothes, they are fine with us. Now, if we filed a claim beside them and started working the stream for gold, it would be a different story."

"Sorry, um, I didn't mean to suggest——"

He smiled faintly. "It's okay, we get used to it." The clerk looked around Jess toward Sallie who stood at the window. "I see you have an Indian woman with you. I suspect you know something of miners' prejudices."

"Oh, yes, I do indeed. Almost daily."

The clerk nodded, finished the tally and wrote the price on a slip of paper. "Coin or dust accepted."

Jess pulled a small bottle from a pocket and handed it to the clerk. He reached under the counter for a scale, placed it on the counter and poured dust carefully from the sack on the scale. He returned the sack to Jess who thanked him and hefted the stack of clothes. Walking to Sallie at the window, he took a canvas bag from her and pushed the clothes into it.

"My, my," he said, "we have sacks of gold and now a sack of new clothes. What's next?"

————

LATE SPRING BROUGHT WARMING SUNSHINE, light rains and green grass, meadows of wildflowers and a rise in water level and current from snowmelt in the high mountains. Jess assumed it also brought a new supply of flakes churned up and washed from rocks and soil along the newly submerged banks.

When he mentioned his assumptions to Sallie, squatting in the cold shallows, she looked blankly at him. "You think about that all you want. I just keep on panning. I still find twice as much gold as you." She smiled. And she *was* taking more. They each kept a bottle into which they dropped their finds, flakes and pebbles of gold. They always compared their takes at the end of the day, and her findings were always more than his, often nearly twice as much as his.

Mild sunny days were followed by cool, crisp evenings, a light breeze whispering in the tall pine trees. They sat on the ground at the fire one cool evening, the low flames flickering, waving. Leaning against the down log, they talked softly. Sallie told stories of her people she heard from oldsters who she encouraged to try to remember tales they had heard as children. Jess responded with reminiscences of his own childhood, growing up on the Kentucky farm.

Then they fell silent, watching the ripples in the stream, the occasional dry leaf washed from banks. Jess studied the large sugar pine nearest the bank on the other side. He leaned forward, frowning.

"Sallie, look at that big pine over there." He pointed. "The trunk is riddled with holes. Looks like a bunch of musket balls hit it. Not likely. Wonder what did that? Maybe a disease of some sort."

"No. Woodpeckers do that. If you dig into one of those holes, you find acorn. Woodpeckers peck out holes before cold weather, before snow, and put in acorns. They come back later and get acorns for food."

"Be damned. Didn't know that." He pulled her

over until she lay across his chest. He kissed her lips, her nose, a cheek. He bit her ear softly.

"Ouch." She reached up and kissed him, then sat up, took his hand and leaned against the log. They stared into the fire.

"Look," said Jess.

He pointed at a fat squirrel foraging in the leaves on the far bank. Jess said he must finally buy a rifle so he could shoot squirrels and hunt deer to supplement the beef he bought at Barney's store. Sallie said she would rather watch the squirrels and deer rather than kill them. He smiled to himself, leaned over and kissed her cheek.

I could spend every day and every evening as we have spent this day. He stood and reached for her, took her outstretched hand and pulled her up. *And this night.*

———

THE WORD PASSED around the diggings a couple of miles each side of Barney's store that there would be music and dancing at a camp a half mile north of the store. All were invited to come to the festive occasion. All were asked to bring food and drink, but if they had nothing to contribute, to come anyway. Jess was encouraged by the tenor of the invitation and decided they would go. They needed the companionship of good people.

On the appointed evening, Jess and Sallie arrived at dusk at the party site and found others were just as interested in some merriment and partying as they. The activities were to take place at a clearing between a thick stand of pines and the beginnings of a small hotel. The structure's frame-work was up, and the room that would eventually be the restaurant was finished and decorated and tables and chairs set up. The tables were loaded with small cakes, bowls of crackers and bottles of wine, gin, and aguardiente. And, wonder of wonders: beer. The hotel proprietors had just received five cases of beer from San Francisco, product of the first distillery in California. Men crowded around the display, eager to taste the first beer they had seen in months, or years.

By sundown, the gathering milled about the yard. There were about eighty men and but five females. Two were middle-aged matrons who were as eager as the men for a bit of carousing. Three of the females were young teenagers, old enough to attract the attention of men who had not seen a white woman in months. The miners had seen Cali-fornian and Indian women, but these were not invited. The oral invitation was clear on that point. You might seek the company of greasers and squaws for sex any time you wish, but not congenial gather-ings of this sort.

The understanding about female companionship did not prevent the men from staring hungrily at Sallie. Jess knew he took a risk bringing her to the party, but he figured he couldn't keep her hidden and deprived of entertainment forever. Besides, she said she was going, and Jess didn't object.

A large fire was kindled in the center of the clearing. The attendees milled about, talking, laugh-ing. They began to wander into the hotel dining room and come back to the yard with drinks. The conversation gradually grew louder and more animated.

The entertainers, a violinist, a guitarist and banjo player stood on the hotel porch, surveying the crowd. They looked at each other, apparently waiting for the signal to begin. When no one seemed to be in charge, the violinist stepped to the edge of the porch and shouted to the yard: "Are you ready for some music?"

The crowd turned in unison to the players and roared their positive response.

The fiddler opened with a rousing rendition of "Betsy from Pike," and the banjo and guitar players picked up on the tune. Some of the men, already feeling fine from the plentiful alcohol, began to dance, alone or with another miner. The bearded, booted dancers stomped and whirled, some gracefully, some stumbling and laughing with the spectators who cheered them on.

The men eventually coaxed the women and girls to join them, and the yard became a frenzy with miners, drinks in hand, jumping in jigs and whirls, the women and girls laughing, eventually withdrawing, breathless, complaining of the fast pace.

Then a brusque grizzled miner, refusing to accept his young partner's withdrawal, pulled her roughly back to the melee. Seriously frightened, she shouted for help to no one in particular, and two young men went to her and began to pull his hands off her. The would-be dancer's eyes opened wide, squinted as he released her, at the same time fumbling, swaying, pulling a pistol and pointing it at the two rescuers. The action galvanized the mob, many of whom shouted, thrashed about, drew pistols and fired wildly. The music stopped, and the players ran inside the hotel.

"Time to go," said Jess.

He and Sallie had watched the festivities from outside the mass of dancers and singers and wild dancing. He had already forcefully discouraged several attempts by drunken miners to pull Sallie into the dancing melee. Early on, he had planned to go inside the hotel for a taste of the first beer since the Boston pub, but the shouting and gunshots changed his mind.

"This is out of hand," he said to Sallie. "Somebody is going to get hurt, and I don't want us to be on hand when that happens." He took her arm, and they withdrew. Walking from the fire's light, they stopped on the dark trail. They would wait for their eyes to adjust to the darkness and the soft moonlight. After a couple of minutes, he put an arm around her waist, and they stepped off.

"Hold it there a minute, pilgrim."

Jess and Sallie stopped and turned around abruptly to see two men who had walked up behind them. Jess winced at the strong alcoholic stench from the men.

"Leave if you need to, pilgrim, but how 'bout leavin' that purty little squaw piece here?" The speaker swayed as he spoke. His companion giggled. "We'll pay."

Jess decided in an instant that he would not even protest. He pulled his Colt quickly and pointed it into the man's face. The man inhaled hard and, open-mouthed, stepped backward.

"Hey, hey!" his companion mumbled. "She's goin' with us!" He grabbed Sallie's arm and pulled roughly. She shrieked and pulled back.

All the trouble he had endured with thugs of this ilk suddenly filled Jess's head. He shouted aloud, raised the pistol and brought the butt down hard on the miner's head. The miner's eyes rolled up, he released Sallie and collapsed.

Jess spoke softly to the drunk standing before him. "Take care of him. If you raise any fuss about what happened here, I'll have both of you before a miner's court that will find you guilty and either send you to the sheriff in Sacramento or send you home to your mama and daddy who may know how to take care of their little boy. Understand all that?"

The man grimaced, weaved, nodded.

Jess and Sallie set out down the trail, leaving the man standing over his pard.

Chapter Ten

JESS STOOD on the sandy bank, scratching his head and tucking in his shirttail, watching Sallie who squatted in the shallows with her pan. She showed him the jar that was over half full. She shook the jar and a pea-sized nugget appeared on top of the flakes.

His jaw dropped. "I swear, Sallie, that little jar might be worth a hundred dollars right now."

She smiled, pocketed the jar and went back to her panning.

"The way this claim keeps producing, I don't think we'll ever have to move. I still think the color is being washed from the ledge. I need to work up there with my knife."

"Yeah, you said that before, 'bout ten times. How 'bout you do it now?"

He smiled, rolled up his pants and squatted in the shallows behind her. He put his arms around her shoulders and squeezed, kissing her neck.

She struck his arm lightly with the rim of her

pan. "Work now! I brought your bottle out. It's there on the sand." She pointed. "It empty."

"Okay, okay, little mother. I'll be a good boy and get to work." He pinched her ear, and she jerked her head aside. He picked up his pan and walked into the water a few feet downstream of Sallie.

"Jess! Jess!"

He and Sallie jerked around to see Dave running down their path. They stood and stepped from the water.

"What's up?" Jess said.

"A miner I don't know came down from the mountain—he was hunting—said he found an emigrant party in real bad trouble about seven or eight miles up. He said they really need help, said they're starving. Reuben and I are going to the store to get supplies. Would you ride up and tell them help is coming? I brought your horse. Yours, too, Sallie, if you'll go as well. You would be a real help."

Sallie took Jess's pan and bottle and ran toward the tent.

"Get our coats, Sallie," Jess called after her.

"The fellow who told me about the party said they were on the emigrant road that comes into the diggings just north of the store," Dave said. "You know it?" Jess nodded. "He said they were about eight miles up the ridge. Said there's some light snow up there, but shouldn't slow you down."

"We'll be off right now," said Jess. Sallie came from the tent carrying their shoes and coats.

"We'll be about an hour behind you with the provisions," Dave said. He handed Jess a bottle of spirits. "Give them a swallow of this, might help until we get there with food." He ran up the path and disappeared into the brush alongside the trail.

Jess looked about the camp, hurried up the path, Sallie following. At the top of the path, they untied their horses. Jess pushed the small brandy bottle into his saddlebag. They mounted and rode at a walk on the rough trail, occasionally loping on the open, level stretches.

They crossed the stream a few miles up at a wide ford that was hardly knee deep to the horses. Beyond, the trail climbed gradually, running through woods and alongside gorges.

It was high noon when they reached the stranded party where they were camped in a scattered grove of pines. The three wagons ringed a campfire whose low flames offered little warmth. Gaunt oxen stood nearby, trying to find grass in a light carpet of snow. The people were as gaunt as their animals, standing listlessly at the fire and beside wagons, staring blankly at the riders.

Jess and Sallie dismounted and walked about the camp, telling the emigrants that help was on the way. "My friends will be here before the end of this day," Jess said, "and you'll have plenty of food."

Sallie called him and beckoned him to come to the wagon where she stood with a man at the tailgate.

They looked at a woman who lay on blankets in the wagon bed. The woman was as thin as a skeleton. She looked at them through eyes that blinked listlessly. Her lips moved as she tried to speak, but no sound came.

"She need help," Sallie said.

Jess lifted her head and pressed the brandy bottle to her lips. She swallowed, squinted, leaned forward for another swallow. She lay her head back on the pillow, eyes closed, nodding slightly.

The man standing with them put a hand to her cheek. "Good, honey, good." He stepped back and beckoned to Jess. "I think it helped. Can you give a swig to Stuart over there?" He pointed to a man who sat on a stone beside the fire circle. He rocked slowly back and forth. "We've almost give up on him."

Jess went to him, held the back of his head with a hand and helped him swallow the brandy. The man looked up at Jess, nodded, held out a hand for another swallow. Jess gave him another drag on the bottle.

"I think it help," said Sallie. "You good doctor."

Jess and Sallie scurried about, gathering fuel and building up the fire, helping the people to come to the fire for warmth.

Dave, Reuben, and two others arrived just as the sun disc touched the horizon. All set to work at once. They prepared a supper that the members of the party proclaimed a lifesaver, the best meal they had ever eaten, they said.

After the meal, members of the party told their story. Their departure from the Mississippi had been delayed at the outset by rainstorms and, they admitted, simply not being prepared. But they decided they could still arrive at the California mountain range in time to get across before snows prevented their passage. They were wrong. Cold and snow in November forced them to camp at the base of the mountains on the eastern side. They consumed most of their provisions during the winter, and they set out in the new year when they thought the worst weather was behind them. They figured they would get across the mountains quickly and reprovision at the first opportunity. They were wrong again. They cleared the crest but were surprised by new snow while still in the foothills on the western slopes.

The leader of the party said their faith had been sorely tested by the predicament. They had given up hope until their rescuers appeared. Now, he said, they were sufficiently revived to complete their journey. They would set out tomorrow. They thanked their saviors, told them that they had restored their hope and their faith and assured them that God would reward them for their kindness. All gathered around the campfire. The emigrants bowed their heads and thanked God for watching over them and sending their rescuers.

Riding down the trail toward the placers, Jess thought on this last. If everything that happens is God's will, as he had been taught in Sunday School, why had He put the poor immigrants in this predicament? He shook his head, deciding that he had no right to question anybody's beliefs, certainly not those of these people who were busy thanking God for their deliverance.

———

DAVE AND REUBEN sat with Jess and Sallie at their campfire on a cool evening, watching the sun's rays play on the foliage of new leaves on the oaks across the stream. The light breeze gently moved the leaves, and an occasional quickening produced a soft swishing in the canopy. Dave pointed at a trio of squirrels rustling about in the dry leaves under the trees.

Jess raised his right hand, his finger pointed at the squirrels, his thumb raised. "Pow," he said softly, raising his hand sharply, mimicking a pistol shot. Sallie slapped his shoulder with a pop.

"Sallie won't let me shoot squirrels, Dave. Says she would rather watch squirrels than eat them."

"I'm with you, Sallie. I'd rather watch God's creatures than eat them."

Jess frowned. "Really? You don't eat beef? Beef comes from a cow, one of God's large creatures."

"Ah." Dave said. "Well, cows aren't very interesting to watch. And they're not wild."

"Deer?" said Jess. "They're God's creature, large and wild."

Dave cut a glance at Jess, frowning. "Sallie, if you should ever get tired of your partner's strange behavior, you can always come down to my place for a while, till he comes to his senses."

"Thank you, Dave. I will remember that." She leaned over and bumped Jess's shoulder. "You remember it too." She smiled.

They stared into the dying fire, the low flames flickering. Jess picked up some short lengths of wood from the stack beside the firepit and placed them carefully, one at a time, on the embers. The dry limbs caught quickly, and new flames erupted.

"Speaking of God's large creatures," said Jess, "I heard up at the store about a bull and bear fight that's gonna be staged in a week or so in the store's yard. These fights are especially popular in the southern mines, and the owner of a prize bear is bringing him up north to put on a fight with a local bull."

Sallie stiffened, frowning. "What! They fight a bull and bear for fun!" She pointed a finger in Jess's face. "No! We not going!"

Jess frowned, punctuated by a hint of a smile. "If you don't want to go, it's okay. Dave and I will—"

She pointed at his face again, almost touching his nose. "No! If you go, you not come back!" She turned to Dave, pointed in his face. "You, too!"

She turned abruptly to Reuben. "You, Reuben?"

"I stay here with you," Reuben said, softly.

Dave and Jess exchanged a glance, trying to suppress smiles.

After a long pause, all studying the fire, Dave stood. "I've been thinking about some building projects we should consider. I'm still working the rocker, but we should consider building a long tom. That is, if I can figure how to set up a good supply of running water. Some people who have diverted water have gotten into trouble with nearby claims. Something to think about.

"And you need a cabin. The four of us, maybe with a bit of skilled help, could put one up in short order. You think about it." He warmed his hands over the fire, buttoned his coat. "You coming, Reuben?"

"I think I sit here just a while," Reuben said. "I be down in a few minutes."

Dave waved his goodbye and walked up the path.

They stared into the flames. Jess added kindling, and sparks rose and swirled.

"I got letter from Talbot Green," said Reuben. "You know, he works for Mr. Larkin."

Jess nodded.

"Barney gave it to me when I went to th' store this morning. I ask him to read letter for me, and he did. I trust Barney. He good man. In letter, Talbot ask me how I'm doing. He say he hear about bad things happening to black people in diggings. He say he talk with Mr. Larkin, and Mr. Larkin say I can come work for him. Mr. Larkin say I can work in his business cutting trees and making lumber. Or I can work for him in his business with Sandwich Islands. What do you think?"

"Hmm, interesting. Reuben, I think working for Mr. Larkin is a very good idea. Larkin is so well known and respected that anyone in his employ is going to be safe. Are you going to accept? Shall I write a reply to Talbot for you? I can show you the letter tomorrow, and you can take it straight away to Barney. You should talk with Dave about this."

"What do you think, Sallie?" said Reuben.

"It's a good idea, Reuben. Mr. Larkin and Mr. Green are good people." She paused, then, softly: "I think you're not safe here."

"I'm going to do it!" Reuben slapped his leg. "I'll talk with Dave tonight and come back here in morning," said Reuben. "Thank you for your help, Jess and Sallie."

———

NEXT MORNING, Jess bent under the tent flap and stepped outside, buttoning his shirt. He was surprised to see Reuben standing there, smiling broadly.

"I talk with Dave last night. He says I should accept Larkin's offer. So everybody thinks I should accept. Me too! I am ready to go." He grinned.

"Wait," said Jess.

He went inside the tent and came out holding a paper. Sallie followed, pulling on a jacket.

"I wrote the letter last night."

He read the letter. In it, Reuben thanks Larkin for the offer and accepts. It goes on to say he will write again when he has arranged transportation.

"I also wrote a letter to Fred," said Jess, "asking him to let me know his schedule so we can arrange for you to ride with him in his boat to San Francisco. He can arrange transport by ship from the city to Monterey. That will be safer than you riding horseback to Monterey from here. Sound okay?"

"Yes! Thank you, Jess. I'm ready to go!" He grinned. "I have enough gold to pay Fred and ship to Monterey and have lots left to spend in Mr. Larkin's store!"

"Good. Fred can tell you where you can sell your gold in San Francisco. Ask him to go with you when you sell it. Just sell enough to get you to Monterey. Mr. Larkin can help you exchange the rest of your gold there." Jess handed the two papers to Reuben. Take the two letters to Barney at the store and ask him to put them in envelopes. I've written the addresses on the backs of the letters. Then we'll wait for replies."

———

JESS AND SALLIE sat with Dave and Reuben at Dave's campfire. Empty supper plates were stacked beside the pile of firewood. They stared into the dancing flames, sipping from coffee cups. All except Sallie.

"That was one fine supper," said Jess, "I do like a little variety from time to time. Never had quail stew before."

"You said you like to watch wild things, not eat them," said Sallie, her eyes twinkling.

Dave straightened. "Well, Johnny down the way, you know Johnny, Johnny gave me these quail. They were dead, and I thought it made good sense to make their lives count for something by eating them rather than just tossing the bodies in the brush." He looked at Sallie, a smile playing about his lips. She looked blankly at him.

"Makes good sense to me," said Jess. "No problem with that delicious apple pie either." He glanced aside at Sallie. "Those apples also lived at one time, but I don't think apples have souls."

Sallie frowned. "What is 'souls'?"

Jess inhaled deeply. "Oh, sweetheart, I'll explain that, but not just now. Too much thinking at the moment might put me off after that good supper."

She took his arm and leaned on him. "Yeah, I think you don't know answer, but okay."

They sat quietly, staring into the fire, Dave drawing on his pipe, smoke curling about his head in the soft breeze. He looked up at the cheep-cheep call of an unseen bird across the stream.

"Hear that?" said Dave. "That's a Spotted Towhee, pretty little thing, if she ever shows herself. Johnny is quite the authority on California foothills birds. He's been in California four years. Worked for Sutter a couple of years, then on the river, lately in the diggings. He's given me quite an education on California birds, songbirds as well as eating birds." He pulled a face at Sallie. "I love birds. I could do without the early morning squawking of Blue Jays, but they're pretty things."

He leaned forward. "Hear that?" He searched the bank across the stream. "There she is." He pointed at the bird that was scratching in the grass just above water line. "Mourning Dove. Watch."

They watched the bird scratching in the grass, pecking at something. Then another dove appeared from underneath a buckbrush shrub, pecking at the grass. "They mate for life. If you see only one, its mate is nearby.

"I love the Mourning Dove's call, but it brings back painful memories. My mother would close her ears when she heard a Mourning Dove. She said it made her remember that she had lost her first child before the baby's first birthday. Would have been my big sister."

He looked up into the canopy across the stream, the sun's rays casting dancing orbs on the leaves. "Received a letter from my father yesterday. He said my mother is ill and begs me to come home." He looked down at the glowing embers in the firepit. He tapped his pipe against a stone, dumped the ashes in the firepit.

Dave stood, flexed his back. "Enjoyed the evening, folks. I hate to end it, 'specially when I'm the host, but I'm headin' for th' barn." All stood and said their goodnights. Dave and Reuben went toward the cabin as Jess and Sallie waved goodbye and walked up the path toward the trail above.

Sallie took Jess's hand, leaned toward him. "What means 'headin' for th' barn'?"

"It just means going to bed. Probably first said by someone who had a bedroom of sorts in a barn. Common expression by country folks. My daddy said it every night."

Sallie reached up and pulled his head down, kissed him on the cheek. "I'm headin' for th' tent."

———

DAVE SAT at dusk on a cool evening with Jess and Sallie at their fire, all staring into the low dancing flames. They looked up when a fish jumped in the deep water just below the ledge. Dave put down his coffee cup, pulled out his pipe and filled it. He picked up a small glowing stick from the fire and lit the pipe, pulling until the tobacco glowed.

"It's on evenings like this," Dave said, "I don't know why, but on evenings like this that I wonder what's ahead. I've been content here, but I wonder whether this will go on forever. Know what I mean?"

"I do indeed," Jess said. "I'm not unhappy— how could I be—but I often ask myself the same question. This can't last." Sallie sat upright, looked at him, frowning. He squeezed her shoulders. "I'm talking about mining." She leaned against him, staring into the flames.

"I've wondered whether we should get some good land north of Sacramento on a reliable stream and get a herd of cows," Jess said. "They're not wild and free for the taking like they were a few years ago but they're still cheap. I've also thought about San Francisco. The lot investments have made us so much money, maybe we should settle on one of the lots and watch the rest of the investment grow."

Sallie looked sternly at him. "You said we would not move to big town. Anyway, what would you do all day? What would you be doing while you watch investment grow?"

"Hmm. Good question." He looked toward the stream. The sun behind the tent had dropped below the horizon, the stream had darkened, the line of oaks across the stream now appearing as a long dark shadow. "Good question."

Dave stirred the fire idly with a piece of kindling, dropped it into the flames. "I have pondered that question for months, what to do after leaving the placers. I think we have all decided that is what we will do before long, leave the diggings. I suppose it's time I tell you about my past since it has much to say about my future." Jess and Sally looked at each other, then at Dave.

"I mentioned some time ago that my marriage went bust. It was all my doing. I had a good marriage, I loved my wife, and she loved me, but I cheated on her. There was this young, pretty nurse in my office. This was in Richmond. My wife found out and confronted me. I apologized, and I was sincere, but she was hurt, she didn't think I was sincere, and she moved out, went to her mother's. I tried to convince her to come back, she refused. I was angry, had to go someplace. I wandered a time and ended up in California.

"I wrote to her last fall. I told her I love her and I miss her, I told her I am so sorry for what I did, and I want to get back together. I meant it. There's not been enough time for her to reply, and I'm waiting and hoping." He took a deep breath, exhaled, staring into the fire. "That's where I am."

———

JESS WAS surprised on his next visit to the store when Barney handed him a letter from Fred, sooner than expected. In the letter, Fred enthusiastically agreed with plans for Reuben's move from the diggings to Monterey. He told about running into Larkin on his last visit to his lots. When each learned that they both knew Jess and Reuben, they had quite a conversation about San Francisco affairs and the price of lots. Larkin confirmed that the value of his lots now had increased to four times his initial investment. He suspected that Fred's and Jess's investments likely increased similarly, probably a bit less since they bought their lots a few weeks after Larkin bought his. Larkin predicted that the trend would only continue. There was no chance, he said, that the value of the lots would decline. He added that he could not say the same about investments of time and money in the diggings.

Jess thanked Barney for the letter, walked outside to the porch. He tarried there, tapping the letter against the porch post. *Is it time to move on? Quo vadis?* The diggings were becoming more crowded by the day. Wherever he went, to Barney's store, to visit the diggings north and south, visits to Coloma and Nevada City, he saw hundreds of people he had never seen before, thousands perhaps.

Fred had reached the same conclusion. He told Jess he was shocked every time he docked lately in Sacramento. The scores of new faces that he customarily used to see on his visits now were in the thousands.

San Francisco growth was even more dramatic. And the word was that, contrary to past experience, the new arrivals were not all rushing to the diggings. Many were staying in the city, held there by new opportunities.

In the diggings, many miners were beginning to ponder the future. Many began to wonder whether it was time to ask the wife or girlfriend or family to join him in California. Others began to wonder whether it was time to think about going home, returning to a settled life among family and friends, doing something of substance, without the constant worry that was an unavoidable component of mining.

Some liked California enough they wanted to stay but not as miners. Bob, one of two miners downstream from Dave, gradually spent less time at the stream and more in the beginnings of a farm just down the hill from his cabin. It was not long before the plantings showed promise: tomatoes, peas, beans, lettuce, melons, corn. He also kept two milk cows and planned to put up a rudimentary fence for a few beef cows. Both Jess and Dave had been buying milk from him for weeks. They both urged him to investigate how to get a deed to the place. Otherwise, they predicted, someday somebody is going to show up with a deed and call him a trespasser, and probably offer to sell him the property.

Unlike Bob's prospects, a miner about a mile north of the store who had plans to augment his mining with a bit of farming on the side did not fare so well. The miner-farmer built a small dam on the stream at his mining claim to impound water for irrigation. He apparently did not explore what effect the dam would do to other claims upstream. Angry miners whose claims were flooded by the dam confronted him and said they were going to remove the dam. In the ruckus that followed, the miners killed him.

———

"Reuben, you are at this moment no longer a miner." Jess, Sallie, and Reuben stood with a smiling Fred and Benny beside their boat at the Sacramento wharf.

"Yeah, I don't know what I am now," Reuben said. "I'll leave that to Talbot and Mr. Larkin."

"Tell Mr. Larkin we'll keep an eye on his San

Francisco lots and let him know what's going on," said Fred.

"How's Reuben getting to Monterey?" Jess said.

Fred and Benny exchanged a sober glance. "You won't believe this," said Fred, "but I almost booked him on the *Yankee Enterprise*.

"What! You what!"

"It's okay, it's okay, I didn't book him. Barney reminded me of your story about the *Yankee Enterprise* and we looked elsewhere. He's sailing down on a Sandwich Islander three days from now. He'll stay with us on board our boat until the Sandwich Islander leaves. We won't let him outta our sight."

"Reuben, it's too bad you won't get a look at San Francisco," said Jess, "but you need to stay below and don't show your face. If any of the *Enterprise* crew sees you, there's bound to be problems."

"I'll stay outta sight. I'm intendin' goin' to Monterey, not Boston. Or Heaven. Or Hell."

Jess pondered. "I wonder why Captain called at San Francisco."

"I asked around," said Fred. "Seems they filled up with hides and tallow earlier than expected, and they hadn't sold all the merchandise they brought from Boston. They wanted to get rid of it before settin' out for home. They didn't figure they would find many buyers in Monterey and didn't want to chance trying to sell in Los Angeles or San Diego, too much competition, so they came to San Francisco to try to unload the stuff."

"Okay, sounds like you have everything in hand, Fred, Benny." He offered his hand and shook with both. He turned to Reuben. "Reuben, my man, it has been a pleasure knowing you. I wish you the best of luck. You'll be in good hands with Mr. Larkin. Ask Talbot to write to us occasionally to let us know how you're doing. Better still, ask Talbot to teach you to write. You've said more than once that you would like to be able to read and write. Dave got you started, so keep it up."

"You are a smart man, Reuben," said Sallie. "I know you will learn fast. Write to us."

Reuben took Sallie's hand in both of his. "Thank you, Sallie. I will learn to write. Thank you for being a good friend."

He turned to Jess. "Thank you for saving my life, Jess. You're a good white man. I haven't known many of those till I got to the mines. You, Dave, Fred, Benny. You're all good white men, good men." He wiped the tear on his cheek with a hand, shook his head, smiling. He straightened. "I won't cry. Captain always said a man who cried unmanned hisself."

"We won't worry about what the captain said. Sallie makes me cry all the time." He shied sideways to avoid her upraised hand. He turned back to Reuben. "We're goin'. Keep in touch with what you're doing in Monterey and the Sandwich Islands. I'm interested. I'm sure Dave will be anxious to hear from you as well." He turned aside. "Fred, Benny, you're a couple of saints. Be careful with this two-legged cargo. Don't let him out of your sight, even if he does want to walk on deck."

They waved as Jess and Sallie mounted and kicked their horses into a lope off the wharf.

———

Jess stood barefoot in the sand just off the water line. Sallie squatted in the shallows at her usual place that continued to yield flakes and the occasional small nugget. He looked into the canopy of the line of oaks across the stream. The new leaves waved and swirled slowly in the light breeze.

Both turned to see Dave coming down the path. He stopped beside Jess, looked down at Sallie's upturned face. "Still taking color from this same spot?"

She took the bottle from a shirt pocket and showed it to him. It was partially filled with about an ounce of flakes. "Jess there hasn't got his feet wet this morning," she said. "I'm still teaching him."

Dave smiled. "I'm going up to the store. C'mon, I'll treat you to coffee and chocolate."

She stood. "Yes, I'll go." She brushed her hands against her pants. "Don't know about him." She bumped against Jess as she stepped from the water.

"Course I'm going. You didn't make coffee this morning for me." She looked at him blankly, realized he was joking and bumped him again as she walked toward the tent.

———

Dave sat with Jess and Sallie at a small round table in the corner at the store. They sipped coffee and chocolate from ceramic mugs.

Dave inhaled deeply, leaned back. "I could sit here all day, but don't see how I can make money doing this." A couple of shoppers smiled at the comment.

A man selecting apples from a box smiled. "Barney there said you have a black man at your claim."

"He was at Dave's claim," Jess said. "He's gone now."

"He's gone away from the diggings?"

"Yes, well away from the gold country."

"Well, he got out just in time. Couple of miles up north of here, somebody stole some dust and pans and some other stuff from a couple of claims. The miners were furious and started rushing around to find the stuff and whoever stole it. They saw a black man on the trail with a sack on his back and hauled him into somebody's camp. Nobody had ever seen him before, and they put two and two together. Some stuff is stolen, and a black man that nobody has ever seen before shows up.

"They dumped the stuff out of his bag and found only old clothes, none of the stuff that was stolen. They figured he had hidden the stolen stuff. They tied him to a tree and said he would stay there till they found the stolen stuff. One of the miners mumbled that they outta kill him right now. I started to say something to them, but since they were so mad, they might decide to kill me, so I went on my way. Feel sorry for the guy. He probably didn't steal anything. He was just in the wrong place at the wrong time. Wish I could do something. I'm Alex, by the way."

Jess looked at Dave. Dave nodded. "We're going up there. Will you go with us?" Alex nodded. "If you know anybody of like mind on the way up, ask them to go as well. The more men we have, the more likely we'll get a hearing."

Jess and Dave stood. Jess went to the counter. "Barney, can Sallie stay with you till we return? Shouldn't be long."

"Sure," said Barney, "wish I could go with you, but you know."

Jess walked back to Sallie. "We won't be long, sweetheart. Stay here."

Sallie stood and put her arms around his waist. "I worry when you go off to help somebody when bad people do things."

"I know, and I'm sorry. But I would blame myself if something happens to the guy, and I could have helped. We'll be careful." He kissed her forehead, beckoned to Dave and Alex.

The three hurried down the stairs to the hitching rail, mounted and kicked their horses into a gallop up the trail. They stopped only once where Alex recruited a friend, Henry, to join them. He ran to his cabin and came out strapping on his pistol belt, went to his horse, hurried to saddle and bridle, mounted, shouted a let's-go, and galloped after them.

After a series of gallops, reining up when encountering walkers, they pulled up when Alex raised an arm calling a halt. They dismounted, tied reins and walked down the path to a clearing between a cabin and the stream. Jess counted six men who stopped where they stood at water's edge and beside a cradle. At the edge of the open space, they saw the old black man sitting at the base of an oak, feet and hands tied and lines wrapped around his chest and the tree trunk. He stared at the newcomers with wide eyes.

"What do you want?" shouted a miner at the cradle.

Jess ignored him. "Cut him loose, Alex." Alex walked toward the captive.

"What! Git away from him!" shouted the miner at the cradle. He reached for a rifle that leaned against a tree beside the cradle.

Jess had already drawn and leveled on the miner. "Leave it," said Jess. "If you touch it, you're a dead man. That goes for the rest of you." The other three men stood mute, glancing at the man beside the cradle, seemingly the leader of the bunch.

"You're in a lot of trouble," said the leader. "This black man stole stuff, and he'll pay."

"Where's the stuff?" said Dave.

"He's hid it. We'll find it and deal with him. If you know what's good for you, you better not interfere."

"We've interfered." The black man stood beside the tree, wide-eyed, watching, rubbing his wrists and stamping to restore circulation. "Do you have any proof this man stole the goods?" Jess said to the miner.

"We'll find the stolen stuff, and that's the proof."

Jess paused, frowned. "Tell you what. I've been thinking about this for some time. We're gonna set up a miner's court. We'll examine your claim that this man stole your stuff. If he's convicted, we'll take him to Sacramento to the authorities. If he's found innocent, he'll be freed, and if you or any of your cronies object, we just might bring you up before the same miner's court. How's that sound?"

"Sounds like a lotta rubbish," said a miner standing in the sand near the stream.

Alex and the black man walked toward the horses. Jess, Dave and Henry pulled back, Jess and Henry still with pistols held at the ready. They untied their horses and mounted, the black man astride behind Alex. They walked their horses down the trail, kicked them into a lope when the trail widened in open glades, walked again when the trail narrowed in brushy lanes.

Dave pulled up beside Jess. "Miner's court?"

Jess laughed. "Nah, not likely, just confusing the issue with the clods back there, give them something else to worry about. If they haven't found the stolen goods by now, they're not likely to find them. We'll see what the black man has to say."

Chapter Eleven

DAVE, Jess, and Sallie sat with the black man around a campfire at Dave's. They had enjoyed a supper of beef, potatoes and beans, and bread. Now they sipped from coffee cups—Jess had brought two from his tent.

They sat quietly, staring into the darkness, looking up into the heavens filled with sparkling stars.

The black man had sat quietly, saying nothing, nodding his thanks for the supper and the coffee. When he spoke, the others, startled, hushed and waited. "I am Abraham. I was owned in Georgia. My master was kind and my mistress taught me to read and write. When my master died, his son, who had begged his father for years to free me, now was my master. He freed me.

"He asked me, a free man now, to go with him to the California gold country. I agreed. I was happy. I liked him. We joined a party that was leaving the Mississippi to go to California. Most had wagons, but we rode horses and had packhorses. He had not planned well, and soon we had nothing and had to beg from others in the train. Most of the people in the train were southerners and did not help us. He became sick, cholera, they said. He died when we were crossing the mountains into California. When I told people in the train I was leaving to go to the gold country, some bad men took my horses and I had to walk. When miners saw me, they ignored me or chased me away. Only one kind old man gave me some bread and dry meat."

"Did you steal the miners' things?" said Jess.

He grimaced. "I stole some potatoes and apples. That's all. I was starving."

They sat silent, staring into the dancing flames, waving, flickering. Dave dropped some kindling on the flames that popped and crackled, sending sparks shooting up from the flames.

"You'll stay with us till we can get you to a safe place," said Jess. He looked around at the others. "Monterey?" All nodded.

"You'll stay with me for a while," said Dave.

———

JESS WROTE to Talbot Green the morning after Abraham arrived in their camp. The reply came in a surprisingly short time, thanks to the dramatic improvement in postal services in recent weeks. Green said that Larkin gave his okay to Abraham's coming to Monterey. He added a proviso. While Mr. Larkin was aware of the ill treatment of black people and sympathized with them, this should be the last referral to him. He did not wish to arouse the sentiments of business acquaintances who did not share his views. Jess replied to Larkin with his thanks for accepting Abraham and said nothing of his proviso.

Jess passed the good news to Abraham and Dave. "Last day on the stream, Abraham," said Dave. "You learned quickly. You'll take an ounce at least with you. Talbot will help you sell it."

Dave and Abraham left the following day at first light, and Abraham boarded Fred's boat the next day. Dave was back in the diggings two days later and went to Jess's claim to report.

They sat with Sallie at the fire circle, sipping their coffee. Sallie surprised them by accepting a cup. Dave told about leaving Abraham at the boat and the solitary ride back to the diggings. "Had too much time to think on the ride back. I've been alone a lot in the past few years, and it's beginning to wear on me. I've been getting used to having somebody with me on the claim, but I'm back on my own again. Never been lonesome before, but I've enjoyed having the boys with me. Now they're gone. Maybe I should get a dog."

Jess reached over and touched Dave on a shoulder. "You're not alone in missing company, pard. The more I talk with other miners at the store or on the trail, the clearer it is that the longer a man is in the diggings, the more he misses people back home. Family, a sweetheart, women in general. There's lots of talk among miners who have been here a long time about going home. And there's the contrary. Miners who have decided they like California, there's talk about bringing parents, or a wife or a sweetheart to California. Maybe you and some of these kindred spirits should organize a wagon train to bring these folks to California." He leaned over and patted Dave's back again, smiling.

Dave looked up into the darkening canopy. "Yeah, I've heard the talk. You know my situation." He drank from his cup. "We'll see."

———

JESS STOOPED and emerged from the tent, barefoot, pulling on a shirt. He scratched his uncombed head vigorously with both hands. He looked at the stream, and there she was. Sallie was in her usual spot, as usual at work before he rose from his bed.

He pushed shirttails into pants, stooped and rolled them up. He would begin his panning before Sallie could berate him for oversleeping. There was his pan on the sandy beach behind her, where she placed it every morning.

He looked upstream and down. The water level was as usual, perhaps down a bit from last week's hard rain which had raised the level and current. He looked at the line of oaks across the stream. There was not the slightest hint of a breeze, and leaves were still.

Then he saw the slightest movement in a dense cluster of leaves in an oak nearest the stream. *Strange, movement at that spot, but nowhere else.* There! A disturbance again in just that one spot. He strained, then saw it when a branch was nudged aside. A huge golden mountain lion crouched on a limb, peering intently at Sallie.

Why didn't I buy the rifle!

He spoke softly. "Sallie. Don't look at me. Don't move." She held the pan, motionless, looking at the water at her feet. He spoke again, hardly more than a whisper. "Now, raise your head slowly and look straight across the stream at the big oak, slowly. Look at the trunk, then at the big branch that reaches out toward the stream. Slowly! What do you see?"

She looked, answered softly. "I don't see…oh! Oh! Oh! It's…"

"It's a mountain lion," he said softly. "Beautiful. Be still. Too bad I didn't get that rifle."

She didn't move. "I talk to you about that rifle," softly.

Then it was over. The lion inched backward up the limb, dropped soundlessly from the limb to the ground and disappeared into the brush on the slope behind the oak grove.

She turned to him, wide-eyed. "That is first time I see mountain lion. He so beautiful!"

"Yeah, I could have bagged him if I had the rifle." A smile played about his lips.

Dropping her pan on the sand, she went to him. She hugged him around the waist. "I know you joke about rifle. I know you like everything about this place and what we do, just like I do." She took his cheeks in her hands, kissed him. "Oh, honey sweetheart, I so happy here, so happy with you." He hugged her as her eyes misted.

———

THEY WORKED the stream this morning with little conversation. She occasionally glanced aside at him, smiled, went back to her panning, carefully removing flakes from the pan and dropping them into her bottle. Mid-morning, she showed him her bottle, holding it up until he showed her his. She smiled when the comparison, as usual, showed hers held about twice as much flakes as his. He frowned, smiled thinly.

When the sun was high, they pocketed their bottles, set pans aside and went to the tent where they collected bread and cheese, fruit and water for lunch. Nooning, miners called it, a respite for mind and body. The day was pleasantly warm, and he did not build a fire. He leaned against the log at the fire circle. She sat a few feet beyond the end of the log, close to the stream. He closed his eyes, dozing. She munched on an apple, running her fingers idly about in the sand at her knees. After a few minutes, she scooted a few feet away, finished the apple as she ran her fingers through the shallow sand.

Sallie stood, tossed the apple core into the bushes and walked toward the tent, pausing a moment before a dozing Jess. She went into the tent, came out and went back to where she last sat. She kneeled and dug in the sand with the knife.

"What are you doing?" Jess had awakened and watched her.

"Come see."

He struggled up and walked slowly to her, scratching his head. He kneeled beside her. She showed him a bottle. The bottom was covered with gold flakes. She smiled and held up a tiny nugget.

His jaw dropped. "Where...where did you find those? Right here?"

"Yes, here and where I sat over there near you. Jess! I think we should work in this ground."

He frowned. "Yes, I agree." He pondered. "We'll need a rocker. I'll talk with Dave."

———

DAVE WAS AS EXCITED as Jess and Sallie about her find. He told them that he had been thinking for months about investigating the possibility of gold deposits in the dry soil near the stream on his claim. He, and other miners as well, had speculated that at some time eons ago, the stream at times was wider and deposited gold near the banks in the wider stretches. If so, that gold was still there in the dry banks well above waterline and could be found by use of a rocker or long tom. Dave said he had thought about a long tom, but didn't have a water source to justify a tom.

He was intrigued about Jess's plan for two reasons. He had decided that his rocker needed repair, or it needed replacement. Now, he could give his old rocker to Jess and watch his progress on mining the dry bank. At the same time, he and Jess could begin building Dave's new rocker.

Here was something new to augment what had become an increasingly routine panning operation. Dave and Jess broke down Dave's rocker and carried the pieces to Jess's claim. There they reassembled it at a convenient spot above waterline near where Jess had chosen to mine. They finished in near darkness.

After a hasty breakfast the next morning, Jess began digging a round hole about three feet wide, depositing shovels of soil on the rocker. Dave poured buckets of water on the trough and helped Sallie work the rocker. This routine continued during the morning, Dave and Jess alternating with the digging and carrying water to the rocker. Sallie was responsible for sifting the soil, looking for color.

Finally, after a long morning of hard work, Sallie looked up at the sun overhead. "Time to stop." Dave offered Jess a hand, helping him climb from the hole which was now almost waist deep.

Jess inhaled and exhaled heavily. "That is the longest morning I have ever lived through," he said. He flexed his back sat slowly at the log.

Dave nodded, sat down heavily at the log. "Agreed. I hope it was worth it."

Sallie came from the tent with a plate of cheese, sourdough bread slices and apples. She sat beside Jess, leaning against the log.

Jess waited, but she said nothing, chewing on a slice of sourdough. "Well?" he said.

She smiled, took a bottle from a pocket and showed it to him. His jaw dropped. The bottle was over half full.

"Dave!" Jess said. "You see this?"

"Yeah. Sallie, are you fooling us? Did all that come from this hole?"

"It did. And these." She held out her open hand that held four tiny nuggets.

"Oooooh, my," said Jess softly. "Let's get back on it."

"You rest, then we get back on it," said Sallie, smiling.

"Well said, Sallie," Dave said. "I'm glad you're in charge here."

After a rest, cut short by Jess's fidgeting, they returned to the dig. They continued the operation until late afternoon when the hole was chest high and Sallie said that the soil had begun to show no color. "How 'bout a new hole?" she said.

"Good idea," Jess said, "tomorrow." He reached up and Dave helped him climb out. "Let's see the bottle," he said. Sallie showed the bottle. It was almost full. "My, my, my," he said. "If my creaking bones are still functioning tomorrow, we'll start a new hole."

During the following two weeks, they dug and worked the soil from eight new holes, filling the old holes from the newly-excavated pits. Jess was fortunate to hire two young fellows who had just arrived in the diggings and had not yet looked for a claim. They were happy to work for somebody else while learning the routine.

Dave helped on the new holes for a couple of days, then decided he had to return to his claim. "You may be on to something with these holes. I heard up at the store yesterday that some miners up above Coloma are working holes that are almost a hundred feet deep. Yeah! That does not sound like fun. I'm not sure the reward would be worth breaking your back. And the risk. What if that tunnel collapsed? That's not for me." He waved and set off up the path.

Jess called after him. "We're not digging a hundred feet for sure. We'll be done soon, and I'll come down to help with the new rocker."

Jess was almost pleased when the latest hole produced little color. The digging was hard work, and he longed to return to the casual panning beside Sallie in the shallows. He realized that gold was not as important as his golden hours with her. He also was so fatigued at night that he retired with little on his mind but sleep. He decided that would not do.

On this last day working the holes, they filled in the last cavity, he paid off his young workers and wished them luck. When they had walked up the path and disappeared in the brush along the trail, he went to Sallie who stood at the waterline, holding their pans. She smiled, leaned up and kissed him.

"Get to work," she said and handed him his pan.

———

Jess recognized from the earliest days he knew Sallie that she was a thinker. He studied her often as they sat at their evening fire, staring into the flames. He admitted to himself that if anyone asked him at that moment, "what are you thinking about?" he probably would answer something like: "that was a good supper; wonder if I need to put more wood on this fire."

But Sallie? He put an arm around her shoulders and asked. "What are you thinking about?" She didn't respond. She stirred the embers with a stick. "Sallie?"

She dropped the stick on the low flames. Putting an arm across his chest, she leaned her head against his arm. "I wonder if I will see my mother in Heaven."

Jess frowned. He had been impressed that, in spite of her compulsory attendance at mission services as a child and attendance at services in following years when the mission gravitated between a semblance of a church and a derelict, she had rarely commented on faith.

"I don't know, honey. You know I'm not a believer, but I don't know if I am right, and I would never tell you what you should believe."

"I know." She stared into the fire, then snuggled against his chest. "I want to go to church." She looked up at him. "Remember when I talked with the woman last time we were at store? She said there would be a church service at dining room of National Hotel, about three miles upstream from store. Can we go?"

———

SALLIE AND JESS walked through the open doors of the National Hotel and into the dining room. Tables were stacked against the windows, and chairs were lined up like benches in a church. The chairs were almost filled with a few dozen in their Sunday finest, probably the only clean clothes they owned. All were men but a woman with her husband and a boy about ten, another woman with husband and two children, both girls, about eight or ten, Jess guessed. The parents and children appeared average American families. *I would like to know them.*

The only accoutrements at the front were a simple lectern and a small table holding a large Bible. *A Protestant service. I hope Sallie is not disappointed.* A minute after they sat, a man walked to the lectern. He wore a dark three-button suit, all buttoned, a white shirt and a gray tie. He picked up the Bible, placed it carefully on the slanted lectern and opened it. He looked up, smiling broadly.

Jess listened long enough to confirm that this was indeed a Protestant service. It sounded like any number of Baptist services he had attended as a young boy. He went with his parents every Sunday and occasional gatherings between Sundays until he was able to persuade them that he would rather be at home, tending to the animals and doing chores, than sleeping on a bench beside them. His mother was indignant, but his father, who agreed with his sentiments for the most part, did not object. So, at age sixteen, he became a practicing nonbeliever. Later, when he understood belief and faith more clearly, he would describe himself as an agnostic since no one could convince him that God did or did not exist.

So far as he knew, Sallie had never wavered in her belief. She had never considered an alternative. On an occasion early on when they had talked about her belief, and Jess had explained his doubts, she had pointed at his chest, touched him lightly and said: "I teach you."

At the end of the service, they stood in the yard

and exchanged pleasantries with other attendees. Now they strolled on the trail southward toward their claim. Neither had much to say about the service. When he asked her what she thought of it, she replied only: "Nice." He took that to mean that she found it less meaningful than the Catholic service they had attended a while ago.

The sun at noon on this early summer day was warm, but not unpleasant as they walked in deep shade. The light breeze rustled leaves in the canopy of the succession of oaks along the stream bank. They looked up at the trill and cheep of unseen birds, then were startled when a trio of birds exploded from branches over their heads, flew across the stream and alighted on limbs of the trees there.

Jess and Sallie stopped when two men who had been walking ahead of them suddenly shouted and turned off the trail, pushing through heavy brush down the incline toward the river. Then they heard excited voices from below. They hurried down the trail, turned and picked their way through the brush toward the stream.

"Oh, Jess," said Sally, her hand over her mouth. They saw three men at the water's edge and two standing in the shallows beside a body that lay face down in the water. The men grasped clothing and arms and pulled the body from the water to the grassy bank. They turned him on his back, and the lifeless eyes stared up at his rescuers.

"Anybody know him?" said one of the men.

"Don't know him properly, but I've seen him on the trail more than once. He was always drunk, any time of day. Probably took a wrong turn and fell in and couldn't stand up. The water's not even knee deep."

"Is he alive?" said Jess.

"No. He's gone."

Sallie, open-mouthed, stared at the body and the men clustered around it. Jess took her arm and climbed up the path back to the trail. "Nothing we can do here. There's plenty men down there to take care of this." He held her arm as they walked on the trail.

They walked in silence. *What a strange thing to say. "He's gone." The body lay on the ground at the speaker's feet, and he says, "he's gone." Strange.*

What possessed a man to become so blind drunk he drowns in knee-deep water? He had heard the stories of miners, even successful miners, who were so addicted to gambling and alcohol that they lost everything at the games that were staged in many camps. And why the addiction? Was it due to the loss of family? Was the absence of family so wrenching one lost all traces of propriety and reason?

Jess stopped when they reached the yard of the store. "Let's stop for a bit," said Jess. "Let's see what new vegetables and fruits they have. I'd sure like to get some corn and tomatoes, but probably too early, even in sunny California. Barney said he should get beets, carrots and peas about now."

They left the trail and walked to the store. Inside, Jess waved to Barney who was accepting cash from a customer who held two filled bags.

Barney made a hurried wave, bent and reached under the counter. He pulled out a couple of letters and held them up. "Jess, here's th' letters you've been looking for." He offered the letters and Jess hurried over to take them.

Jess turned to Sallie, sober. "They're from my daddy." He looked at the dates. One was post-marked ten days after he left home, the other dated a month later. He went to the window, stood in the sunlight and opened the letters, his hand shaking. Sallie went to him, stood behind him, put her arms around his waist and rested her head on his back.

He read silently, then stared through the window, holding the letters at his side. He wiped his eyes with a sleeve and turned to Sallie. "The first letter was just them wondering when I was coming home. The second was them wondering why I hadn't written, saying this was not like me, not telling them what was happening with me. It didn't say it in so any words, but they were wondering whether I was still alive. It said my mama had been sick with worry-ing." He put his arms around Sally and held her. "I hurt them. I really hurt them." He leaned back, wiped his eyes again. "But they've received my letters by now, so they'll know I'm alive. They'll know I'm a California miner." He smiled. "And they'll know I'm in love with a California woman named Sallie."

He frowned, looked at the letters again. "It's a wonder these letters ever reached me. They knew only the name of the hotel where I stayed in Boston. Just before leaving for dinner at the pub, I wrote a short letter to them and asked the hotel clerk to post it for me. I mentioned the name of the pub in the letter. I wrote a longer letter from Chile and another from Monterey. They'll have them all by now."

He showed her the envelopes. There were forwarding addresses on both sides, smudged and obliterating the writings underneath. "They were posted before they received my letters. I will keep the letters and ask them when I see them. I *will* see them."

"Oh, how I wish I could have seen their faces when they read my letters. I'll write this evening and post it with Barney tomorrow." He frowned, pondering, tapping the letters on the windowsill. "I've an idea. I hear every now and then about a miner who is giving it up and going home. I'm going to write a copy of the letter I'm giving to Barney. If I can find somebody who's returning home overland, I'll pay him to carry the letter and drop it to the first post office he sees that carries regular mail to Kentucky. That'll be much faster than mail carried by ships."

He brightened. "Now let's see what we can find for a big happy supper! I'll invite Dave to come over and tell him the good news." He noticed Barney was watching them. "Barney, I need a bottle of good Zinfandel!"

———

THE SUN WAS high at late morning, and warm in spite of the soft whisper of a breeze. Sallie squatted on the sandy bank at the upper end of their claim. Jess stood thigh deep at the ledge that crossed the stream and marked the boundary of their claim. He and the owners of the claim above the ledge had reached an agreement that each would search the ledge only on their respective sides. Jess had shown them the nuggets he had gouged from the stony surface. They were mostly pea-sized, but one was the size of a plump cherry.

And then there was the colossus that he had gouged from the ledge. It weighed almost two pounds. He had danced like a madman on their beach and showed it to no one but Sallie. He had heard about bigger nuggets in the diggings, but this was the largest he had heard about in the vicinity of his claim. He had buried this one apart from the stash of dust bottles.

Sallie stood, stretched, and wiped her hands on her trousers. "Stop for lunch now. I'm hungry." He accepted her outstretched hand, and she pulled him from the water. They walked toward the tent.

He kissed her softly, pinched her bottom. "What's for lunch," he said.

She jerked aside, brushing his hand away. "I don't know. What's for lunch? I got breakfast. You get lunch."

"Yeah, I know." He grinned. She sat by the fire circle, leaned against the log. He walked to the tent.

He came back in a moment, carrying a smaller version of a gold pan. It held slices of bread and cheese, chunks of last night's beef, and two apples.

"Looks good," she said. "You can fix supper too."

"Supper may be more of this. We'll eat early. We're going up the trail to a camp I heard about. Every Friday night—that's tonight—a bunch up there sit around a campfire, and somebody talks about what he did before coming to the diggings. A couple of old boys I talked with at the store said it can be really interesting. We tend to think about people we meet in the diggings as, well, miners. But they had lives before coming here. They said the fellow who will talk tonight has a really interesting past. I'm looking forward to it. Dave is coming, and we'll go up together."

———————

JESS, Sallie, and Dave sat with about three dozen others, all men but Sallie and a young woman whose arm was wrapped around a girl about four years old. The spectators were arrayed near a large circle of stones that surrounded a most welcome fire on this cool evening. Sallie was surprised when Jess accepted the pipe, already filled with tobacco, offered by Dave. She smiled as Dave lit Jess's pipe with a glowing stick, and Jess puffed contentedly as if this were something he did on every evening.

She looked around and saw that almost all the men puffed on pipes, silent, staring into the flames. She pulled Jess's hand down, the hand holding the pipe. She looked up at him and laughed out loud. He smiled, drew on the pipe and blew a puff of smoke toward her.

She leaned against him, her lips at his ear, and spoke softly. "I think I get a pipe." She smiled thinly. He offered her the pipe. She made a face and pulled back.

They started at the voice of a man standing on the opposite side of the fire circle. "Thanks for coming tonight, folks. I s'pose it's gotten around that we're going to hear from a man who has lived a bit of history that will make our own lives seem humdrum by comparison. I refer to my friend here." He gestured to the man who sat at his feet. The man nodded soberly. "Now I'll sit down."

He sat, the man nodded again, and did not stand. "I've sat around campfires for most of my life and I'll sit here as well. I take exception to my pard's suggestion that my life makes yours humdrum. Every one of us here is exceptional in one way or another. Including the pretty lady sittin' over there." He gestured with a nod toward Sallie. Everyone turned to look at her as she shrank halfway behind Jess. He moved aside so she was visible.

The speaker smiled, turned back to face the throng. He was in his early sixties, dressed in clean, simple worker's clothing. His face was browned and almost leathery, suggesting a life spent outside.

"My name is Jean-Baptiste Charbonneau. The most important thing about me is that my mother was Sacajawea who helped Lewis and Clark in their expedition to the Pacific Ocean early in this century. If you haven't heard of her, you've probably heard of them. My father was a French Canadian, and the most important thing about him is that he married my mother." Chuckles from around the circle. "When the expedition was finished, William Clark adopted me, and I was educated in white men's schools back east. When I decided I had learned enough, I wanted to return to the wild country. I became a trapper and guide. I got involved during the late war with Mexico, serving as guide to Philip

St. George Cooke's Mormon Battalion and General Kearny's Army of the West.

"In California, Colonel Cooke appointed me magistrate of the San Luis Rey Mission near San Diego where I was happy to start a school for the Indian children there. Sometime later, I went north to Sutter's Mill and finally settled on the Middle fork of the American River near Auburn where I live now."

He paused, inhaled deeply, looked around the fire circle at the listeners who leaned forward, wide-eyed and jaws hanging, expecting more. "If any of what I said is of interest, I'll be happy to answer questions."

For a moment, there was only silence. No one said a word. Then, as if a dam had exploded, a barrage of questions came, excited questions. Charbonneau responded slowly, and soon the discussion was measured and most interesting. All came to realize that this man had played a large part in the opening of the West by Americans, culminating in the conquest and acquisition of California.

The miner who had opened the gathering eventually stood and held up a hand to signal an end. He thanked Charbonneau for his comments, thanked the group for coming and waved his goodbyes. All stood, many going quickly to Charbonneau to thank him and shake his hand before he had a chance to leave. He acknowledged the compliments and thanks, smiled and withdrew with his friend.

Jess looked at Dave. "Whew, that was interesting, like we had the last fifty years replayed in an hour." He turned to Sallie. "Sallie, I think you should speak to this group. You have seen change in the past fifteen years or so that this bunch of miners know nothing about, and—"

"No!" She pointed a finger in his face, almost touching his nose. "No," she said softly. She looked away, into the darkness. "No. It hurts too much. I can talk with you about my past, and Dave, but nobody else. They would ask questions that I could not answer, or questions that I don't want to talk about."

"I understand," said Jess. He bent and tapped his pipe on a stone, emptying the ashes. He handed the pipe to Dave who had listened quietly to Charbonneau. "What about you, Dave? I bet you've had an interesting life. I'll bet half these rowdies never saw the inside of a doctor's office."

Dave held up a hand, palm outward. "If I tell these rowdies I'm a doctor, I'll have a lineup at my claim every morning. No, I'll not reveal that I'm a doctor, and don't you do it."

"They'll not hear it from me, pard. I'll tell 'em you were a sailor, and we jumped ship together."

"You both liars," Sallie said.

Chapter Twelve

THE BALMY DAYS of spring gave way to hot summer, still cool at night but scorching on some days. Not as hot as the valley, said oldtimers. You want hot, they said, go to Sacramento. You want cool, go to San Francisco. The summer fog in the bay cools the city so you have to wear a coat, even in July.

Jess looked up through the oak canopy at the hot sun ball directly overhead. "We need to go to San Francisco, sweetheart," said Jess. They sat in shade near their tent, finishing bowls of beans and fresh tomatoes, supplemented by chunks of bread.

"If you too hot, I fan you." She fanned him with her gold pan.

He smiled, pulled her hand down to stop the fanning. "We need to see what's happening to our investment. If the lots have increased in value as the realtors predicted, maybe we should buy more. We have gold that's lying idle. I'll talk to Dave."

"I don't want move there."

He smiled, threw an arm around her neck and

pulled her to him. He kissed her cheek, lightly bit her ear. She pushed him away, smiling, patting his cheeks with both hands, the last pat a gentle slap.

"Okay, wildcat, you want to rassle?"

She pulled back. "I don't know. What's 'rassle'?"

"Well, I guess the correct word is 'wrestle'. It means to fight without hitting, just hugging tight and squeezing."

"Sound like fun, not fight."

He smiled. "We'll rassle tonight. Let's go down to talk with Dave now."

———

JESS AND DAVE sat opposite Thurston in his office. Sallie stood in the back, looking through the window to the street.

"Yessir, your lots have increased as I predicted. Well, not *exactly* as I predicted. I said they would triple in value. They have *quadrupled* in value! What d'you think of that?"

"Most encouraging," said Dave. "Has the new value been tested by someone selling his lots?"

Thurston leaned back, grinning from ear to ear, his arms outstretched over the desk, his palms flat on the desktop. "I figured you would ask that. Yes! Two owners who were returning east sold their lots at *four times* what they paid for them. I'll show you the figures if you doubt me."

"All right," said Jess, "I would like to invest two thousand dollars in lots in the same locale."

"Sorry to say, there are no lots available in that section. They have been picked up by eager investors who have heard about their increase in value." He paused, smiling, watching Dave's and Jess's reaction. "However, we are now selling lots in a newly surveyed area. We call it the Mission District. It has the same potential as the bay view section. Perhaps greater. As the city expands, this section will almost surely become the heart of the business district. *And,* gentlemen, don't take my word for it. Mr. Larkin was among the first to invest in the Mission District."

"Okay," said Jess, "I'll put down two thousand dollars on lots as close to Larkin's as you have."

"Thank you, sir." He waved to Wally seated at his desk against the wall, who nodded, his face solemn. Thurston, smiling broadly, turned to Dave. "And you, sir?"

"The same." Thurston thumped the desk with his fist. He pointed at Wally who nodded again, still straight-faced.

"I trust you know, Mr. Thurston, that we'll have your hide if your prediction does not materialize," said Jess with a straight face.

Thurston straightened, mouth agape. Then Jess smiled slightly. Thurston relaxed, smiled. "Gentlemen, you know the workings of business as well as I. I predict what I think will happen, based on evidence; I do not control what happens. I think you understand that."

"Of course," Jess said. "We have faith that you will invest our money wisely." Jess smiled, and Thurston smiled thinly.

"And that your forecast will make us rich men,"

said Dave. Thurston nodded, shook hands with Dave, then Jess.

"We'll keep in touch," said Dave, waving over his shoulder as they walked to the door.

Outside, Dave and Jess looked at each other, chuckling.

Sallie looked solemnly at them. "Sometime both you sound dumb."

———

AT DUSK on the evening of their return from San Francisco to their claim, Sallie and Jess sat at their usual place, staring at the dying embers of the fire. Both drank from coffee cups, though Sallie's cup contained only warm water.

"Too bad we missed Fred and Bennie's new steamboat," said Jess. "Fred said the upgrades should be finished before we go San Francisco again." When Sallie didn't answer, he turned to her.

"What were you doing before we sat down here?" Sallie said. "You runnin' everywhere around camp."

He sipped his coffee, hesitated, frowning before answering. "Sallie, it's almost scary to say it, even to think about it, but we're worth almost forty thousand dollars. That includes the gold we've taken here, the gold from the mission, and the San Francisco lots. That is a *lot* of money. Actually, and I hate to even say it, but we're rich. One of these days, we're going to have to talk seriously about the future."

She stared into the fire, looked across the stream

at the woods that were now dark. "I think you decide you finished with California, and you leave me and go home to Kentucky." She leaned forward, picked up a stick and stirred the embers. "And I kill myself."

He recoiled. "What! Why would you say such a thing?"

"I hear you and Dave talk about home far from here, and I think you miss it and people back there. You have money now and you can go back and buy anything you want."

He frowned, shook his head. "I thought you were joking, but…Sallie, the only way I would go back to Kentucky would be with you at my side. You're stuck with me, woman. I'll never leave you, and if you try to leave me, I'll give you a thrashing. As for the money, it's as much yours as mine, maybe more so."

"Okay." She took his arm and held it tightly. She leaned against the shoulder, looked up at him, frowning. "What means 'thrashing'?"

He smiled. "It means I would beat you with my hands and sticks and whips until you say you will do anything I want."

She took his cheeks in her hands. "I do anything you want, but no thrashing!" She pointed a finger into his face and kissed him. She snuggled against his chest. "I go to Kentucky with you for visit, if you promise come back to California. I don't want move to Kentucky."

He shook his head slowly. *Okay, so she's in charge. And I think she knows it. Fine with me.*

SALLIE AND JESS sat at a table on the store porch. Their table was shaded by a large oak, most welcome in the sunshine at high noon. Each sipped from a cup of chocolate. A small plate on the table held only crumbs.

The door opened, and Annie came out. "Buenos dias," she said.

Sallie's eyes opened wide. "Buenos dias! Ahora hablas español! You speak Spanish now!"

"I want to learn. I've been talking with a young man named Jorge who is working with the Jews building the cabin behind the store. He doesn't speak much English, so we're teaching each other."

"Wonderful, I will help too. I've been trying to teach Jess, but he is not good student."

Jess grimaced. "Why should I learn Spanish when I've got Sallie in camp?"

"Annie," Sallie said, "we can tell stories in Spanish about Jess and Barney, and they won't understand."

Annie smiled and shot a glance at Barney who stood in the open doorway, listening. He shrugged his shoulders.

"More chocolate?" Annie said. "Cakes?"

Sallie shook her head, so Annie picked up the plate and went inside.

Jess stood. "All done, sweetheart? Let's be on our way. I'd like to collect a thousand dollars of dust before supper." She stood, drank the last swallow of chocolate, and they went down the stair to the trail.

She hooked a thumb on his belt at his back,

swung her other arm to match her gait, almost skip-ping. "Thousand dollars? *You* can't find thousand dollars in a *month*." She looked up at him, smiled. "I find thousand dollars in a week!"

"Hah!"

"Watch. You see."

———

JESS AND SALLIE walked down the path to their claim.

He put an arm around Sallie's shoulders. "I started to say it's always good to be—and almost said 'home'."

She bumped his side. "Well, it is home now, isn't it, and—"

He stopped, held out an arm to stop her. "Whoa," he said softly.

She looked abruptly at him. "What's wrong?"

Then she saw it. Under the manzanita near their tent, a hole in the soil, two feet wide. They went to the hole, looked inside to the bottom, about three feet down. Then they saw another. Beside the adja-cent chamise, a second hole the same width and depth. Jess pushed through the branches of the two shrubs to a smaller manzanita where he saw a third hole.

He looked down. "Oh, my."

"What is it?" said Sallie.

"They found a sack of dust."

"Oh, Jess. Was it much?"

"Seven or eight hundred dollars."

They stared into the hole. Jess shook his head. "I

should have sent it to the bank in Sacramento long ago. Dumb, dumb, dumb."

"I wonder why only three holes?"

He looked up into the canopy, his eyes shut. He opened his eyes and looked again at the hole. "Might've heard us coming. They're either dumb or lucky, maybe both, digging around a claim in broad daylight."

"What can we do?"

"I'll ask around. Maybe somebody else has had something like this goin' on. Maybe somebody has seen some characters they haven't seen before. Likely it's somebody passing through, looking for an opportunity."

"But how would they know you buried gold in camp?"

"Good question. Many miners have told me they've buried sacks of gold on their claim, so maybe they just took a chance. More likely, somebody saw me burying it." He drew his Colt, checked the cartridges, and pushed it back into the holster. "Let's take a walk, and I'll talk with people about strangers they might have seen today."

He headed toward the path. He stopped, looked back to see Sallie at the hole near the small manzanita, moving the soil and leaves aside with her foot. She bent and picked up a small piece of cloth. She held up the cloth, showing it to Jess. She sniffed it, wrinkling her nose.

He went back to her and took the piece, holding it up with two fingers. He inspected it, turning it over to see both sides. It was about a foot square, soiled, it seemed, with mucous and spittle, a faint touch of blood. "Probably passed for a handker-chief." He looked at the stream, pondering. He pushed the cloth into a pocket. "Let's go."

They went first to Dave's claim. Jess told him about the incident, said he and Sallie were going to walk north along the stream asking miners if they had seen anyone carrying a sack of any sort. Or someone they had never seen before. Dave volunteered to walk south and make the same inquiries in that direction.

———

NEXT DAY, first light. Jess and Sallie stood before their tent, fully clothed. Jess buckled the pistol belt and pulled his hat tight.

"I don't know how long I'll be, but Annie said you're welcome to stay with them as long as it takes. I think she's real happy to have you there. She said not many Californians come to the store, and she thinks it's because nobody there speaks Spanish. She said having you at the store will be good for business." He smiled. "Well, she likes you too. I know Barney will like having you around."

He smiled, tapped her nose with a finger. "You watch out for yourself, sweetheart." He kissed her. "Stay put at the store. Don't go to the claim. Dave will take care of it. Okay? You all right with all this? You promise to stay with Annie and Barney?"

"Yes, but I worry already."

"It'll all be okay. The tracker I've hired was recommended by half a dozen miners who have used him in the past. They say he can smell a thief a mile away. Well, it's his dog doing the smelling. Speaking of smelling..." He reached into a shirt pocket and pulled out a corner of the thief's soiled handkerchief, wrinkled his nose. He pushed the cloth back into the pocket. "Okay, let's go."

Sallie and Jess each shouldered a small bag, and they walked up the path.

———

JESS AND SALLIE stood before their tent with the tracker they had fetched and brought back to their claim. Matt, the tracker, introduced his dog, Pard, as if he were introducing a person. Pard wagged his tail wildly, acknowledging the courtesy. Jess pulled out the handkerchief and gave it to Matt who dangled the cloth before Pard's nose. The dog sniffed, moving his head up and down, right and left, to sniff every inch. Matt pocketed the handkerchief.

Pard looked at Matt who nodded. The dog bounded around the camp, sniffing the ground in all directions, pausing at each of the holes and settled on the one Jess had identified as the location of the stolen bag. The dog sniffed the ground in all directions a few feet from the hole, then sniffed the ground as he bounded for the path that led upward to the trail.

"We're off," said Matt.

———

ANNIE MET Sallie and Jess on the store's front porch. She hugged Sallie and assured Jess that she could stay with them as long as she liked. She would be a big help in the store, she said, and would be most welcome in her determination to learn Spanish.

Jess kissed Sallie on the cheek, hurried down the steps and walked to the trail where Matt waited with Pard. He waved to Sallie who stood on the porch, her hands clasped beneath her chin. She returned the wave as Annie put an arm around Sallie's shoulders.

Matt offered the soiled cloth to Pard. The dog sniffed and sniffed, pushing his nose into the folds, and he was off. Matt had to call him back often as he bounded ahead. They had walked hardly an hour when Pard turned off the trail and scurried down the path to a claim both Matt and Jess recognized. The claimant was well known for offering his services in rowing people across the stream for a fee. The boat was tied up at streamside.

The miner saw them coming and waved. "You fancy a crossing this morning? Better'n swimmin'." All three were startled at Pard's bark. The dog stood in the shallows, sniffing the boat's gunwales, reaching over the side and sniffing inside.

"That dog's onto somethin'," said the miner.

"Somebody stole from my claim. Did you row anybody across yesterday carrying a bag, maybe a stranger?" said Jess.

He squinted. "Matter of fact, I did. Two fellas I never seen before."

"Can you give us a description?" Jess said.

He frowned. "Yeah. Middle-aged, scruffy. One was wearing blue pants, the other faded brown pants. One of 'em was wearing a sombrero, but he didn't look like a Mex. Each of 'em carried a little bag, not the sorta bag you carry your things in when you're travelin'."

"Did you hear them say anything that might indicate where they were going?"

'No, not really. One of 'em mumbled somethin' about Coloma, but I don't know whether he said that was where they was goin'. I can describe the road to Coloma if you like."

"I know the road," said Matt.

"Thanks, okay, we need to cross," said Jess. He and Matt climbed in and Pard jumped in. The dog scurried fore and aft in the boat, sniffing vigorously on the sides and bottom.

"They were in the boat, for sure," Matt said.

The miner pushed off, climbed in, and picked up the oar. As he rowed, he laughed at Pard's sniffing and apparent eagerness to reach the shore, with his front paws on the gunwale.

On the other side, Jess and Matt climbed out, and Jess paid the miner. They were startled by Pard's bark. He was impatient. On bounding from the boat's bow, he sniffed right and left on the bank and headed up the incline. Matt called him back, and he and Jess climbed the bank behind the dog. It was but a short climb to a well-worn road.

Pard sniffed on the road, trotted ahead. "Coloma's that way." Matt pointed.

Jess wished they had horses, but it was too late for that. Matt called Pard back, and they hitched a ride in a filled goods wagon. After a couple of hours, Matt said they should get down in case they were off the scent. As the wagon pulled away, he offered the handkerchief to Pard. After a thorough sniffing, the dog set off on the road, sniffing the ground and being restrained by Matt.

Rounding a turning, they saw in the distance a motley collection of a couple hundred frame buildings and tents. Coloma. Jess had been near the town when he and others investigated the ruckus caused by the Oregonians who wanted to kill Indians, but he had never actually visited the town. He was relieved at Matt's comment that he had occasion to visit a couple of times. Jess looked behind and saw the sun halfway below the horizon. He would be glad to find a place to get refreshment and spend the night. He said as much to Matt.

Matt wasn't listening. He had stopped beside Pard who was busy sniffing the ground. The dog ran back on the road a few yards, then went across the road to a trail that headed northward. He sniffed in the trail as he walked slowly away from the road.

"Our men didn't go to Coloma," said Matt. "They turned off here, headin' north."

"Oh, my," said Jess. He pondered. "Well, it's too late to head up that way today. Let's stay in Coloma tonight and get back on the trail in the morning." They walked toward the town, Matt having difficulty persuading Pard that they were off the scent trail now.

As they approached the outskirts, Jess recalled the story he heard at Sutter's about the origins of the town's name. It was named after the Cullumah valley where it was built. The name meant "beautiful" in the language of the local Nisenan Indians.

Jess shook his head. *It sure isn't beautiful today.*

Except for the main street, it obviously had grown without much planning. As they walked the streets, he was surprised to see a number of stores, a variety of shops and hotels and boarding houses. He was not surprised to see a sizable selection of saloons.

Jess went inside a small hotel to book a room. Matt waited outside on the plank walk until Jess gave him the signal that the clerk had stepped out of the lobby. Matt rushed in with Pard on a lead and ran up the stairs in the direction pointed by Jess. Matt returned in a few minutes and followed Jess outside. They had drinks and supper at the saloon next door. They were content to cut the evening short and retire to the hotel room. It had been a long, tiring day.

———

AT FIRST LIGHT the next day, Jess and Matt had a quick breakfast and were back on the road. At the path where they stopped last evening, Matt gave Pard a sniff of the handkerchief. The dog buried his nose in the cloth, then dropped his head to the ground and he was off, sniffing each side of the trail. He wanted to run but was restrained by Matt.

The trail led north, sometimes along streams and claims, sometimes through meadows and open country. At times Pard halted, sniffed the trail, the air and in the vegetation alongside the trail. Each time, he returned to the trail and moved ahead. On occasion Jess wondered whether the dog had lost the trail, but each time he doubted, Pard seemed to find the scent and move ahead on the trail.

When the trail merged with a well-worn dusty road, they hitched a ride on a heavily- laden goods wagon bound for Nevada City. Jess told the driver about their mission. The driver thought about it a bit, then opined that the men probably were not local and likely were bound for Rough and Ready or Nevada City. Rough and Ready was a small burg, he said, without many attractions, particularly being short on places to stay, and it contained only one dinky saloon. He guessed the thieves were bound for Nevada City.

The driver was in no hurry and became caught up in their pursuit. He was content to stop occasionally to permit Matt to let the dog down, nuzzle the cloth and sniff the ground. Then Pard would bound off on the road ahead, only to be called back by Matt who hauled him back up on the wagon.

"Must be confusing for the pup," said the driver.

"Yeah, probably so," said Matt, "but he seems to still have the scent."

———

THE SUN BALL rested on the western horizon. Dark shadows from a line of oaks lay across the road. The wagon was stopped on the outskirts of Rough and Ready. Matt and Pard had climbed down from the wagon, Pard nuzzled the proffered handkerchief, sniffed the ground in all directions, moved off, stopped, bounded in another direction, stopped, looked back at Matt.

"He ain't sure," said Matt.

"Hmm. Maybe we should spend the night here. Maybe the trail will be fresher in the morning."

"Uh, fellas," said the driver, "I'd be careful about spendin' the night in Rough and Ready. Things are a bit uncertain hereabouts right now. The town declared its independence from the United States a while ago so they wouldn't have to pay no federal minin' taxes. At least, that's what they intended. People here are a bit on edge about what's gonna happen. I'm goin' on to Nevada City now. You can go with me if you want and spend th' night there. If you want to come back here tomorrow in daylight, it's only a few miles walk. Just sayin'."

Jess pondered. "That's probably a good idea. Matt?"

"Okay with me. Pard would probably agree since he's a bit confused at the moment."

———

Jess had never visited Nevada City and was not prepared for the size of the town. Even in darkness, dispelled by the few lamps on posts and walls, he was impressed with the appearance of a town unlike any he had seen in California east of Sacramento. Exercising the subterfuge that had proved successful in Coloma, he procured a room for the night in a small hotel followed by a light supper in the hotel café that was in the process of closing for the night.

———

Jess was awakened by bright sunlight streaming through the open window, curtains waving gently in the soft breeze. He threw back the covers, saw Matt still asleep on the pallet beneath the window, Pard snuggled alongside him. Matt stirred, patted the dog's back and pushed the quilt aside. He sat up, scratching his head.

"Let's be off," said Jess. "I feel good about this day."

Pard stood, shook all over vigorously, went to Jess who patted his head. As they dressed, Jess noticed Pard sniffing the thief's handkerchief at his feet. It had fallen from his pocket as he was pulling up his pants. He picked it up and stuffed it into a pocket. The men collected their gear and went down the stairs to the hotel café.

After a light breakfast, they went outside to the almost empty street. They looked up and down the street. "Now where would a stranger likely go in this place?" said Jess, more to himself than Matt.

"Don't ask me," Matt said. "Ask him." He was watching Pard. The dog was sniffing the dusty road. With his nose to the ground, he walked slowly toward the boardwalk on the far side of the street, then back to the near side, constantly sniffing. He bounded up the boardwalk ahead and sniffed as he walked, scurrying right and left on the walk. Jess and Matt followed.

Pard stopped at the door of the Crazy Mule Saloon. He looked back at them, barked once, tail wagging. Jess and Matt looked at each other, walked to the door. Jess opened it slowly, and they went inside.

The large room contained half a dozen round tables and a long bar at the wall. A bartender stood behind the empty bar, frowning at them. Only one table was occupied. Six men sat at the table, all holding cards, staring at the intruders.

"No dogs!" said the bartender.

Matt looked at the bartender. Jess ignored him. Pard sniffed the floor, walked slowly toward the table, sniffing right and left. The card players watched the dog. Pard stopped behind a chair, sniffing. Then he bent forward, spraddle-legged, and barked loudly, startling the players.

"I said no dogs!" the bartender shouted. He strode toward Jess and Matt.

Jess drew the Colt slowly, held it at his side. "Stay where you are," he said to the bartender who stopped and took a step backward. Jess turned to the table to see the players all stand slowly, pushing chairs back, watching him. Pard continued to bark, then grabbed the man's pants in his teeth and jerked side to side, growling.

"I said no dogs, sumbitch!"

Jess whirled to see the bartender striding toward him, carrying a shotgun loosely. Jess raised the Colt and fired at the floor at the bartender's feet. The bartender, startled, threw the scattergun into the air and ran back to the bar.

"Jess!" Matt shouted.

Jess turned to see the man from the table running toward a back door, Pard in pursuit, barking loudly.

"I'll get him!" said Matt. Pistol in hand, he ran after Pard.

Jess ran to the front door, went outside, ran down the boardwalk, turned around the side of the building to see the thief standing in the alley, kicking at Pard and shouting. Pard clamped on a leg with his teeth and shook.

"Ow, damn dog!" The man dropped the bag he carried, drew a pistol quickly, and fired at Pard. The dog recoiled, and the thief fired again. Pard was blown backward and lay trembling.

Matt stopped behind the thief. He fired into his back, and he fell forward. "Damn you! Damn you to hell!" He fired again at the prostrate thief. The bullet tore into his forehead.

Matt knelt beside the dog. "Pard," he said softly. He stroked the dog's side, touched his head. Matt stood, leaned back, and shouted at the top of his lungs, an anguished wail. He turned to the thief's carcass and fired into the dead man's head, then kicked the body repeatedly, sobbing.

Jess holstered the Colt, walked slowly to Matt, and put an arm around his shoulders. "Sorry, old man, so sorry." He patted his shoulder.

Matt looked up. "What about the other guy? There were two."

Jess put a hand on Matt's shoulder. "We're not going to worry about him. We have the gold. We need to be on our way. Somebody might know the dead guy back there and come looking for us."

"I'm takin' Pard with me," Matt said. "I ain't leavin' him."

"Are you sure? He looks heavy."

"I ain't leavin' him. I'm buryin' him at the

claim." He knelt and picked up the dog, grunting. "I'm ready." Tears coursed down his cheeks.

Jess picked up Matt's bag and the bag dropped by the thief. He opened it, looked inside and confirmed that it held the stolen gold sacks.

They went back to the main street and walked in the center, ignoring the stares of curious towns-people who had come out of stores at the sounds of gunshots.

By the time they reached the town's outskirts, Matt was grunting under the heavy burden. Jess took his arm, giving him moral support but little else. They turned at a creaking sound from behind and saw the wagon they had ridden in yesterday.

The driver pulled up. "How 'bout a ride, fellas. I saw it all back there. Hope you found what you was lookin' for. Sorry for what happened to your dog. Too bad."

Matt mumbled his thanks. Jess let the tailgate down, and Matt gently laid Pard in the empty bed. He climbed into the wagon to sit beside the dog, and Jess replaced the tailgate. Jess patted Matt on the shoulder, went forward and climbed up to the wagon seat.

"Thanks, man," Jess said to the driver.

He nodded, shook the lines and the horses moved ahead.

Jess looked back to see Matt gently stroking the dog's side, tears rolling down his cheeks.

Chapter Thirteen

JESS SAT with Sallie on the sand at the edge of the stream. He told her everything that happened since leaving her at the store, including the return from Nevada City in the empty goods wagon.

The driver of the wagon had been delighted to share his wagon. From the time they climbed aboard, the driver related everything that had happened to him from the time he left Missouri in spring 1849. He told about the overland trek, including the names and stories of everyone he knew in the caravan, settling into hunting gold in the placers, early success followed by disappointment and departure, hiring on with the Sacramento merchant for whom he drove supply wagons to gold rush towns, chiefly Nevada City. He's happy as a lark with the job, he said. Driving through the beautiful California countryside of meadows and wildflowers and sunny days, talking with hitchhikers he welcomed in his wagon.

"He was still talking when Matt and I got down

where we would cross the stream," Jess said. "As he drove off, he yelled that he would finish his story the next time he saw us. He was one happy fellow, content with his lot. Matt got a little annoyed with his banter. He had a lot on his mind. But I enjoyed his stories."

"What about the gold?" Sallie said.

"He spent less than a half of one small sack. He must have won at cards, or he would have spent lots more. He must not have been a very smart fella, or he would have left the country. With that much dust, he had all the money he needed for a long time." He pondered, making ripples in the water with a stick, back and forth, side to side. "Didn't do him any good. He's crow bait now."

"Was it just one man?"

"I wondered about that. Seemed to be two at the start. Either I was wrong, or the other guy disappeared, or the thief got rid of him. Or...could he have been one of the men at the card table? Hmm. If so, I hope he's scared off and doesn't come looking for me. We'll have to keep our eyes open."

They stared at the stream, quiet, the occasional leaf carried by the slack current, two small birds flitting about the lower branches of the pines across the stream, lacy light gray clouds against a cobalt sky.

"Annie learn Spanish fast," said Sallie. "She can already speak some sentences. She told me to ask you to go away again soon, so I will stay with them and she will learn more Spanish."

"Hmm." Jess continued stirring the water with the stick.

"I think you not listening to me. What you thinking about?"

He turned to her, dropped the stick. "Sorry. My mind was somewhere else. After we were dropped off by the wagon driver, we started walking and fell in with a couple of men who had just arrived from Sacramento. They talked about a law that the new state government in San Jose passed that has a lot to say about how the state is going to treat native people.

"It's not good. I don't completely understand the details, but the law is meant to remove Indians from their ancestral lands in favor of white people. It will disrupt Indian families and separate them from their cultures and languages. It will even make it possible for a white person to go to a legal authority and indenture Indian children to work for them."

"What means 'indenture'?"

"It means the children would be removed from their parents and forced to work for the white person."

She frowned. "That sound like slavery. Even the missions didn't remove children from parents."

They fell silent, staring into the languid stream.

"I've been thinking," he said. "We've talked a lot about what we might do after we leave the diggings." He looked at her. "It's time to do it, Sallie, move on. I'm sure neither of us ever intended to spend our lives in the gold country, but the time spent has been good for us. We now are worth about forty thousand dollars in gold and thousands more in San Francisco property. Sallie, that's enough to do whatever we want to do." He waited.

She looked aside at him, looked back to the stream. "Okay. I don't want to stay here all time. I don't want move to San Francisco. I don't want leave California."

"I agree on all counts. I may want to go visit my parents. Or ask them to come here. But I want to live in California." He paused, pondered.

"I've been thinking a lot about this lately, sweetheart, where we're going from the diggings, what we're going to do. Here's what I'm thinking." He inhaled deeply. "We could settle near the San Miguel mission. We buy land and cattle and build a ranch. We employ local people, Salinan people."

As she listened, she leaned toward him, her eyes opening wide, her jaw dropping. She clasped her hands under her chin, and the tears came, streaming down her cheeks.

"Would this work, you think?" he said.

She threw her arms around his neck, then pulled back. "Oh, Jess. Would you? I can't think of anything I would rather do." She threw her arms around his neck again and hugged tightly, sobbing.

He pulled at her arms. "Hey, ease off, you'll strangle me, and you'll be on your own."

She pulled back, dropped her arms, and wiped her cheeks with a sleeve. She smiled faintly, wiped her cheeks again. "I love you, honey sweetheart."

She straightened, sober, looked past him to the oaks behind the tent, pursing her lips.

He leaned toward her. "Uh-oh, I can hear that brain churning."

She looked at him. "Jess. You remember I have talked about how the Salinan have lost our past, our culture, and our language. The Spanish and Mexicans took them from us. They said we should be like them, accept their culture and language and believe in their God. We had no choice. We became Spanish and Mexican. I tried to find out about our past, but nobody I talked with knows."

She took his hand in both of hers. "But Jess, *somebody* knows. The Spanish, when they came so many years ago, they found Salinan people speaking their own language and living in their old ways. The Spanish must have written down what they found. Their bosses in Spain would have wanted to know. Those writings must still exist. They must be in libraries or offices somewhere, in Mexico or Spain. "

"Sallie, I think you are on to something."

"You said we have enough money to do whatever we want to do."

"I did, and I meant it."

"Jess, we could look for these writings. If we don't find them in California, could we hire someone to go to Mexico, or maybe to Spain, to search for the writings?"

"We can. What a wonderful idea. I would like to do this, Sallie."

She looked at him, eyes filling and tears flowing. "I think I dream." She lunged at him, toppling him, lying on top of him. She smothered him with kisses.

———

JESS AND SALLIE sat with Dave at a small table on the store porch. Empty plates lay on the table, and they sipped from cups, coffee and chocolate. Dave had listened quietly, pondering, staring into his cup, to Jess's recounting their plans for leaving the placers and building a cattle ranch in Sallie's homeland.

"What do you think?" said Jess.

Dave continued to stare into his cup, his face blank. Jess and Sallie glanced aside at each other. Then Dave looked up, smiling. "I think that is absolutely, positively fantastic. I have learned a lot about you two since becoming neighbors. I sensed that you would be leaving soon, but I didn't dream you would settle on this. Congratulations. It sounds perfect. For both of you."

Jess and Sallie relaxed, smiled. "Thanks, Dave," said Jess. "You've been a good friend. We owe you a lot. We'll miss you."

Dave leaned back in his chair. "Maybe not as much as you might think." Sallie and Jess frowned. "You're not the only one with news. Before you arrived this morning, Barney gave me a letter. It was from my wife." He paused, sober. Then he grinned. "She's coming!"

"That's wonderful, Dave!" said Jess. He slapped Dave on his back.

"That's good!" Sallie said.

"Yep. There's more. Remember when I said I might someday set up a practice in San Francisco? Been thinking a lot more about it lately. Now your news makes me rethink. Maybe I don't want to move to the big city. Maybe Monterey instead. What do you think about that?"

Jess threw up his hands. "We'll almost be neighbors! And you'll get to know Larkin. He will introduce you to all his friends, and you'll have a filled practice overnight. I'm sure of it."

"Hey, Jess!" The shout came from the yard.

They all looked down and saw Matt striding toward the porch. A small long-haired pup trotted beside him, tongue lolling.

"Hey, Matt," said Jess. "Come on up." Matt climbed the stair, and Jess introduced all around.

"I figured I might catch you here," said a grinning Matt. "I wanted to show you my new little buddy." He pointed at the pup. "This here is Pardie, my new sidekick. Don't know if she'll have as good a nose as old Pard, but she's as sweet as sugar. Just wanted to check in with you to let you know that all's right with the world." He smiled at Sallie. "Nice to meet you folks."

He went down the steps and waved over his shoulder as he walked across the yard. Reaching down, he patted the little dog on the head. The pup wagged her tail and frolicked beside him. Matt stopped, braced himself spraddle-legged, leaned forward and said something to the pup. She whirled, faced him, went down on her front legs, tongue hanging, and barked. Matt reached down and patted her head, strode down the path, Pardie dancing alongside.

Jess upended his cup, set it on the table. He watched Matt and the pup reach the trail and turn north. "Nice fellow, Matt."

"Yes," said Sallie. She looked at Jess, frowning. "What means, 'all's right with the world'?"

Acknowledgments

The setting and story in this volume were inspired by a suggestion from Mike Bray, president of Wolfpack Publishing. Thanks to the staff at San Miguel Arcángel, the California mission featured in the story. I am grateful to Anne Schroeder and Michael Erin Woody for their insights on the Salinan people. Thanks to Dugan Miller for Spanish translations and to Pamela Pan for Chinese translations. Members of the Mount Diablo Critique Group made useful comments. Thanks to Cary Hague Henoch for her careful proofreading.

I am enormously indebted to the many authors who wrote about California in the mid-nineteenth century, particularly the hide and tallow trade, California missions, Sutter's Fort, Sacramento and San Francisco, and the gold rush. I am particularly grateful to the diarists who told about their personal experiences—and their dreams—in the diggings.

A Look At: This Promised Land

A WESTERN ROMANCE

Award-winning author Harlan Hague takes readers on an unforgettable journey of loss, resilience, and the search for a new beginning.

After the devastating loss of his beloved wife, Wes Haag finds himself grappling with grief and the daunting task of starting over. Determined to create a fresh start for himself and his young son, he embarks on a treacherous cattle drive from Texas to Kansas—and a land of new possibilities.

Amidst the unforgiving landscapes and unpredictable weather, Wes encounters Christina Browning, a young schoolteacher burdened by her own demons. As they forge a connection amidst harsh challenges, they find solace in each other's company. But their hopes for a peaceful life are threatened when a ruthless rancher sets his sights on their land, unleashing a battle for survival.

Bound by a shared sense of justice, Wes and Christina befriend an old Kansas Indian who seeks solace in his ancestral lands, and they lend their support to a group of black Exodusters—former slaves yearning for their own Promised Land. As racial prejudice and violence escalate, Wes and Christina become determined to protect those who are marginalized, challenging the injustices that plague their community.

AVAILABLE NOW

About the Author

Harlan Hague, Ph.D, is a native Texan who has lived in Japan and England. His travels have taken him to about eighty countries and dependencies and a circumnavigation of the globe, thereby proving the earth is round.

Hague is a prize-winning historian and biographer and award-winning novelist. His history specialties are exploration and trails, California's Mexican era, American Indians, and the environment. Early on, while a professor of history, he wrote history articles published in scholarly journals. His novels are mostly historical Westerns with romance themes. One Western includes a time travel twist. Two novels are set largely in Japan, with a novella in Belize. Some titles have been translated into Spanish, Italian, Portuguese and German. In addition to history, biography, and fiction, he once wrote travel articles, as well as a bit of fantasy. His screenplays are making the rounds.

For more information about what he has done and what he is doing, visit his website at harlanhague.us. Hague lives in the San Francisco Bay area.